A stray bead of water lazily trailed down his
neck toward the hard grooves in his chest,
making me moisten my lips at my
sudden urge to trace its path with my tongue . . .

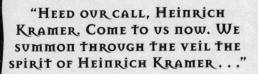

"HEED OUR CALL, HEINRICH KRAMER. COME TO US NOW. WE SUMMON THROUGH THE VEIL THE SPIRIT OF HEINRICH KRAMER . . ."

I tensed, feeling the grate of invisible icicles across my skin again. Bones's gaze narrowed at a point over my right shoulder. Slowly, I turned my head in that direction.

All I saw was a swirl of darkness before the Ouija board flew across the room—and the point of the little wooden planchette buried in Tyler's throat. I sprang up and tried to grab Tyler, only to be knocked backward like I'd been hit with a sledgehammer. Stunned, it took me a second to register that I was pinned to the wall by the desk, that dark cloud on the other side of it.

The ghost had successfully managed to use the desk as a weapon against me. If it wasn't still jabbed in my stomach, I wouldn't even believe it.

Bones threw the desk aside before I could, flinging it so hard that it split down the center when it hit the other wall. Dexter barked and jumped around, trying to bite the charcoal-colored cloud that was forming into the shape of a tall man. Tyler made a horrible gurgling noise, clutching his throat. Blood leaked out between his fingers.

"Bones, fix him. I'll deal with this."

By Jeaniene Frost

ONE GRAVE AT A TIME
THIS SIDE OF THE GRAVE
ETERNAL KISS OF DARKNESS
FIRST DROP OF CRIMSON
DESTINED FOR AN EARLY GRAVE
AT GRAVE'S END
ONE FOOT IN THE GRAVE
HALFWAY TO THE GRAVE

JEANIENE FROST

ONE GRAVE AT A TIME

A Night Huntress Novel

AVON

An Imprint of HarperCollinsPublishers

AVON BOOKS
An Imprint of HarperCollins*Publishers*
10 East 53rd Street
New York, New York 10022-5299

For my grandmother, Kathleen.
Though you are no longer with us,
you are no less loved.

Acknowledgments

I will again try to keep this short, but I never have before and this may not be the exception. Before anyone else I have to thank God for continuing to give me inspiration and determination—two things no writer can survive without. Thanks to my editor, Erika Tsang, and the rest of the wonderful team at Avon Books for all your hard work. Additional thanks go to Thomas Egner, for yet another gorgeous cover. Nancy Yost, my agent, has my continued gratitude for keeping my head above water professionally. To my husband, friends, and family, I love you and would be lost without you. Thanks to Tage, Carol, Kimberly, and the rest of the incredible team at Frost Fans for spreading the word far and wide about my books. Endless gratitude also goes out to my readers, who've amazed and humbled me with your support. I could never thank all of you as much as you deserve.

A final note of thanks goes to Theresa and the Lock Haven Paranormal Seekers for answering my questions regarding paranormal investigations. It should be mentioned that I took "artistic license," which is a nice way of saying I twisted the information they gave me to suit my plot, so any errors were derived from my imagination and not their feedback.

Author's Note

The *Malleus Maleficarum*, or *Hammer of Witches*, is a real book written by Heinrich Kramer and Jacob Sprenger (though some scholars suggest Sprenger's contribution was more ceremonial than authorial). For the purposes of my plot, however, I chose to credit the creation of the *Malleus Maleficarum* to only one author, Heinrich Kramer. Jacob Sprenger, you got off lucky this time.

ONE GRAVE AT A TIME

PROLOGUE

Lasting Peace Cemetery
Garland, Texas

DONALD BARTHOLOMEW WILLIAMS, GET YOUR ass back here *now*!"

My bellow still hung in the air when movement drew my gaze to the right. Just behind a headstone shaped like a small, weeping angel stood my uncle. Don stared at me as he tugged on his eyebrow in a way that expressed his discomfort more eloquently than a litany of words. In his suit and tie, gray hair combed back in its usual impeccable style, Don would look like your average middle-aged businessman to anyone observing him, except for one thing. You had to be undead or a psychic to be able to see him.

Don Williams, former head of a covert branch of Homeland Security that guarded the public against rogue supernatural creatures, had died ten days ago. Yet there he stood. A ghost.

I'd sobbed at his bedside when that fatal heart

attack struck, seen to his cremation afterward, been like a zombie at his wake, and even brought his ashes back to my home so I could keep him near me. Little did I know *how* near to me Don had actually been, considering all those times I'd thought I caught sight of him out of the corner of my eye. I'd chalked up those brief glimpses of my uncle to nothing more than grief-induced mirages until five minutes ago, when I realized my husband, Bones, could see him, too. Even though we were in the middle of a cemetery that still had bodies strewn about from a recent battle, and I had silver bullets burning inside me like agonizing little bonfires, all I could focus on was that Don hadn't wanted me to know that he was still grave-side up.

My uncle looked none too pleased that I'd discovered his secret. Part of me wanted to throw my arms around him while another part wanted to shake him until his teeth rattled. He should have *told* me, not skulked in the background playing a phantomish version of peekaboo! Of course, despite my dual urges, I could neither shake nor hug Don now. My hands would slip right through his newly diaphanous form, and likewise, my uncle couldn't touch anything—or anyone—corporeal anymore. So all I could do was stare at him, battling confusion, joy, and disbelief combined with some irritation at his deception.

"Aren't you going to say anything?" I finally asked.

His gray gaze flicked a few feet beyond me. I didn't need to turn around to know that Bones had come up behind me. Since he'd changed me from a half-breed into a full vampire, I could feel Bones like our auras were supernaturally intertwined. Which they were, I supposed. I still didn't know everything about what made up the connection between vampires and their sires. All I knew was that it existed, and it was powerful. Unless he shielded himself, I could sense Bones's feelings as though they were a continuous stream threaded into my psyche.

That's how I knew Bones was a lot more in control than I was. His initial shock at discovering Don as a ghost had given way to guarded contemplation. I, on the other hand, still felt like my emotions were in a whirlwind. Bones drew even with me, his dark brown gaze on my uncle.

"You see that she is safe," Bones stated, an English accent coloring his words. "We stopped Apollyon, so ghouls and vampires are at peace once more. You can go in peace. All is well."

Understanding bloomed along with a spurt of heart-wrenching emotion. Was that why my uncle hadn't "crossed over" like he should have? Probably. Don was even more of a control freak than I was, and though he'd rejected my repeated offers to cure his cancer by becoming a vampire, maybe he'd been too worried about the brewing undead hostilities to let go entirely when he died. I'd seen at least one ghost stay on long enough to ensure the safety of a loved one. Making sure I'd survived this battle and protected humanity by preventing a clash between vampires and ghouls was no doubt the anchor that had held Don here, but now, like Bones said, he could go.

I blinked past the sudden moisture in my gaze. "He's right," I said, my voice rasping. "I'll always love and miss you, but you're . . . you've got somewhere else to be now, don't you?"

My uncle gazed at both of us, his expression somber. Even though he didn't have actual lungs anymore, it sounded like he let out a slow, relieved breath.

"Goodbye, Cat," he said, the first words he'd spoken to me since the day he died. Then the air around him became hazy, blurring his features and obscuring his outline. I reached for Bones's hand, feeling his strong fingers curling around mine with a comforting squeeze. At least Don wasn't in pain like the last time I'd had to say goodbye to him. I tried to smile as my uncle's image faded entirely, but grief hit me in a fresh wave. Knowing he was going on to where he belonged didn't mean the ache of losing him went away.

Bones waited several moments after Don vanished before turning to me.

"Kitten, I know it's wretched timing, but we still have things we must do. Like getting those bullets out of you, removing the bodies—"

"Oh shit," I whispered.

Don appeared behind Bones while he was talking. A fierce scowl darkened my uncle's features, and he waved his arms in an uncharacteristic display of emotional excess.

"Does anyone want to explain why the *hell* I can't seem to leave?"

Oне

I CRUMPLED UP THE INVOICE IN FRONT OF ME, not throwing it away only because it wasn't the minister's fault that burying Don's ashes in hallowed ground didn't do jack toward sending my uncle to the Great Beyond. We'd now tried everything that our friends—alive, undead, or otherwise—had suggested to get my uncle to cross from this plane to the next one. None of it worked, as evidenced by Don pacing next to me, his feet not quite touching the floor.

His frustration was understandable. When you died, unless that was just a precursor to changing into a vampire or ghoul, you rather expected *not* to be stuck on earth anymore. Yeah, I'd been around ghosts before—a lot lately—but considering the number of people who died compared to the number of ghosts that existed, the odds of getting your Casper on were less than one percent. Yet my uncle seemed to be stuck in this rare between-worlds stasis whether he liked it or not. For someone who had been almost Machiavellian in his ability to manipulate circumstances, his current helplessness had to rankle that much more.

"We'll try something else," I offered, mustering up a false smile. "Hey, you're a pro at overcoming insurmountable odds. You managed to keep Americans from finding out about the supernatural world despite complications like cell phone video, the Internet, and YouTube. You'll find a way to move on."

My attempt at cheerfulness only earned me a baleful look. "Fabian never found a way to cross over," Don muttered, a swipe of his hand indicating my ghostly friend who lurked just outside my office. "Neither did any of the countless others who've found their way to you since you've become a spook magnet."

I winced, but he was right. I'd thought being born as the offspring of a vampire and a human was the height of improbability, but that only showed my lack of faith in Fate's twisted sense of humor. My turning into a full vampire put me firmly in first place as the World's Weirdest Person. I didn't feed off human blood like every other vampire. No, I needed undead blood to survive instead, and I absorbed more than nourishment from it. I also—temporarily—absorbed whatever special abilities the owner of that blood contained. Drinking from a ghoul who just happened to have incredible ties to the grave had made me irresistible to any ghost who happened to be in the same area code as me. Privately, I worried that my new, borrowed abilities might be one of the reasons Don couldn't cross over yet. I'm sure the thought had occurred to him, too, hence his grumpier-than-usual attitude with me.

"Ask them to keep it down, Kitten," Bones muttered when he came in the room. "Can't hear myself bloomin' think."

I raised my voice to be sure that it carried not just around the house, but the porch and backyard, too.

"Please, guys, a little softer with the chatter?"

Dozens of conversations instantly become muted even though I'd made it a request instead of an order. I was still uncomfortable with how my new, unwanted ability meant that ghosts had to obey whatever I commanded. I didn't want that kind of power over anyone, so I was very careful in how I phrased my communications with the spectral dead. Especially my uncle. *How things have changed,* I mused. For years when I worked as one of Don's team of elite soldiers, I'd chafed at having to follow his orders. Now he'd have to follow mine, if I chose, something I'd longed for back then—and couldn't wait to get rid of now.

Bones sank into the chair nearest me. His lean, muscled frame exuded a heady mixture of sexiness and coiled energy even though he sat in a casual sprawl, one bare foot propped against my thigh. His dark hair was damp from his recent shower, making his short curls cling even tighter to his head. A stray bead of water lazily trailed down his neck toward the hard grooves in his chest, making me moisten my lips at my sudden urge to trace its path with my tongue.

If we were alone, I wouldn't have needed to suppress that urge. Bones would be all too willing to indulge in some afternoon delight. His sex drive was as legendary as his dangerousness, but with two ghosts watching us, my tongue explorations would have to wait until later.

"If more noisy ghosties keep showing up, I'm going to plant garlic and weed 'round the entire house," Bones stated in a conversational tone.

My uncle glowered at him, knowing that both those items in large quantities would repel most ghosts. "Not until I'm where I should be."

I coughed, something I didn't need to do since breathing became optional for me.

"By the time it would grow in, this power should be out of my system. The longest I wielded borrowed abilities was two months. It's been almost that long since . . . well."

It still wasn't common knowledge that Marie Laveau, voodoo queen of New Orleans, was the reason I was now the equivalent of a ghostly den mother. It had been her blood I was forced to drink. Yeah, I understood later why she'd made me do it, but at the time, I'd been more than a little pissed.

"I knew a ghost who once took three weeks to cross over," Fabian spoke up from the doorframe. At my grateful smile, he came all the way in. "I'm sure Cat will think of something that will help you make the journey," he added with supreme confidence.

Bless Fabian. True friends came in all forms, even transparent ones.

Don wasn't convinced. "I've been dead for over five weeks," he replied shortly. "Did you know anyone who took *that* long to cross over?"

My cell rang, giving Fabian an excuse not to reply as I answered it. Good timing with the interruption, too, because from his expression, Don wouldn't have liked Fabian's answer.

"Cat."

I didn't need to glance at the numbers to recognize Tate, my former first officer, just from that one syllable. He was probably calling to talk to Don, but as a ghost's voice didn't travel well through technology, I'd have to act as relay.

"Hey, what's up?" I said, waving Don over while mouthing, *It's Tate*.

"Can you come to the compound tonight?" Tate's voice sounded odd. Too formal. "The team's operations consultant would like to meet you."

Operations consultant? "Since when do we have one of those?" I asked, forgetting that I hadn't been part of the team's "we" in a while.

"Since now," Tate replied flatly.

I glanced at Bones but didn't wait for his acquiescing shrug before answering. We didn't have important plans, and my curiosity was piqued. "All right. I'll see you in a couple hours."

"Don't come alone."

Tate whispered the last part right before hanging up. My brows rose, more that he'd made the sentence inaudible to anyone without supernatural hearing than the words themselves.

Something else was clearly up. I knew he wasn't asking me to bring Bones since Tate knew he always accompanied me on trips to my old workplace. Tate must mean someone else, and there was only person I could think of.

I turned to Don. "Feel like going on a field trip?"

* * *

From the air, the compound looked like a nondescript single-story building surrounded by a lot of wasted parking lot space. In reality, it was an old military nuclear fallout shelter that had four extensive sublevels underneath its deliberately plain exterior. Security was rigid here, as you'd expect for a secret government facility that policed the activities of the undead. Still, I was surprised when we had to hover for ten minutes before our chopper was given clearance to land. It was not like we were dropping in unexpectedly, for crying out loud.

Bones and I exited the chopper but were stopped by three helmeted guards when we attempted to go inside the roof's double doors.

"ID," the guard closest to us barked.

I laughed. "Good one, Cooper."

The guards' visors were so dark that I couldn't see any of their features underneath, but they all had heartbeats, and Cooper was the only one of my old human friends who was smart-ass enough to attempt such a stunt.

"Identification," the guard repeated, drawing the word out enough to determine that his voice was unfamiliar to me. Okay, not Cooper, and not a joke, either. The flanking guards tightened their grips ever so slightly on their automatic weapons.

"I don't like this," Don muttered, coming to float on my right. None of the guards even flinched in his direction, but of course, as humans, they couldn't see him.

I didn't like it, either, but it was obvious these guards were bent on seeing our ID before letting us enter. I began to dig through my pocket, having learned the hard way to always carry a wallet even if I didn't think I'd need it, but Bones just smiled at the trio.

"Want my identification?" he asked silkily. "Here it is." Then his eyes changed to glowing emerald green while fangs slid out from his upper teeth, extending to their full length like mini ivory daggers.

"Let us pass, or we'll leave, and you can explain to your boss that the visitors he expected had better things to do than have their time wasted."

The guard who'd demanded our ID hesitated for a loaded moment, then stepped aside without another word. The twin fangs gleaming from Bones's teeth retracted, and his eyes bled back to their normal dark brown color.

I put my wallet back in my pants. Guess I wasn't going to need my driver's license after all.

"Wise choice," Bones commented. I brushed past the guards, with him following behind me, my uncle still muttering that he didn't like this. *No shit,* I thought, but didn't say it for more reasons than not wanting to appear like I was talking to myself. This was Don's first trip back to the building he'd run for years and ultimately died in. Now he was returning in a supernatural form that most of his colleagues couldn't even see. That had to be discomfiting in more ways than I could imagine.

We went down the hallway toward the elevator, and I mentally catalogued the differences since the last time I'd been here. There used to be two busy offices in this section, but now the only sounds of activity were our steady footfalls on the linoleum floor.

When we got in the elevator, I pressed the button for the second sublevel, where the staff offices were located. A poignant sense of déjà vu washed over me as the shiny doors closed. The last time I'd ridden this elevator on the way down, I had been rushing to Don's bedside to say goodbye. Now he stood next to me, the other side of the elevator hazily visible through his profile. Life certainly had some bends in the road that I never would have anticipated.

"Just so you know, if I see a bright light while I'm here, I'm running into it without waiting for you to say a damn word," my uncle said, breaking the silence.

The wryness in his tone made me laugh. "I'd be cheering you the whole way," I assured him, glad his sardonic sense of humor hadn't vanished despite the roughness of the past several weeks.

The elevator stopped, and we got out. I instinctively wanted to turn toward what used to be Don's office but made a left instead. Tate said he didn't feel right moving into Don's old office even though it was the largest and had a mini command station in it. I didn't blame him. It would feel like grave robbing to strip Don's things out of his office when he was still technically *here*, though only a handful of people in the building were aware of that. My uncle hadn't wanted anyone to know of his new, ghostly status, but I'd refused to hide the information from any undead team members who could still see and talk to Don.

Tate's door was ajar. I went inside without knocking though I knew he wasn't alone. Someone with a heartbeat was in there with him. A heartbeat, and too much cologne for a vampire's sensitive nose.

"Hey, Tate," I said, noting how stiff his posture was despite the fact that he was sitting. The reason for his tenseness must be the tall, thin man who stood a few feet away from Tate's desk. He had graying hair cut in the same high-and-tight style Tate favored, but something about his bearing suggested his hair was the only military influence he had. His stance was too relaxed, his hands boasting calluses that I'd bet came from pens versus weapons. His startled glance up revealed that he hadn't known we were here until I spoke, either, and while vampires *were* stealthy, I'd made no attempt to conceal the sound of our approach.

The arrogance in his stare once he recovered from his surprise made me mentally reclassify him from *civilian* to *government desk jockey*. Usually just two things accounted for such an immediate, overconfident attitude at a first meeting: a wealth of bad-ass undead abilities, or a person who firmly believed that his connections meant he could make his own rules. Since Mr. Cocky was human, that left the latter.

"You must be the new operations consultant," I said, smiling in a way that would look friendly to someone who didn't know me.

"Yes," was his cool reply. "My name is—"

"Jason Madigan," Don completed the sentence the same time as the gray-haired government contractor. My uncle's voice sounded strained, almost shocked. "What is *he* doing here?"

two

I KEPT MY ATTENTION ON MADIGAN, NOT LOOK-
ing over at Don even though it was my first instinct. Mustn't let on that there was a ghost in the
room, and the question had been rhetorical since Don
knew Madigan couldn't hear him.

"Cat Crawfield . . . Russell," I introduced myself.
Okay, Bones and I weren't married according to
human law, but by vampire standards, we were bound
together tighter than a piece of paper could ever make
two people.

A wave of pleasure brushed against my subconscious, drifting out from the shields Bones had erected
around himself as soon as our helicopter landed. He
liked that I'd added the last name he'd been born with
to my own. That was all the officiating I needed to
decide that I'd be Catherine Crawfield Russell from
this day forth.

Even though I hadn't needed Don's reaction to

deduce that Madigan was going to be a pain in my ass, years of strict farm-bred manners made it impossible for me not to offer my hand. Madigan looked at it for a fraction too long before shaking it. His hesitancy revealed that Madigan had a prejudice against women or vampires, neither of which endeared him any further to me.

Bones stated his name with none of my hand-offering compulsions, but then again, his childhood had been spent begging or thieving to survive the harsh circumstances of being the bastard son of a prostitute in eighteenth-century London. Not being endlessly drilled about manners and respecting your elders like mine. He stared at Madigan without blinking, his hands resting inside the pockets of his leather coat, his half smile more challenging than courteous.

Madigan took the hint. He dropped his hand from mine and didn't attempt extending it to Bones. The faintest expression of relief might have even crossed his face, too.

Prejudice against vampires, then. Perfect.

"You were right, weren't you?" Madigan said to Tate with a joviality that rang false. "He did come with her."

For a second, my gaze flicked to Don. Good God, could Madigan *see* him? He was human, but maybe Madigan had some psychic abilities . . .

"With vampires, if you invite one spouse, the other is automatically included as well," Bones replied lightly. "That's an age-old rule, but I'll forgive you for not knowing it."

Oh, Madigan meant Bones. I stifled my snort. What

he said was true, but even if it weren't, Bones wouldn't have stayed behind. I didn't work here anymore, so it was not like I could be threatened with anything if Madigan didn't like my attitude. And he wouldn't, I could promise him that.

"What's up with the ID check on the roof?" I asked to steer things away from the staring contest between Madigan and Bones that the consultant would lose. No one could outstare a vampire.

Madigan shifted his attention to me, his natural scent souring ever so slightly underneath its preponderance of chemical enhancement.

"One of the oversights I noted when I arrived two days ago was that no one checked my identification when I landed. This facility is too important to be compromised by something as simple as sloppy security."

Tate bristled, hints of emerald appearing in his indigo eyes, but I just snorted.

"If you're arriving by air, they kinda figure that after they've double-checked the identity of the aircraft, the crew, and the flight plan, whoever's inside is who they're supposed to be. Especially if you invited those people here. But if they weren't, and they still pulled all the rest of that off, fake ID would be the easy part. Besides"—another snort—"if anyone got here by air that *didn't* belong, you think they'd be able to get away with their aircraft in weapons range and several vampires able to track them by scent alone?"

Instead of being made defensive by my blunt analysis of how useless a roof ID check was, Madigan stared at me in a thoughtful way.

"I heard you had difficulty with authority and following orders. Seems that wasn't exaggerated."

"Nope, that's true," I replied with a cheery smile.
"What else did you hear?"

He waved a hand dismissively. "Too many things
to list. Your former team raved about you so much I
simply had to meet you."

"Yeah?" I didn't buy that as the reason I was here,
but I'd play along. "Well, whatever you do, ignore
what my mom has to say about me."

Madigan didn't even crack a smile. Uptight prick.

"What *does* an operations consultant do, I
wonder?" Bones asked, as if he hadn't been busy
using his mind-reading skills to eavesdrop in Madigan's mind from the moment we arrived.

"Ensures that the transfer of management in a
highly sensitive Homeland Security department is as
smooth as it needs to be for the sake of national security," Madigan said, that smugness back in his tone.
"I'll be reviewing all records over the next few weeks.
Missions, personnel, budgets, everything. This department is too critical to only *hope* that Sergeant
Bradley is up for the task of running it."

Tate didn't so much as twitch a brawny muscle
even though the implied insult had to burn. For all the
issues I'd had with him in the past, his competence,
dedication, and work ethic had never been among
them.

"You won't find anyone more qualified to run this
operation now that Don's gone," I said with quiet steel.

"That's not why he's here," Don hissed. He'd been
quiet for the past several minutes, but now he sounded

more agitated than I'd ever heard him. Did becoming a ghost give my normally urbane uncle less control over his emotions, or did he and Madigan have a nasty history together?

"He's after something more important than auditing Tate's job performance," Don went on.

"I'm particularly interested in getting caught up on *your* records," Madigan said to me, oblivious to the other conversation in the room.

I shrugged. "Knock yourself out. Hope you like stories about the bad guys—or girls—getting it in the end."

"My favorite kind," Madigan replied with a glint in his eye that I didn't care for.

"Are Dave, Juan, Cooper, Geri, and my mom in the Wreck Room?" I asked, done with playing stupid word games. If I spent much more time with him, my temper might overcome my common sense, and that wouldn't be good. The smartest thing would be to play docile and let Tate find out if Madigan was really sniffing around this operation for ulterior motives.

"Why do you want to know their location?" Madigan asked, as if I had nefarious intentions he needed to protect them from.

My smile hid the fact that I was gritting my teeth. "Because since I'm here, I want to say hi to my friends and family," I managed to reply, proud of myself for not ending the sentence with *dickhead*.

"Soldiers and trainees are too busy to drop what they're doing just because a visitor wants to chat," Madigan stated crisply.

My fangs jumped out of their own accord, almost aching with my desire to tear the snotty expression right off Madigan's lightly wrinkled face. Maybe some of that showed, because he followed that comment with, "I must warn you, any hostile actions toward me will be taken as an attack against the United States itself."

"Pompous prick," Don snapped, striding over to Madigan before stopping abruptly, as if remembering there wasn't a single thing he could do to him in his current state.

A thread of warning edged into my furious emotions, Bones's silent reminder for me to get control of myself. I did, forcing my fangs to retract and my eyes to return from sizzling green to their normal shade of medium gray.

"Whatever would give you the idea that I'd attack you?" I asked, making my voice as innocent and surprised as I could while mentally folding him into the shape of a pretzel.

"I might be new here, but I've extensively studied reports on your kind," Madigan said, dropping his patronizing G-man façade to show the naked hostility underneath. "All of them show that vampires' eyes change color right before they attack."

Bones laughed, a caressing sound that was at odds with the dangerous energy starting to push at his walls. "Bollocks. Our eyes turn green for reasons that have nothing to do with intent to kill—and I've seen vampires rip throats out without the slightest change in iris color. Is that the only experience you've had with vampires? Reports?"

The last word was heavy with polite scorn. Madigan stiffened.

"I've had enough experience to know that some can read minds."

"Shouldn't concern you. Men with nothing to hide have nothing to fear, right, mate?"

I waited to see if Madigan would nut up and accuse Bones of prying into his mind during this conversation, but he simply adjusted his wire-rim glasses as though their location on his nose was of prime importance.

"Your mom and the others will be done with training in an hour," Tate said, the first words he'd spoken since we'd come into his office. "You can wait here, if you'd like. Madigan was just leaving."

"Are you *dismissing* me?" Madigan asked with a touch of incredulity.

Tate's expression was bland. "Didn't you say right before Cat got here that you'd had enough of me for the day?"

Faint color rose in Madigan's cheeks. Not embarrassment, from his scent spiking with hints of kerosene. Carefully controlled indignation.

"I did," he replied shortly. "You'll have those reports for me in the morning? I assume staying up the rest of the night should be no hardship for someone like you."

Oh, what an *asshole*. My fangs did that *let me at him!* thing again, but this time, I kept them in my gums while also stifling the nosferatu green from leaping into my gaze.

Then Madigan turned back to us. "Cat. Bones." He said our names like we should apologize for them, but I just smiled as though I hadn't already eviscerated him in my fantasies several times.

"*So* great to meet you," I said, holding out my hand again only because I knew he didn't want to touch it.

He took it with the same faint pause he'd shown last time. I didn't squeeze once I had him in my grip, but oh, it was tempting.

As soon as I let him go, Madigan swept out of Tate's office, trailing a cloud of aftershave and irritation behind him.

"I'm following him," my uncle said flatly. "And I'm not going back with you later, Cat."

I glanced at Tate, who gave me a barely perceptible nod. In truth, I was relieved that he didn't attempt to argue. Don could snoop on Madigan a hell of a lot more effectively than anyone else. Maybe Madigan was here because Uncle Sam *was* just being paranoid at having a vampire in charge of an operation that hunted and concealed evidence of the undead. If so, Madigan would waste a lot of taxpayer dollars by scrutinizing this operation only to come to the conclusion that Tate was an outstanding replacement for Don. His record was spotless, so I had no fear of Madigan's unearthing any skeletons in Tate's closet—real or metaphorical.

But that wasn't why I was glad my uncle was focusing more on Madigan than on finding his way to the eternal doorway for the other side. If Madigan had a more sinister reason for being here, Don could alert us faster than anyone else. I had faith in Tate, Dave, and Juan being able to get themselves out of here if Madigan's dislike of the undead took a more menacing turn; but my mother, for all her bravado, wasn't as tough as they were.

And this wasn't a regular building that she could just bust through a wall to escape from. The fourth sublevel was built to contain vampires against their will. I should know. I designed it back when I was capturing vampires so Don's scientists could make a synthetic wonder drug called Brams. That drug, derived from the healing compound in undead blood, had kept several members of our team alive after they'd sustained grievous injury. Then Bones joined the operation, and Don got over his fear that raw vampire blood—far more effective in healing than Brams—would turn anyone evil who drank it. Bones donated enough of his blood for Don to parcel out to injured team members as needed, and the vampire cells on the fourth sublevel had remained empty for years as a result.

But that didn't mean they couldn't be put back into use if Don was right and Madigan was here for other reasons than a routine evaluation.

Or maybe I'd had so much shit happen lately that I assumed the worst about everyone now, whether I had valid reason to or not. I gave my head a shake to clear it. For all that Madigan pissed me off, it wasn't too long ago that Don had had the same prejudice about vampires. Hell, it was just eight years ago that *I'd* thought the only good bloodsucker was a dead bloodsucker! Yes, Madigan's attitude screamed Suspi-

cious Bureaucratic Bastard, but hopefully his spending some time with Tate, Juan, Dave, and my mother
would make him realize there was more to supernat-
urals than what he'd read in the pages of classified
murder reports.

"So, what do you think of him?" Tate drawled, the
former tightness now gone from his tone.

"That he and I won't be BFFs," was all I said. No
need to say more when this room could be bugged.

Tate grunted. "I'm getting that vibe, too. Maybe it's
a good thing that . . . circumstances are what they are."

By Tate's careful allusion to Don's condition, it was
obvious that he, too, was taking no chances over our
words being played back to Madigan later.

I gave a concurring shrug. "I suppose everything
does happen for a reason."

THREE

BY THE TIME BONES AND I GOT IN OUR CAR
on our last leg home, it was only an hour before
dawn. We could've gotten back to our Blue Ridge
house quicker if we'd flown the whole way, but it was
less flashy to keep our helicopter at the local private
airport. Even though our nearest neighbor was over
two dozen acres away, a helicopter coming and going
tended to attract a lot more notice than a car. The
lower our profile in our home area, the better.

Once in our car, however, Bones and I could speak
freely. The first item on my To Do list after I got some
sleep was to have the helicopter swept for bugs, and I
didn't mean of the insect variety. Madigan struck me
as the type who'd consider it standard operational pro-
cedure to have listening and tracking devices planted
on our chopper while Bones and I were at the compound. Hell, when I first started with the team and
everyone worried that I'd turn to the dark side, Don

had bugged my vehicle *and* had me followed twenty-four/seven. It took my uncle years to trust me enough to drop the surveillance and wire taps. Something told me Madigan would take even longer.

"So what's it like in his mind?" I asked.

Bones gave me a sideways glance as he navigated up the winding roads. "Murky. He clearly suspects my abilities and has fabricated a decent defense against them."

"Really?" Madigan hadn't struck me as having the exceptional mental fortitude necessary to prevent Bones's mind reading, but guess that meant I'd under-estimated him.

"He repeats rhymes nonstop in his head, making that the majority of what I hear," Bones replied with grudging admiration. "Managed to pick up a few things past them, like how he believes dousing himself in cologne will negate a vampire's ability to scent his emotions and that he despised Don. The mere mention of your uncle's name caused a spate of insults to appear in his thoughts."

"Don didn't seem too fond of him, either."

I'd have to ask my uncle about their history the next time I saw him. Maybe it was as simple as ri-valry over a woman; that had been enough to start the Trojan War, after all. Still, as long as Madigan kept his actions aboveboard, whatever had happened be-tween him and Don in the past didn't matter. Madigan thought my uncle was dead and gone. He didn't know he was right on only one of those counts.

"He also deeply distrusts vampires, as you had guessed yourself," Bones added. "Aside from that, all

I heard was enough repetitions of 'how many chucks could a woodchuck chuck' to make me want to stake myself."

I laughed. Maybe underneath Madigan's pompousness and prejudice, there lurked a sense of humor. That gave me hope. Pride wasn't the world's worst flaw, and vampire prejudice could be overcome with time. But the lack of a sense of humor was an insurmountable defect, in my opinion.

"Makes me grateful my mind-reading skills were on the fritz earlier."

Bones grunted. "Lucky you, pet."

Since I'd made Bones's blood my regular diet, I had more days where I could read humans' thoughts than not; but every once in a while, that ability blinked out. I chalked it up to mind reading being a power Bones had only recently inherited when his co-ruler, Mencheres, shared some of his formidable abilities through a blood bond. Too bad I didn't also catch occasional breaks from my inner ghostly paging system, but then again, the spectral juju juice in Marie Laveau's blood had had centuries to ferment.

At last, we turned onto the final gravel road that led to our house. Since it was at the top of a small mountain, it still took a few more minutes until we pulled into our driveway. Numerous ghosts lounged on our porch and in the surrounding woods, their energy making my skin tingle with a faint pins-and-needles sensation. Every head turned my way when our car came to a stop, but at least they didn't rush me when I got out. I'd had to explain several times that while I appreciated their enthusiasm, only my cat was allowed to twine around me when I came back from an outing.

"Hello, everyone," I said in greeting, turning in a circle to encompass the lot of them. Then I held out my hands, my signal that whoever wanted could do a fly-through on them. At once, a steady streak of silvery forms came at me, my hands almost burning from the multiple contacts the ghosts made with them.

This still felt like a very odd version of giving a group high five, but I'd come to discover that ghosts craved contact even though they passed through whoever—and whatever—they touched. And at least my hands were a far more appropriate body part for them to poltergeist than other areas that some of them had "accidentally" flown through. Implementing an automatic eviction order on any ghost who did a flyby below the belt put a stop to those incidents.

Bones gave a sardonic snort as he strode past me into the house. I knew I wasn't the only ones count-ing down the days until the voodoo queen's borrowed powers faded from my blood. Even though he under-stood the reasons behind it, Bones liked a bunch of different men and women zinging through my flesh about as much as I liked running into his countless former flings.

Once I was done with my unique form of saying hello, I went into the house, dropping my jacket onto the nearest chair. Bones's voice stopped me from flop-ping my body there next, his English accent sharper with annoyance.

"Fabian du Brac, I trust you have a good reason for this?"

Uh-oh. Bones didn't use Fabian's full name unless he was ticked, and there were only a few rules we'd set down when we agreed to let Fabian live with us. When I came into the living room, I saw which one of those rules Fabian had broken.

"Um, hi," I said to the female ghost floating by Fabian's side. She wore a dark, rather shapeless dress that did its best to conceal what must have been a Marilyn-Monroe-like figure when she had skin, and her severe bun only highlighted how naturally beautiful her face was.

Bones didn't appear impressed by the new ghost's lovely visage. He continued to give Fabian a quelling look, dark brow arched in challenge. Fabian knew that only he and my uncle were allowed to float inside our home. We'd had to set some ground rules to protect our privacy, after all. Otherwise, we'd have ghosts trailing us from room to room, even following Bones and me into the shower or running a stream of commentary about our bedroom activities. That whole traveling through walls thing made most ghosts forget about what was appropriate and *in*appropriate behavior.

"I can explain," Fabian began, throwing me a beseeching look over Bones's shoulder.

"Allow me," the female ghost replied in an accent that might have been German. "First, let me introduce myself. My name is Elisabeth."

She dipped into a curtsy, first to Bones, then to me as she spoke, her voice even despite her obvious unease.

Some of the tightness left Bones's shoulders as he bowed in return while extending his leg in a manner that had gone out of style centuries before I was born.

"Bones," he replied, straightening. "Pleasure to make your acquaintance."

I hid a smile. Bones might be able to snub Madigan's extended hand without a second thought, but he'd always had a soft spot for women. I settled for giving Elisabeth a smile and a welcoming nod while I told her my name. Hey, curtsying wasn't something I'd ever done before, but I'd learn just to see Bones do that courtly bow again. He somehow managed to make even the formal gesture look sexy.

"Fabian did not think it wise to reveal my presence to the others," Elisabeth went on, yanking my attention away from my musings. "That is why he bade me to wait inside for your return."

She spoke mainly to me though her gaze flicked to Bones more than once in mild consternation. Guess word had traveled that Bones was less than thrilled with my new popularity among the living-impaired.

"Why is it a big deal if the others know you're here?" I wondered out loud. Sure, some of the ghosts might grumble about Elisabeth's being inside when they'd been given strict orders not to breach the house's walls, but it wasn't every day that Fabian enticed a hot babe to come home with him—

"I am considered an outcast by many of my kind." The words were whispered so low, I almost wasn't sure I heard her.

"An outcast?" I repeated. I hadn't even known

ghosts *had* outcasts. Jeez, looked like no group could totally get along no matter what side of the dirt they were on. "Why?"

Elisabeth squared her shoulders as she met my gaze. "Because I am trying to kill another ghost."

Both my brows went up while a dozen questions sprang into my mind. Bones let out a low whistle before turning to give me a slight, jaded smile.

"Might as well be comfortable to hear the rest of this, so why don't we have a seat?"

Fabian nodded toward the curtained windows. "Perhaps you could arrange for more privacy first, Cat?"

Right. The other ghosts might not be able to see our new, enigmatic visitor, but if they floated too close to the house, they might accidentally overhear the rest of our conversation with Elisabeth. I sighed.

"Wait here. I'll be right back."

Once I'd politely insisted that all transparent persons vacate the premises for the next hour, I returned to the family room. Bones sat on the couch, a half-empty whiskey glass in his hand. Vampires were one of the few who could honestly claim to drink for the taste since alcohol had zero effect on us.

Fabian and Elisabeth hovered in sitting positions above the couch opposite Bones. I sat next to my husband, tucking up my legs more for warmth than comfort. Predawn in the early fall at these altitudes meant chillier temperatures. If I hadn't hoped to be in bed soon, I would've started a fire. Luckily for me, my cat, Helsing, took my seated position as a cue to jump from his window perch onto the couch next to me.

His furry body was like a mini furnace as he settled himself across my legs.

"So," I said, drawing the word out while I gave Helsing a few scratches around his ears, "how do you two know each other?"

"We met in New Orleans several decades ago," Elisabeth murmured.

"June, 1935," Fabian supplied before giving one of his sideburns a self-conscious rub. "I remember because it was, ah, unusually hot that year."

I almost bit the sides of my cheeks to keep from laughing. Fabian had a crush on the lovely ghost! His lame explanation for remembering the exact month and year they had met when ghosts didn't even *feel* temperatures was topped only by the cow-eyed look he darted her way before schooling his features to faux blandness.

Yep, he had it bad, all right.

"Okay, you two have been friends for a while, but you're not here just for a social visit, so what brings you, Elisabeth?"

I assumed it had something to do with the ghost she wanted to kill, but if so, she'd be shit out of luck. For one, I wasn't a contract killer of any species, and Bones had long since retired from that business himself. For another, I couldn't even help my uncle willingly find a way to the other side. So offing a phantom was way outside my abilities even if I did have a sudden urge to go ghostbusting, which I didn't.

She folded her hands in her lap, fingers twisting together. "Back in 1489, at the age of twenty-seven, I was burned at the stake for witchcraft," she began softly.

Even though that was over half a millennium ago, I winced. I'd been burned before, and both times had been excruciating experiences.

"I'm sorry," I said.

Elisabeth nodded, not looking away from her hands. "I wasn't a witch," she added, as if that made any difference in the horrific nature of her execution. "I was a midwife who challenged the local magistrate when he accused a mother of deliberately strangling her baby with its own cord. The fool knew nothing of the complications that birthing often wrought, and I told him so. Soon after, he sent for Heinrich Kramer."

"Who was he?"

"A murdering bastard," Bones replied before Elisabeth had a chance. "He wrote the *Malleus Maleficarum*, the *Hammer of Witches,* a book responsible for several centuries' worth of witch hunts. According to Kramer, anyone in a skirt was like as not to be a witch."

So Elisabeth had been killed by a homicidal zealot with a serious case of misogyny. I knew what it was like to be singled out by a zealot, and that made me even more sympathetic toward her.

"I'm sorry," I said with even more sincerity this time. "However Kramer bought it back then, I hope it was long and painful."

"It wasn't," she said, bitterness edging her tone. "He fell off his horse and broke his neck instantly instead of being stomped on and left to suffer."

"Not fair," I agreed, while thinking that at least Kramer would've gotten a taste of his own fiery medicine in hell.

Bones gave Elisabeth a long, speculative look. "Know quite a few details about his death, do you?"

Elisabeth met his gaze. In her half-hazy state, her eyes were medium blue, making me wonder if they had been as dark an indigo as Tate's when she was alive.

"Yes, I'm the one who spooked his horse," she replied defensively, oblivious to the pun in her words. "I wanted revenge for what he'd done to me, and to put a stop to the deaths of more women in the town he was traveling to."

"Good for you," I said at once. If she'd expected judgment, she hadn't heard much about me. Or Bones. "Wish I could shake your hand."

"Too right," Bones said, raising his whiskey in salute.

Elisabeth stared at both of us for several seconds. Then, very slowly, she rose and floated over, holding out her hand to me.

I shifted self-consciously. Guess she didn't know what a metaphorical statement was. Then I stuck out my hand, reminding myself that this was no different than all the other times I'd let ghosts pass through my flesh in greeting. But when her hand closed over mine, that usual tingling feeling followed by my fingers poking right through her didn't happen. Unbelievably, an icy-cold grip squeezed back with the same firmness and consistency as my own flesh.

"Son of a *bitch*!" I exclaimed, jumping to my feet. My cat hissed and leapt to the side of the couch, miffed at being unseated.

Elisabeth suddenly stood before me in vibrant

color, like she'd been switched from being broadcast in a fuzzy channel to high def. Her hair, which I'd thought had been a nondescript brown, shone with rich auburn highlights, and her eyes were so deep blue that they looked like the ocean at midnight. Her cheeks even had a pink flush to them, highlighting a complexion that could only be described as peaches and cream.

"Bloody hell," Bones muttered, standing also. His hand shot out to grasp Elisabeth's arm, his expression mirroring my shock as his fingers closed around solid flesh instead of passing through vaporous energy.

"I told you some of my kind were stronger than others," Fabian murmured from behind Elisabeth.

You weren't kidding, were you? I thought numbly, unable to stop myself from squeezing Elisabeth's very cold, very firm fingers to verify once more that she was really solid.

But soon after I did, I felt a pop of energy in the air, like an invisible balloon had burst. Pins and needles broke out across my skin while the hand I'd been clasping vanished. In the next instant, Elisabeth's appearance dulled back into muted colors, and the arm Bones had been holding melted under his grip, leaving his fingers curled—like mine were—around nothing more than a transparent outline of flesh that was no longer there.

"The longest I can merge into solid form is a few minutes, but it is very draining," Elisabeth said, as if what she'd done wasn't incredible enough. "Yet Kramer is stronger than I am."

I felt like my brain was still playing catch-up from everything I'd just witnessed. "Kramer? You said he died centuries ago."

"He did," Elisabeth replied with frightening grimness. "Yet every All Hallows' Eve, he walks."

FOUR

IF A PIN HAD DROPPED IN THE ROOM, IT would have shattered the sudden silence with the same effect as a bomb. I had a good idea of what Elisabeth meant by "he walks" but because it was too far-fetched for me to conceive of, I had to make sure.

"You're saying that after the homicidal asshat died, Kramer became a ghost who could walk around *in solid flesh* every Halloween?"

Elisabeth's brow furrowed in confusion at *asshat*, but she addressed the rest of my query without hesitation.

"As far as I know, it has only been the past few decades that Kramer has been able to manifest flesh for an entire evening."

"Why just Halloween night?" Sure, it was the time where many people celebrated the *idea* of ghosts, ghouls, vampires, or other creatures, but most of them didn't believe such creatures existed.

"It's the time when the barrier between the worlds is the thinnest," Bones replied. "The celebration of Samhain harkens back long before humans made a candy and costume holiday out of it."

Elisabeth's mouth curled. "The irony that Kramer is strengthened by an evening dedicated to what he once considered heretic worship is lost on him. He still believes himself to be acting on God's side, as if the Almighty hadn't made it clear that He wants nothing to do with Kramer."

"And what does he do on Halloween?" I'd bet every drop of blood in my body that Kramer didn't spend it trick-or-treating.

"He extracts 'confessions' of witchcraft from three women whom he's coerced a human accomplice into kidnapping, and then he burns them alive," Elisabeth replied, a spasm of pain crossing her features.

It was official. I now wanted to murder a ghost, a notion I'd discarded as unlikely only twenty minutes before. Problem was, killing vampires and ghouls was my specialty. Not people who were already *dead* dead.

"How long beforehand does he get an accomplice to capture these women?" Bones asked.

"I'm not sure," Elisabeth replied. She glanced away as if ashamed. "Perhaps a week? I've followed Kramer as best I could these many centuries, trying to discover a way to end him, but he is wily. He evades me much of the time."

Yeah, that whole ability to disappear would make him hell to follow, even for another ghost. Tracking him would be like trying to put handcuffs on the wind.

Which brought up another question. "You said a lot of other ghosts consider you an outcast for trying to kill one of your own kind, who obviously had to be Kramer. How did you, ah, attempt to do it?" A mental image of two transparent figures trying to throttle each other flashed in my head.

"Over the centuries, I made contact with several mediums, convincing them of Kramer's evil in the hopes that one could banish him. They tried many different ways, but each attempt failed. Once word of what I'd done spread, I was shunned by many of my kind . . . except those like Fabian."

The smile Elisabeth gave him as she finished that sentence was filled with such poignancy, I felt like I was intruding just watching. Maybe his interest in her wasn't only one-sided.

"Kramer's a murdering sod. Why wouldn't other ghosts want him dead as well?" Bones asked, sticking to the practicalities.

"Think about it," Fabian replied, dragging his gaze away from Elisabeth's face. "Most humans can't see us, vampires and ghouls ignore us, and we've been rejected by every god ever worshipped. All we have is each other. Most might sympathize with Elisabeth's reasons, but trying to kill one of our own is considered abhorrent no matter the cause."

"But not to you," I said, proud of him for being one of the rebels against that warped spectral version of diplomatic immunity.

Fabian ducked his head. "Perhaps others like me cling to our lost humanity more than the rest of them."

No, I thought. *Strongly principled people like you*

do the right thing regardless of whether you're made of flesh or fog.

"Kramer's only been killing for decades, yet you've attempted to destroy him for hundreds of years?"

Bones's tone was mild, but his gaze had narrowed.

"Oh, he killed long before he acquired the ability to burn people again," Elisabeth said flatly. "He would torment those who had the ability to see him, driving them to insanity or death. Then once he was able to manifest himself, he singled out the most vulnerable: children, the elderly, or the sick, driving them to the same bitter resolution. And no one believed them. Just like no one believed me when I was denounced as a witch and sentenced to burn."

Chills ran up my spine at the bleak resonance in the ghost's voice. If Elisabeth had watched this same brutal pattern play out all these years, unable to do a thing to stop it, I was amazed *she* was still sane. I couldn't always get the bad guys, but one of the things I clung to was the hope that one day, they'd get their just deserts whether it was in this life or the next. Yet Kramer had managed to escape punishment on every side of the grave. Even though I had enough to deal with from my unwanted powers from Marie, my uncle's quest to cross over, and the suspicions over the new operations consultant, the injustice of Kramer's wandering free to torture and murder more innocent people was too much for me.

Yet it wasn't just my anger that made up my mind. It was the way Fabian stared at Elisabeth. Then he turned his gaze to me, and the pleading in that single glance confirmed my decision.

"I'll help you," I said to Elisabeth, holding up my hand in anticipation of Bones's protest. Fabian had come through for me many times in the past, but the only way I'd been able to show my appreciation was a mere thank-you. Well, here was my chance to let Fabian know he was as dear to me as any of my other friends, even if he was the only one of them without flesh. Helping Elisabeth wasn't only the right thing to do; it was also important to Fabian. Really, what other choice did I have?

Cool fingers curled around my hand, squeezing once. I looked away from Fabian to meet Bones's steady gaze.

"You're not the only one who feels indebted to him," Bones said quietly. Then his mouth curled as he focused on Fabian. "Though you could've set an easier task before us."

"I'll do whatever you need to assist you," Fabian vowed, his expression brightening with such hope that my heart twisted. I might feel confident in our abilities to deal with Kramer's accomplice if we found out who the newest acolyte was in time, but I didn't even know if it was *possible* to kill a ghost. Bones had threatened exorcism on a couple of them before; but according to Elisabeth, that probably wouldn't work. Seeing Fabian's obvious faith made me afraid for more reasons than the idea of a murderer going free. I was afraid I'd let him down after all he'd done for me.

"We know you will, mate. You've already proven that," Bones replied.

"Thank you," Elisabeth said, her voice very soft. Something shone in her eyes that I'd swear were tears on any other person. "I came here with little hope. Your kind usually doesn't bother with mine no matter the circumstances."

"Yeah?" My smile was wry. "Just call me an equal opportunity ass-kicker, because Kramer and his assistant deserve to be taken out no matter what species they are."

"Perhaps it's best if you stay in Fabian's room while we determine our first course of action," Bones suggested, giving Fabian a slanted look before returning his attention to Elisabeth. "Safer if energy's emitting from a room in the house that other ghosts are used to its coming from."

"Of course," Elisabeth replied, smoothing her long skirt as she floated into a standing position. "I will be very discreet."

"Fabian can also fill you in on the house rules. We'll talk more once my wife and I have rested for the day."

Both ghosts took the hint, vanishing with more murmured thanks. I waited until I felt the energy in the room dissipate before turning to Bones.

"You sly matchmaker, you."

His grin held more than a hint of wickedness. "If I didn't give the bloke an edge, he'd likely spend the next century working up the courage to pay her a compliment."

"Shameless," I teased him, being sure to keep my voice low since I didn't know how far Fabian and Elisabeth had spoofed off to.

Bones's laugh flowed over me, dark and promising. "Indeed, as I intend to prove once we're in bed."

Tired I might have been, with too many things on my mind *and* on my plate, but only an idiot passed up that kind of invitation.

"Race you there," I whispered, and dashed up the stairs.

FIVE

I SNAPPED THE COVER OVER MY IPAD, NOT crumpling up the device in a fit of anger only because it was too damn expensive.

"What a sick, crazed *ass*hole!" I spat.

Bones glanced over at me before returning his attention to the road. "Told you not to start reading that book."

Yeah, well, it was a long drive to Washington, D.C., the book was available to buy online, and studying my target was my first step when I began a hunt. I knew the *Malleus Maleficarum* would be filled with superstitious bull crap, but I had underestimated the depths of its viciousness. I didn't know what disgusted me more: the precepts set forth by Kramer, or the knowledge that hundreds of years and countless deaths occurred before the average person stopped believing that he was correct.

"The accused had *no* chance," I continued to fume.

"Evidence was something none of them cared about. All someone needed to do was get a 'feeling' that a person was a witch, and boom, an Inquisitor could take her. Confessions were extracted by torture—described in sickening detail, I might add—and even if the poor woman confessed *before* being tortured, she'd be tortured anyway just for 'confirmation.' And if any of the accused managed *not* to confess no matter what horrific things were done to them, they were burned to death anyway because then they were considered to be unrepentant. Jesus!"

A grunt. "Don't think He had anything to do with it, luv."

"Bet your ass," I muttered. Religion might have been the excuse, but power and depravity were the real culprits. "Do you know Kramer considered women responsible for everything from impotence to failed crops—and that's not getting started on his obsession with their inherently evil, insatiable slutty natures, of course."

Bones's mouth curled. "Want to kill him a great deal now, do you?"

"Oh, so much." My hands itched with the urge to do violence to Kramer, but since he'd only be solid when he was burning new victims alive on Halloween, that would be too late. I'd have to settle for finding a way to dispatch him while he was still in vaporous form, and that—sadly—wouldn't involve dismemberment, I'd bet.

The look Bones threw my way said he could guess my thoughts. Or maybe he noticed me clenching my hands into fists.

"Chin up, Kitten. Perhaps the chap we're meeting will find a particularly brutal way to banish the sod for good."

"You seem pretty relaxed about this whole situation," I said with mild exasperation, noting the nonchalance in his tone and vibe.

Bones all but rolled his eyes. "Why wouldn't I be? For the first time in years, our relationship is solid, no one's actively trying to murder us, and our closest mates are happy. Blimey, Kitten, if I were any more relaxed, I'd need a smoke."

I was about to point out that things were hardly rosy considering my uncle's stuck-in-between state, the potentially troublesome Madigan, and a murderous ghost on the loose, but then I paused. Wouldn't there *always* be something stressful going on in our lives? If I didn't learn how to savor the positives—and everything Bones pointed out was a big positive— then I would march through life with a permanent case of Glass Half-Empty syndrome.

"You're right," I said, reaching out to squeeze his thigh. "Things have never been better."

Bones caught my hand and raised it to his mouth, lips brushing over my knuckles in a whisper of a kiss.

We'd always have challenges, but like everyone else, we would tackle them one at a time. Right now, Kramer was first on the list, and for all the problems the spectral schmuck represented, there were also positives. He might be able to terrorize and harm humans, but once I had Kramer in my sights, he'd be picking on someone his own size. I didn't scare easily, and a ghost could never beat a vampire in a fight. He couldn't even throw a punch until Halloween, and we'd lay the smackdown on him well before that. My mood improved even further.

"I bet this medium is going to give us great news," I added, voice throatier from Bones's tongue flicking between my fingers with the barest of touches.

Elisabeth had said mediums couldn't get the job done before, but she'd only been able to get a few to try, and the last attempt had been over fifty years ago. Bones's best friend, Spade, knew some noted demonologists who'd recommended the medium we were on our way to see, and if we were lucky, he'd prove more efficient than the others. If he didn't pan out, we still had a few other tricks up our sleeves. Good thing, too, because October wasn't far away.

At least we had an ace in the hole. As a ghost, Elisabeth was limited to traveling long distances by either physically hitching a ride on a car or using a ley line, which was a supernatural version of a speed train. Ley lines usually led to various supernatural hot spots, so then she'd have to pit stop at each one during her attempts to locate Kramer, but put me within a hundred mile radius of him, and I could use the borrowed power in my blood to lure Kramer to me. Then, once he was there, I could command him not to leave until we were done exorcising him. I'd detested that one of the side effects of drinking the voodoo queen's blood—in addition to becoming catnip for spirits—was the ability to strip ghosts of their free will, but that ability would come in handy in this situation. I didn't feel comfortable using that power on the ghosts who found their way to me, but on a prick like Kramer, I'd wield it with a smile. And a distinctly witchy cackle.

As for the accomplice, well, a human would be so easy to dispatch, it took the fun out of contemplating it.

"We're here," Bones said, letting go of my hand to pull into a strip mall parking lot.

I glanced around, looking for any afterlife-themed names in the businesses lining the front of the L-shaped complex. The closest thing I found was Deena's Heavenly Cheesecake, but I doubted that was the place.

"Are you sure this is it?"

Bones pointed. "Helen of Troy's Garden is right over there."

"But that's a florist," I said, as if the obvious had escaped him.

He answered me as he parked the car. "Maybe he fancies communing with flowers as well as ghosts."

It shouldn't surprise me that a medium would have a regular day job, but it did. Then I gave a mental shrug. Several years ago, I'd gone to college during the day and hunted vampires at night. Just because people were connected to the paranormal in one way didn't mean they had to be involved with it in all parts of their lives.

When I got out of the car, a smash of voices assaulted my mind, as abrupt as a switch being flipped. My hand flew to my head in an instinctive yet totally useless gesture of defense against the sudden deluge of chatter.

"Aw, crap," I muttered. "Give me a second."

Bones came over to me without asking what was

wrong. He'd seen this response enough before to know. His gaze flitted between me and the rest of the parking lot while coiled, dangerous energy leaked from his aura—a warning to anyone without a pulse that approaching us would be a bad idea. I was at my most vulnerable in those first few moments, when I used all of my concentration to turn down the roar of voices in my mind, courtesy of my mind-reading abilities suddenly kicking in.

Once I was able to dim the carousel of conversations to a level similar to annoying background music, I gave Bones a thumbs-up.

"What's my time?"

"Seventy-two seconds," he replied.

Bones didn't have a stopwatch, but I knew his quote was accurate. I blew out a sigh. On the plus side, that was my fastest recovery time to date. In the negative column, if we'd been under attack during those seventy-two seconds, I could've been killed several times over. Not by another human, sure, but a midlevel vampire or ghoul could clean my clock while my attention was so dangerously divided.

"You were right. The voices are easier to control when I'm used to them being there. Wish this on-again, off-again garbage would stop already."

He ran his hands down my arms in a slow, firm caress, his touch conveying both strength and resolve.

"It's happening less, and you're rebounding faster. Soon you'll master it completely, just like you've done with every other challenge that's been thrown at you."

I wish I had half his confidence in my abilities, but there wasn't time for me to wallow in uncertainties.

For now, I'd follow the sage mantra of *fake it 'til you make it.* I smiled and changed the subject.

"There's a man inside the florist's shop thinking you're *way* too hot to be straight. Think he's our medium?"

Bones's mouth curled, but he didn't bother looking over my shoulder at the shop behind me. No doubt he'd picked up on those same thoughts himself, but was too polite to admit it.

"Let's find out."

The plethora of scents inside Helen of Troy's Garden had me breathing almost as often as I had before I became a full vampire. Fresh floral fragrances washed away the acridness of oil, exhaust, and chemicals from my occasional breaths on the drive over, making me feel like my lungs had just gone through a quick cleaning. For practicality's sake, it also gave me a chance to scent out any potential dangers. Undead Masters might be able to cloak their auras, but no one could fully erase their scent. A couple sniffs told me that no other vampires were in the store but me and Bones, and I didn't catch the earthy scent of any ghouls, either. Sure, we were here on Spade's referral, but waltzing in without our guard up was akin to asking Fate to send us an unpleasant surprise, in my opinion.

Once I established that the only danger the florist shop represented would be to someone with allergies, I turned my attention to the chicly dressed, smiling African-American man who continued to check Bones out as if he was an orgasm for the eyes.

In fairness, he was, but it still raised my instinctive vampire territorialism even though Bones was faithful, not to mention he didn't swing that way.

"You Tyler?" Bones asked at the same time that I loudly cleared my throat. Both served to cut off the beginnings of a mental fantasy the man was having about Bones that would take days to scrub from my mind.

"That's me," Tyler replied with a quick, engaging grin.

"We have an appointment," I said, fighting my urge to grip Bones's arm while hissing and flashing fang. "I'm Cat, and this is my *husband*, Bones."

Amusement wafted over my subconscious, but Bones's expression didn't change from its mask of cool inscrutability as he regarded Tyler.

"Just my luck you couldn't be a brother and sister shopping for some flowers for Mom," Tyler said in a disappointed tone. Then he winked at me. "That's right, honey, state your claim on Mr. Yummy Pants. I'd do the same if I were you."

A grin ticked at my mouth. I swept my gaze over the muscled roundness of Bones's ass, which his black jeans only highlighted. Then I gazed at the snug fit of the front that had nothing to do with the cut of the denim. Finally, I met Tyler's chocolate-colored eyes and winked back.

He laughed.

"Nice shop," I said to change the subject. "Everything's so fresh and beautiful."

Tyler waved a hand. "Being a medium might sound glamorous, but creditors are only impressed with one thing, sweetness. Payments. Besides"—he shuddered dramatically—"when they find out about my *other* job, they always want proof that I'm not faking, and telling someone their dead Aunt Tilly hates their skanky new girlfriend just leads to your power getting shut off."

I couldn't stop my laugh at that. Bones's mouth quirked. "Indeed. Now, mate, you know why we've come. Shall we chat here, or elsewhere?"

"Here. Just let me close up."

Tyler bustled over to the entrance, flipping the sign from OPEN to SORRY WE MISSED YOU! before locking the door. On his way back, he gave another open leer at Bones's ass before meeting my gaze and fanning himself.

"Rawr!" he stage-whispered.

My initial spurt of territorialism had changed to humor. Tyler reminded me of another affable pervert—my friend, Juan. If it was female, Juan was attracted to it. Aside from a switch in gender, Tyler seemed to be the same way. From his thoughts, I knew he had no serious interest in hitting on Bones now that he knew he was married. He just couldn't seem to help himself. Tyler's thoughts bounced around between wondering what sort of ghost was giving us trouble, to pondering whether we were human, to guessing that Bones tasted like vanilla frosting.

Two out of the three musings weren't slutty, at least.

"All set now. Follow me," Tyler said.

We headed toward the back room of the shop. Another heartbeat came from there, making me wonder if Tyler had a partner. I wasn't worried that he hadn't mentioned anyone else being here, though. If one human proved too much for Bones and me to handle, we didn't deserve to have fangs. More plants and boxes were stacked along the short, narrow hallway, as well as bags of fertilizer and other greenery accessories. As predicated, this clutter ended in a small office with no windows and walls that had seen better days. It was also empty of anyone that I could see, but from the rapid heartbeat—and some nasally grunting—an animal was in here.

Bones and I sat in the two folding chairs opposite a desk that had duct tape wrapped around one corner. Tyler pulled a comfier-looking chair out from behind the desk to sit closer to us.

"Sorry for the surroundings," he said, still in that same cheery way. "Have to make it pretty in front for customers, but that means skimping back here where it's just me and Dexter."

At that, a white-and-tan dog with rolls of flesh decorating his shoulders and a face that looked perpetually smashed came out from underneath the desk.

"Aww, who's Daddy's little baby?" Tyler cooed, patting his lap.

More nasally grunts ensued, sounding joyous this time, before the bundle of flesh and fur landed on Tyler's lap hard enough to elicit an "oof" from the medium.

"Baby needs to lay off the burgers or he'll break daddy's hip one day," Tyler continued in the same singsong manner.

I tended to agree. With his leanness and Dexter's size, the dog had to be about a third of his master's weight. The medium didn't seem to mind, though. He beamed at Bones and me.

"Isn't he gorgeous?"

With those rolls, the wet-sounding grunts, bulbous wiggly tail, and smashed face—not to mention the fart the dog let out once he situated himself—he was gorgeous in a way that only a parent could appreciate. But the open joy in Dexter's furry countenance as I stuck my hand out to pet him made me forget his less-than-aesthetic qualities.

"Who's a good, pretty boy?" I asked, scratching Dexter's ears and getting my wrist thoroughly licked in the process. The dog shuddered in delight, barely staying on Tyler's lap as he shifted to get closer.

"You have a friend forever now, sweetie," Tyler said, gripping Dexter more firmly so the dog didn't topple over. "So tell me, what sort of haunting are the two of you experiencing?"

"We're looking for someone who can summon and kill a ghost," Bones stated.

Tyler's brows went up, and some of that flirtatious sparkle left his gaze. "Why?" he asked bluntly.

I pulled out my iPad, a few taps bringing up the text of the *Malleus Maleficarum*. Then I held it up so Tyler could see it.

"Because the asshole who wrote this came back after he died," I replied. "And he's found a way to keep murdering people."

Tyler took the tablet from me with one hand while the other still held the dog. Somehow he managed to brace it against a knee and scroll down through the pages without dislodging Dexter from his perch.

Great, a crazy couple, ran through Tyler's mind as he read some of the text. *They actually think they've got the ghost of an infamous witch hunter haunting their house!*

Bones leaned forward, his smile showing the tips of his fangs. "We're not crazy, and this sod isn't haunting our anything."

Tyler's head whipped up, his expression changing as he spotted the new pointy canines in Bones's teeth and realized he hadn't said that last sentence out loud.

"Oh," he said at last. "Sorry. My friends didn't mention certain . . . details about you, and you wouldn't believe how nutty some people are. Just last week, I had a woman convinced her trailer was haunted by Tupac, as if he'd want to spend eternity in a double wide that smelled like cat piss."

That made my lips twitch, but Bones stayed on topic. "Now that we've cleared up the issue of our sanity, let's move on to our query."

Tyler gently shooed Dexter from his lap with a "Daddy's got to work" explanation that nevertheless drew a whine before Dexter went under the desk again. A loud exhalation, like a sigh, preceded the sound of the dog's plopping down on something soft. Spoiled rotten, I noted in amusement, but that only raised my opinion of Tyler. Kindness toward the voiceless or the vulnerable, like animals and children, usually denoted good character in a person.

"How do you know you're dealing with the shade of Heinrich Kramer and that he's able to kill people?" Tyler asked, all business now.

"Ghostly informant," Bones replied.

Tyler nodded as if that response wasn't unusual. "Is that the only confirmation? Ghosts lie sometimes."

The glance Bones cast my way said he'd considered this possibility. "All we have is the ghost's word."

Tyler gave both of us an unblinking look. "I can't kill a ghost, but I know some people who might be able to. Before I give you their names and put in a good word for you, I need to make sure I'm not setting up an innocent person."

I doubted that Elisabeth had made all this up, but I'd been lied to convincingly before. Just because she seemed nice and Fabian had a crush on her didn't mean we should blindly trust a virtual stranger when we had the chance to confirm the facts for ourselves. I exchanged a long, wordless look with Bones. We could green-eye the information out of Tyler, but from the brush of his emotions, Bones also wanted further corroboration on the identity of the ghost Elisabeth had sent us after.

"If you have a way to make sure that what we've been told is true, do it," I told him.

Tyler stood, brushing Dexter's hair from his pants. "All right," he said, his tone chipper once more. "Time to talk to the dead."

Six

I STARED AT THE CARDBOARD BOX TYLER RE-
turned with.

"A Ouija board? *That's* how you intend to prove
we're dealing with a murderous Heinrich Kramer instead of Casper the Friendly Ghost?"

If this was his method of identity verification, five
bucks said Tyler's idea to dispatch Kramer would involve playing "light as a feather, stiff as a board." Or
calling forth Bloody Mary from a mirror to send *her*
after the witch hunter.

"When used properly, Ouija boards open doors to
the other side," Tyler replied, setting the box on his
desk. "All we have to do is knock on the right one."

He began to clear things off to make room, humming the whole time. I looked at Bones, surprised he
hadn't offered an instant objection to this tactic, but
all he did was tap his chin thoughtfully.

"Spade said his demonologist mates spoke highly

of Tyler, so we'll trust that he knows what tools to work with."

Or Spade is just paying us back for exposing Denise to what he considered "dangerous circumstances" recently, I added, but didn't say out loud. Might as well see where this led us, though a session with a Ouija board in a flower shop was hardly the way I imagined we'd summon a potentially evil spirit. Holding a séance in a graveyard at midnight with some ancient relics seemed far more appropriate.

Tyler had the board opened up on the desk, its symbols looking more hokey than supernatural, heart-shaped planchette pushed to the side. Then he disappeared into the main part of the shop before returning with some fragrant potted plants and a box of matches.

"All right, ready," Tyler declared, giving us both an appraising glance. "Bones is a vampire, and I'm guessing you are, too, but who's more powerful?"

"She is," Bones replied at once.

I was about to argue since Bones was a damn sight stronger *and* faster than me, plus had centuries more fighting experience; but with a start, I realized he was right. With Marie Laveau's control over the grave still residing in my body, I was more powerful than even most Masters.

Until that borrowed power wore off, anyway.

I cleared my throat, feeling a stab of uneasiness as I realized for the first time in our relationship, I ranked higher than Bones ability-wise—and he knew it.

"Are you okay with that?" I blurted, forgetting

for a moment that we had an audience. Bones had never been the insecure type, but an abrupt shift in a couple's dynamic had caused rifts in lots of relationships before ours.

His amusement wafted through my emotions even before he started to grin. "The last thing you need to fret about is my feeling emasculated, Kitten; but talk is cheap, so I'll be sure to show you later."

His voice was rich with so many undercurrents, I grew warmer just listening to him. Then Bones's expression became serious, and he leaned forward to brush my hand.

"I've watched you barely escape death several times, and each instance killed me a little inside. They may be dormant now, but we have enemies both cunning and cruel. Knowing you possess the power to defeat most of them doesn't threaten me, luv. It relieves me to my very core."

Bones also knew that power wasn't permanent, but as he'd pointed out in the car, the present was what mattered. For the present, I had these abilities. For the present, things were good. That was what I'd dwell on.

"So honest and sure of yourself." Tyler licked his lips. "You get sexier by the minute, sugar."

"Ahem." I pulled my gaze away from Bones to give Tyler a pointed look. "Mine, remember?"

Tyler waved a hand. "Yeah, yeah." *But I'm having GOOD dreams tonight,* he mentally finished.

I rolled my eyes. Bones just snorted. "Can't sleep until you finish with us here, Sandman, so let's get on with it."

Tyler scooted his chair closer to the edge of the desk, the Ouija board between me and him.

"Put your fingertips on the planchette, Cat," he instructed.

I copied the placement of his fingers on the small device, noting that my nails could use some attention, but a manicure had been way low on my list of priorities. Even though I didn't exert any pressure, the planchette jerked beneath my light touch, causing Tyler to cock his brow.

"Lots of juice in you, hmm?" he noted.

I wasn't about to explain the reason behind it, so I just shrugged. Tyler started to recite a series of invitations to any spirits who were nearby. Crackling energy filled the air as the planchette began to edge around the board in irregular circles, powered by something other than our touch. Bones sat back, watching us with a hooded expression, his gaze flickering between the board and the rest of the room.

A drawn-out, keening noise made me jump before I realized that it came from the canine underneath the desk. You'd think since I lived with a ghost and had dozens more camped around my house, engaging in a séance wouldn't rattle me, but it did. Maybe because it felt like I was trespassing somewhere that I didn't belong instead of just having some unusual friends or visitors.

"Does that mean Dexter has to pee?" I muttered, as the dog's whine grew into a loud bark.

"No." Tyler's voice was tighter than before. "Animals can sense the supernatural better than most people. It means someone's coming."

Right after the words left his mouth, I felt the shift in the air, like a freezer door had abruptly blown open. Icy needles ran along my skin, prickling me with power that wasn't of this world. Someone wasn't *coming*—he or she was *here*.

The planchette spun around the board the same time as a hazy figure materialized behind Tyler. He shivered.

"I think someone's here now," Tyler whispered. Then louder, "Who is with us? Tell us your name."

"Beth Ann," the cloudy figure replied while the planchette raced to land over the letter "B," then "E."

"Someone's definitely here," Tyler said under his breath as "T" was the next letter highlighted.

"She's right behind you," Bones replied.

Tyler jerked around in his seat, his face level with the midsection of the ghost. From her high-necked garb and long, wide skirt, she wasn't a newbie. That style had gone out well over a century ago.

"I don't see anyone yet," he mused.

"Really?" I asked in surprise. The ghost had manifested fully, even revealing slight pockmarks on her cheeks along with salt-and-pepper hair.

"It takes mortals longer to see us, even the gifted ones," Beth Ann replied, looking back and forth between me and Bones. "Not so with those of *your* ilk."

Her disdain for vampires came through crystal clear, too. Most ghosts who were drawn to me because of my borrowed power seemed not to mind the fact that I was a vampire, but this one obviously did.

"Hey, sorry if we bothered you, but there's no need to be snippy."

"Did she tell you her name?" Tyler asked low.

"Yeah. It's Beth Ann, and she's a little grumpy."

Tyler leaned forward as if to see better. It put his face squarely at the apex between Beth Ann's legs. She jumped back, incensed, even as I struggled to stuff back a laugh. Evidently he still couldn't see her yet.

"Filthy reprobate!" the ghost spat.

"Beth Ann, give us a sign of your presence," Tyler said in a commanding way, oblivious to what had just happened.

The ghost slapped his face, her hand passing right through. Tyler frowned.

"I felt a cold breeze just then. Did she do something?"

"She gave a sign of her presence," Bones replied, his lips twitching.

"Normally it takes longer for one to appear and interact with us," Tyler said, sounding bemused. His gaze slid to me. "You must be the wild card."

If he only knew. "Okay, well, now what?"

Tyler replied, but it was drowned out by Beth Ann's loud, indignant response. "If you presume I will do anything for a group of disgusting ruffians such as yourselves—"

"Shh," I told her, trying to make out what Tyler was saying.

She quieted instantly, her eyes widening in shock. Damn, I'd just taken away her ability to speak. Guess shushing her was the same as giving her an order to be silent.

"—that the door's open, we can attempt to summon your witch hunter," Tyler finished.

"So Beth Ann doesn't need to stay?" I asked, feeling guilty as her mouth opened and closed in a series of futile attempts to talk.

"No. I'll send her away—"

"You can speak again, and feel free to go back to where you were before," I told her with an apologetic wave.

The ghost vanished after snarling out a sentence that raised my brows. Well. She'd certainly learned some colorful phrases in her time.

"Prim-looking ladies always were the dirtiest," Bones commented, chuckling at my expression.

Considering his former occupation, he should know. I shook my head, answering, "Yep" to Tyler's question if the ghost was gone.

"All right, let's try for the main event." Tyler sounded enthused. "Keep touching the planchette, Cat."

I put my fingertips on the device again, feeling the pulsating throb that came from it. Maybe that was why it was shaped like a heart. Symbolism for what it felt like when it was properly activated.

"What's the witch hunter's name again?" Tyler asked.

"Heinrich Kramer."

"Heinriiich Kraaaaaaaaamer," Tyler drew out in dramatic fashion. He even lolled his head back and closed his eyes. "We summon you into our presence. Heed our call, Heinrich Kramer. Come to us now. We summon through the veil the spirit of Heinrich Kramer—"

Dexter let out a sharp noise that was part whine, part bark. Tyler quit speaking. I tensed, feeling the grate of invisible icicles across my skin again. Bones's gaze narrowed at a point over my right shoulder. Slowly, I turned my head in that direction.

All I saw was a swirl of darkness before the Ouija board flew across the room—and the point of the little wooden planchette buried in Tyler's throat.

SEVEN

I SPRANG UP AND TRIED TO GRAB TYLER, ONLY to be knocked backward like I'd been hit with a sledgehammer. Stunned, it took me a second to register that I was pinned to the wall by *the desk*, that dark cloud on the other side of it.

The ghost had successfully managed to use the desk as a weapon against me. If it hadn't been still jabbed in my stomach, I wouldn't even have believed it.

Bones threw the desk aside before I could, flinging it so hard that it split down the center when it hit the other wall. Dexter barked and jumped around, trying to bite the charcoal-colored cloud that was forming into the shape of a tall man. Tyler made a horrible gurgling noise, clutching his throat. Blood leaked out between his fingers.

"Bones, fix him. I'll deal with this asshole."

Dexter's barks drowned out the sounds Tyler made

as Bones slashed his palm with his fangs, then slapped it over Tyler's mouth, ripping out the planchette at the same time.

Pieces of the desk suddenly became missiles that pelted the three of us. Bones spun around to take their brunt, shielding Tyler, while I jumped to cover the dog. A pained yelp let me know at least one had nailed Dexter before I got to him. Tyler's gurgles became wrenching coughs.

"Boy, did you make a colossal fucking mistake," I snarled, grabbing a piece of the ruined desk. Then I stood up, still blocking the dog from any more objects the ghost could lob at him. He'd materialized enough for me to see white hair swirling around a craggy, wrinkled face. The ghost hadn't been young when he died, but the shoulders underneath his dark tunic weren't bowed from age. They were squared in arrogance, and the green eyes boring into mine held nothing but contempt.

"*Hure,*" the ghost muttered before thrusting his hand into my neck and squeezing like he was about to choke me. I felt a stronger than normal pins-and-needles sensation but didn't flinch. If this schmuck thought to terrify me with a cheap parlor trick like that, wait until he saw *my* first abracadabra.

"Heinrich Kramer?" I asked almost as an afterthought. Didn't matter if it wasn't him, he would regret what he did, but I wanted to know whose ass I was about to kick.

"Address me as Inquisitor," the ghost replied in a heavy accent. At least he spoke English; I didn't know a word of German.

I smiled nastily. "You know that witchcraft you pretended to try and stamp out when you were alive? I've got it running all through my veins." Then I sliced open my wrist with the ragged edge of a piece of desk, blood dripping in slow plops before the wound healed.

If I wanted to summon a legion of regular ghosts to my side, I'd shed tears, but blood, combined with my inner roar of *come and get him, boys!* was shed to summon a different kind of spectre, all courtesy of my borrowed abilities from New Orleans' most famous voodoo queen. Cold, seething power streaked through my body, electrifying my nerves and filling the room with an abundance of supernatural energy. The ghost could feel it, too, I could tell. A frown replaced the sneer on his face. Dexter squeaked and limped out of the room.

In the next instant, shadows sprang up from the floor, flinging themselves upon the ghost with all of the hunger that the grave held within it. It wasn't her expertise with spells or potions that made vampires and ghouls alike fear Marie Laveau. It was her ability to call forth Remnants and bend them to her will, just like I was doing now. As one, the Remnants began to rip through the ghost's body, eliciting a howl from Kramer that I savored like candy. Remnants fed on pain, and it sounded like the Inquisitor was serving up a banquet. I didn't know if they could kill the ghost, Kramer lacking the flesh that they could eventually explode, but I was willing to let them do their best to find out.

My wishful thinking was short-lived, however. Just as abruptly as Kramer appeared, he vanished, leaving the Remnants twining their diaphanous, deadly forms through nothing more substantial than air.

"Come back here!" I yelled.

Nothing stirred except the dozens of Remnants who turned toward me with hazy expressions that all seemed to be asking the same question.

Now what?

Damned if I knew. "Go get him!" I tried, but they only swayed like reeds in a strong wind while their bodies stayed anchored in the demolished room.

Great. I shivered, fighting off the combination of hunger and cold that raising Remnants always brought about. My most lethal, secret weapon couldn't follow Kramer, and I'd neglected to order him to stay put before I unleashed them on him.

"Wait," I told the Remnants. Maybe Kramer would spoof back for another assault. I doubted it, but I could hope he'd be that stupid.

"How's he doing?" I asked Bones, kicking pieces of the desk out of my way to reach the opposite corner of the room.

Bones stood and moved aside, revealing Tyler crouched in a ball on the floor. He clutched his neck, but blood no longer streamed out between his fingers, and his breathing was ragged but unhampered.

"He'll be fine," Bones replied. "Just a bit traumatized."

"I was dead." Tyler's voice was no more than a croak. "I saw a bright light, felt myself floating away—"

"You did nothing of the sort," Bones interrupted. "Your heart didn't stop once though your larynx was crushed, and you were choking on your own blood."

"Oh, God," Tyler moaned.

"Maybe you shouldn't attempt to reassure him," I said dryly, fighting a shiver for a different reason. The Remnants tugged on my emotions, the chill and hunger of the grave permeating my defenses.

Bones cast a glance at the Remnants, his mouth curling down. He'd experienced firsthand what they could do when Marie unleashed them on him in order to blackmail me into drinking her blood. To say it hadn't endeared them to him was putting it mildly, but they couldn't help themselves. They were like supernatural missiles drawn to whatever target they were pointed at—or whatever target was the closest.

"Pity they didn't do the trick."

I lifted my shoulder in an apologetic shrug. "Not their fault. I jumped the gun."

He gave me a level look. "All of us underestimated what Kramer could do, but we won't make that mistake again. At least now, we have confirmation of Elisabeth's claims."

Oh yeah. I'd say Tyler's near-death experience, the wreckage of this office, his injured dog, and my being bulldozed by a desk were all very definitive forms of *confirmation*.

I sighed, brushing some wood shards off Bones's shirt. "How long do you want to wait here to see if he comes back?"

"Wait here?" That alarmed Tyler into standing. "Hell no, we're not waiting here. We're leaving, and I'm not coming back until that thing is taken *care* of. Mama didn't raise no damn fool."

"He's not interested in you, Tyler, so there's no reason he'd come back once we're gone—"

"You see that Ouija board?" he interrupted me, pointing at pieces littered among the ruins of the desk. "I didn't get a chance to turn it off before he broke it. That means the gateway's still open, so no way am I gonna work here while a ghost who's obviously pissed that I summoned him has a ticket straight to my door. I'll have my assistant run things for a while. Ghost's got no issue with *him*."

"Okay, you want us to give you a ride home?" He looked too wound up for me to trust him to drive.

"That's not safe, either. I've opened gateways there before. That ghost could sneak in through one—and I don't have any vampires in my apartment who can heal me if he tries to kill me again."

"So where do you want to go? A friend's house?" Hunger and a bone-deep inner chill sharpened my tone. Only being a vampire kept my teeth from chattering. I couldn't wait to cut my connection with the Remnants by sending them back, so I could feel normal again.

Tyler looked at me, then Bones. And smiled.

"No way," I said, not needing to read his mind to figure out what he intended. "No. Way."

"Forget it, mate," Bones replied sternly. "We have enough unwanted guests already without adding one more."

Tyler's smile vanished, and he sank to the floor as if our rebuffs had sapped his strength.

"I'm sorry, but you can't stay with us," I said,

making my voice a lot kinder because Tyler hadn't done anything to warrant my snippiness.

"He's going to find me and kill me," Tyler said again.

I shifted uncomfortably. Maybe it was too dangerous to leave him on his own. Besides, even though he'd dealt with ghosts long before meeting us, we were the reason one had almost put him in the grave just now.

Out of the corner of my eye, I saw Dexter limp over, whining even though he also wagged his stubby tail. Tyler pulled him onto his lap, wincing when the dog let out a sharp cry as his injured leg was jostled.

That was all I could take. I turned to Bones, who was already shaking his head with a distantly jaded expression.

"It'll just be until we take care of Kramer, and he did say that he knew some people who might be able to off a ghost . . ." I began.

Tyler's mournful expression vanished as if by magic. He sprang up, still holding the dog.

"Wait right here. It'll just take me a minute to get my and Dexter's things."

Eight

SEVERAL HOURS LATER, WE PULLED INTO OUR driveway with two more passengers than we'd left with. Dexter's left hind leg was secured in a cast, and his eyes were distinctly glassy because of the pain-killers the vet had administered.

"This is where you live?" Tyler cast a look around at the steep, forested terrain surrounding our Blue Ridge cabin. "I'm amazed I don't hear banjo music."

I ignored the quip, reminding myself that near-death experiences were very traumatic for people who weren't used to them. Besides, it wasn't news to me that our home was in the middle of picturesque nowhere. That had been the intention, so Bones and I would have more privacy. Little did we know that having privacy would prove to be wishful thinking. At least our lack of close neighbors meant Tyler's thoughts were the only ones inside my head aside from my own.

Dexter let out a low whine, picking his head up. "Are you sure it's safe?" Tyler asked. "Dexter's telling me there are ghosts nearby."

Bones let out a sardonic snort as he got out of the car. "Too right."

Tyler had mentioned that he could see ghosts, just not right away. I'd better prepare him for life at Casa Russell. My cat had gotten so used to the ghosts here that he almost never hissed at them anymore.

"There are a lot of ghosts here. All friendly," I hastened to add. "They just, um, like to hang out around our house."

Liar, Tyler thought, his gaze narrowing. Dexter chuffed like he didn't believe me, either. Too bad. Only a select handful of people knew why I was so popular with ghosts, and it wasn't information I was about to share.

"Maybe we built on a former burial ground, and that's why this place is such a hot spot," I improvised as I got out. "You know. Like in *Poltergeist.*"

Lying her pasty white ass off, Tyler thought, but smiled blandly. "Could be, sugar."

I debated telling Tyler that Bones wasn't the only one who could read minds, but decided not to. For all that we'd brought Tyler home with us, we still didn't know him. Getting a peek into his thoughts would go miles toward determining if he was someone we could trust. I didn't perceive him as a threat, but we still had to be careful. We'd already taken a risk by showing him where we lived, but that information could be erased from his memory if need be.

Who was I kidding? With how vigilant Bones was

about my safety, he would probably insist on doing that regardless of how trustworthy Tyler proved to be.

"Go on inside, I'll be there in a minute," I said, heaving a mental sigh as I spread out my hands and waited for the barrage of transparent greeters. I still felt off kilter from summoning the Remnants, but it wouldn't be fair to march into the house without saying hello in the manner that my ghostly acquaintances preferred.

Tyler gave me a strange look but hefted Dexter and went into the house. Five minutes later, my hands tingling, I did as well. Bones wasn't in sight, but I could hear him upstairs on the phone with Spade, and his tone was less than pleased. *That's right, honey, give him hell,* I thought wryly.

I found Tyler in the kitchen, checking out my refrigerator's contents with dismay.

"I know you're both vampires, but a few packets of cheese and some tonic water *can't* be all you have."

"I'll go shopping tomorrow, but you'll have to make do with some canned soups and crackers from the pantry in the meantime." It was not like we'd been expecting company, and I didn't feel like driving forty minutes to get to the grocery store tonight. It would probably close before I arrived, anyway.

Fabian floated up to me, leaning down near my ear.

"I don't know if I like this man," he whispered. "He made a comment questioning your decorating skills upon entering, and now he disparages your hospitality. He won't be staying long, will he?"

"If we're lucky, no," I replied. Tyler's staying a long time would mean we'd failed to stop Kramer, not to mention wreaking havoc on my patience. Neither option was acceptable to me.

Fabian frowned. "Are you well, Cat? You look tired."

"I'll be fine after a shower." A lingering chill still clung to me, and the thought of banishing that under a steady stream of hot water sounded heavenly.

My cat chose that moment to come sauntering down the stairs but stopped short when he spotted Dexter. The dog spotted him, too. He got to his feet—the three that worked, that is—and wagged his tail while emitting a friendly-sounding chuff.

Helsing hissed, his dark hair fluffing out to stand on end. That hiss turned into a garbled, extended growl, with a distinctly threatening undertone while his ears went flat.

"No, no. Be a nice kitty!" I ordered. Poor Dexter had stopped cold and cringed even though he outweighed my cat by about thirty pounds.

Helsing's growl ended with a final hiss before he turned to give me a look that could best be summed up as *A dog? How could you?* Then he ran back up the stairs, tail twitching in agitation the whole way.

Okay, so no one was thrilled about our new guests, but it was only temporary.

"Ohhhh," Tyler drew out, staring to my right. "You've got a ghost floating next to you."

"You can see me?" Fabian asked in surprise.

I left the kitchen to start closing the drapes. "Tyler, meet my friend, Fabian. Fabian, this is Tyler, the medium we went to see today. Things didn't go as

planned, but we'll get into that after I take a shower
. . . and pet my cat until he forgives me."

After a blissfully long, hot shower—and some grov-
eling to my cat that I doubted Helsing understood—I
came downstairs to find Tyler on the couch, wearing
nothing but my favorite blue robe.

"My clothes are in the wash, and it was this or a
towel," he said with a shrug.

Of course Tyler would want to change out of his
bloody outfit. I should've thought to offer him some
of Bones's clothes. "Sorry, I'll get you something else
to wear."

His casual wave stopped me from heading back
upstairs. "This is fine for now."

Fabian buzzed over to me, almost twitching in
anxiety. "It is unseemly that he wears your robe, Cat!"

I bit back a laugh at the ghost's scandalized tone.
Nineteenth-century formalities must be hard to shake
even after death.

Tyler shot Fabian a patient look. "Keep your panties on, ghostfriend, it's only temporary."

Fabian threw up his hands. "You see? He is incor-
rigible!"

"We'll get him some proper clothes straightaway,"
Bones reassured Fabian as he descended the stairs.

"Elisabeth, the man in the robe is Tyler," I introduced when I saw Tyler's gaze fasten on her, finally
noticing her after a few minutes. "Tyler, meet Elisabeth, but don't mention her to any ghosts aside from
Fabian. She's kind of hiding out here."

Tyler smiled. "Charmed to meet another refugee like me."

Elisabeth looked a little confused, but she curtsied, reminding me that I wanted to learn how to do that as gracefully as she.

"Tyler's hiding from Kramer, too," I said in explanation.

"Oh." Her face pinched with compassion. "You poor man."

"Finally, some genuine sympathy." He patted the spot next to him. "Sit here, sweetie, and tell me all about yourself."

"Um, you and Elisabeth can chat later. You mentioned people who might be able to help with Kramer. Do you mean another medium?" I prodded him.

"You are hell and gone from anything a medium can do. Good mediums can open gateways, summon and commune with spirits, clean a house of presences, and sometimes help a ghost cross to the other side. What *you've* got is a nasty, free-range phantom that can poltergeist like nothing I've ever seen."

"We told you that," Bones pointed out.

Tyler rolled his eyes. "Believe me, I wish I'd listened, but that's what most people say. I had no idea you'd be the only ones telling it like it was, and you weren't sure yourselves, either. No medium can help you, but maybe the best damn ghost hunters money can buy will be able to."

"Yeah, well, I hear Bill Murray and the gang don't do that anymore," I countered in growing frustration.

He waved a hand. "Not the Hollywood version.

The real ones, and lucky for you, I happen to know some."

"Give us their names and how to contact them," Bones directed.

Tyler's look grew pointed. "I'll set up a meeting and go with you. Otherwise, just like me, they won't believe how powerful that ghost is until it's too late, and you might not be fast enough to save all of them."

My inner cynic calculated the odds of ghost hunters being able to help us at twenty to one . . . in Kramer's favor. Still, I'd sworn that I would try to see the silver lining instead of only the ominous clouds, so I fetched my cell phone from the counter and handed it to Tyler.

"Make the call."

Tyler rose. "Right after I take a piss."

Once he disappeared into the bathroom, Bones spoke very softly. "Keep trying to tail Kramer, Elisabeth. If there's a particular place he frequents, or any humans he's attentive to, I want to know."

Bones must not have high hopes for the ghost hunters, either. Elisabeth nodded solemnly. "I saw him earlier today. He was not far from the largest ley line in Iowa, at Oktoberfest in Sioux City, but he left quickly. Too quickly for me to see if he'd been interacting with any humans."

"What time was this, do you know?" Bones asked, suspicion edging his emotions.

"Right after midday," she replied.

One-ish Iowa time would've been about 2:00 P.M. in Washington, D.C. Right about the same time that Tyler broke out the Ouija board.

"I think Kramer left in a hurry because he got a page," I said wryly.

Bones's gaze was speculative before he returned his attention to Elisabeth.

"Keep trying to find him, then follow him when you do, but don't let him tail you back here."

I knew how important it was for Elisabeth to find out who Kramer's intended victims were, not to mention the identity of his human accomplice; but after meeting the former Inquisitor, I *really* didn't want him to know where we lived. Sure, I could summon Remnants to our defense if Kramer tracked Elisabeth back here despite her best efforts, but what if he snapped Tyler's neck before I sicced the Remnants on him? Even if I were fast in calling forth my spectral guards, it only took a split second to kill a human, as I well knew.

And sometimes, it only took a split second to kill a vampire, too. We had plenty of silver knives at our house, for obvious reasons. What if the malevolent ghost poltergeisted one of those through Bones's heart before either of us even knew he was near? I shivered at the thought.

"What's wrong, Kitten?" Bones asked, his sharp gaze picking it up.

I forced a smile. No more what-if thoughts of worst-case scenarios. *Silver linings and glasses half-full, remember?*

"Nothing."

Nine

A HUGE BUILDING LOOMED IN FRONT OF us, dark exterior looking ominous even with the many gold-edged leaves on the trees surrounding the grounds. Hundreds of windows reflected the moonlight as if in stark rejection of any illumination penetrating the structure's interior. Every so often, shadows would pass by those windows, and voices would drift out on the crisp autumn air, but the former hospital was empty.

Well, empty of anyone who was solid. All the members of N.I.P.D., the Northeastern Investigative Paranormal Division that Tyler had recommended, were still outside with us. They'd just finished setting up their equipment in various rooms of the former Waverly Hills Sanatorium. Now they were huddled up in a final group pep talk before they started their documentation of everything that went bump in the night here.

The sanatorium might have closed decades ago, but it was quite the popular attraction, as it turned out. The curious paid for guided tours of the facility, hearing all about its history and the many anecdotes of ghostly encounters. Amateur or professional paranormal buffs could opt to have the hospital all to themselves for a night of investigation, provided they paid the proper amount and booked in advance. Waverly Hills Sanatorium had a waiting list, and the owners didn't give refunds if a group missed its scheduled appointment.

That was why Bones and I were meeting the investigators—they didn't like the term "ghost hunters," as it turned out—here instead of at a local coffee shop or somewhere else normal. They'd planned their evening at Waverly weeks ago and weren't about to lose their time slot—or their money—just to talk to Tyler's new clients, as they considered Bones and me. For our part, we weren't willing to waste another day and night before finding out if they could help with Kramer. After Tyler set up our chat, we hopped in the car for a road trip to Louisville, Kentucky. Taking a plane would have been faster, but we weren't about to go anywhere unarmed, and airport security frowned on suitcases filled with a stockpile of weapons.

Tyler refused to leave Dexter behind, saying the dog would give us precious seconds of warning if Kramer was about to spoof up. Dexter did seem to have an uncanny radar for ghosts; he'd begun to whine in that eerie way of his as soon as we pulled up to the sanitarium. By comparison, it took Tyler a few minutes *after* we arrived to even see the shadows passing by the windows. Of the two of them, I had to admit that Dexter seemed to be the more qualified medium. *Maybe Spade's demonologist friends really recommended Dexter, and the message somehow got garbled,* I thought ruefully.

"Let's get this party started!" Chris, N.I.P.D.'s team leader, finished his pep talk with.

"Finally," Bones muttered, too low for anyone but me to overhear.

We'd promised not to start with our questions until all of their prep work was done, having been told that setting up was too crucial for distractions. Little did we know how much prep work they were talking about. We'd been standing outside for a good two hours. If left to himself, Bones might have green-eyed Chris and the others into forgetting about their set-up-first conditions, but he knew I would have objected to that. We were here because we wanted their help, not the other way around. Besides, two hours of polite waiting wasn't going to make or break our circumstances with Kramer.

Unless he showed up soon in another murderous mood.

"So," Chris said, sizing us up as he approached. I didn't mind that he'd barely glanced our way before this. All his attention had been on making sure his team was prepared, and that was a plus in my book. "What's this big, urgent issue that Tyler tells me can't wait until tomorrow?"

Bones glanced at the van with N.I.P.D. painted on the side, the endless cords for their equipment, and the dozen team members bustling about before he replied.

"You doing this because you truly believe in activity on the other side, or because you want to make a bit of profit off the gullible?"

Chris bristled, his cheeks becoming ruddier above his beard while his scent flared with anger. That wasn't what I paid attention to. It was his spate of thoughts.

So sick of dealing with ignorant pricks who can't see beyond what society tells them to believe. Never should've agreed to let Tyler bring them here tonight; we've got too much work to do.

"I have a Master of Science in Engineering from Stanford, so I can make more money with a hell of a lot less effort in about a hundred different fields," he replied evenly. "If that doesn't answer your question, then you're wasting my time."

Satisfaction flitted across the edge of my emotions. Someone smart who was passionate about his work and dedicated to his team was more than I'd hoped for. Maybe Tyler had hit a home run directing us here.

"Make sure you do EVPs and take lots of pictures on five," Chris called out to a young woman who hurried past us.

I glanced up toward the sixth floor, where I'd seen the most shadows pass by the windows. This facility primarily contained residual ghosts; brief, repeating snapshots of people who had long since passed on, no more sentient than a splice of frames from a film reel. Judging by the levels of energy emanating from the building, a couple sentient spirits also called Waverly Hills home, but they didn't stick to one place in this huge facility. The sixth floor would yield the best chance for pictures of unexplainable shadows or orbs. Not anything that would make headline news, but at least it'd be something tangible that Chris's group could take home with them. They'd rented this place for the night; might as well help steer them into getting their money's worth.

"Try six instead," I suggested. "You'll have better luck."

Chris's gaze narrowed. "Five has had more reported cases of incidents," he countered.

I smiled blandly. "Six will net you more solid data, but hey. It's your show."

Chris looked at Tyler, who nodded in confirmation. Bones just folded his arms, his coolly detached expression revealing nothing. The young woman balanced her tripod camera on her hip, and I didn't need to tap into her thoughts to know it was heavy. Chris gave a last, musing glance at me before he spoke again.

"Start on six first, Lexie."

Fucking tourists should just keep their mouths shut, Lexie thought, but her "sure thing!" was as cheerful as it was false. I wasn't offended. She could take orders and knew when to keep her opinions to herself. Again my hopes lifted about this group.

"Follow me," Chris said after a measured silence. "We'll talk while I work."

* * *

We had covered most of the first floor by the time I finished telling Chris what we were looking for, and why. He kept his verbal comments to a minimum; but from his thoughts, Chris had trouble believing who Kramer was, not to mention the extent of the Inquisitor's abilities. Just like Tyler predicted. That was okay. Two sentient—and chatty—ghosts had been not-so-stealthily following me from the moment I crossed through Waverly Hills' doors. From their matching, dated clothes, I deduced that they were former patients of the facility. Their comments to each other revealed that since they'd died, they liked to pass the time by playing pranks on visitors, especially ghost investigators. Perfect.

I waited until Chris paused in front of what looked like a large, lengthy tunnel before I put my plan into action.

"You, hiding behind the support beam, what's your name?" I said to the ghost currently skulking a few yards off. He came out with a "busted" expression on his filmy countenance, twisting the edges of his long-sleeved, pale pajamas.

"Herbert."

"Who are you talking to?" Chris wondered, looking in that direction but, of course, seeing no one.

"One of Waverly's former residents," I replied, thinking the ghost was too young and cute to be named Herbert. "Can you do me a favor, Herbert? Fly through the bearded man's body. *Only* the bearded man."

Herbert obeyed without hesitation. Dexter barked once at the ghost's zooming approach, but before

Chris finished muttering, "What kind of joke is this?" the ghost dove right through his upper torso and appeared out on the other side.

Chris stood absolutely still. Thoughts skidded across his mind almost too fast for me to read. *Guts feel cold. Tingly, but she couldn't actually be able to direct a ghost to do what she wants, could she? No fuckin' way.*

"Stomach feels a bit unusual? A little icy and shivery, maybe?" I asked softly.

"How do you know that?" he asked.

"Ooh, that looks fun!" the other ghost cried, abandoning his attempt at hiding in the ceiling ducts to dive through Chris's upper right side. More chaos sounded in Chris's mind. Dexter barked again.

"You just had that same icy, prickling feeling in your right shoulder this time," I said in a matter-of-fact way. "There's another ghost in the room, and he's a little playful. But if you need more proof that this isn't a coincidence, I can tell them to do more demonstrations."

The word "no" resounded in his mind, but Chris swallowed hard and nodded.

"Yeah. One more."

Had to admire his courage. Chris might have studied paranormal phenomena and believed in ghosts for years, but I knew firsthand that having a ghost repeatedly bullet through your flesh was an unsettling experience.

"Herbert, one more time, please."

The ghost complied, choosing Chris's left calf to zip through this time. He was quickly followed by his buddy, who took the same path. Two shudders rocked Chris before his widened hazel gaze met mine. I shrugged.

"You felt that in your lower left leg. Twice, because his friend thought it looked fun, too."

"Who *are* you people?" Chris asked with a touch of incredulity.

Bones draped an arm around my shoulder, smiling languidly at the investigator.

"We're wealthy and on a timetable. Any more questions?"

Chris swallowed again as his mind spun to compartmentalize all that had just happened. *What if she isn't wrong about who this other ghost is, and what he can do? Still, even if it's risky, there's too much to learn to say no.*

"One more question," he said at last. "When do you want my team to get started on your problem?"

"Tomorrow," Bones stated, his arched brow hinting that objections wouldn't be acceptable.

Chris cleared his throat, a businesslike composure replacing his former uncertainty. "So we're clear, I don't know how to kill a ghost. I don't even think that's possible. What I do know, in theory, is how to imprison one, but for that you'd need to supply me with a lot of limestone, naturally running water, quartz, and moissanite."

"Not a problem, you'll have everything you need when you start tomorrow," Bones replied without hesitation.

"He will?" Okay, I knew Bones approached every

challenge with confidence, but it's not like we could buy all those things at our local Walmart tonight.

He gave me a bland look. "Yeah, he will, Kitten."

I stared at him in confusion until understanding dawned. "*Oh*," I drew out. Then I grinned at Chris. "Not a problem at all."

Ten

I SHIELDED MY EYES FROM THE BRIGHT BEAM on Chris's hard hat as he swung around in my direction. The glare was almost painful, but without those streams of light, Chris and his team would have been completely sightless in the cave. Bones and I had no need of artificial aid to see, and in any event, we both knew this place like the back of our hands. After all, this was where our relationship had begun.

"Reckon there should be enough limestone and running water for you here, and five hundred pounds of quartz and moissanite will be delivered later," Bones stated, his wave encompassing the rocky underground riverbed we were gathered on. "Will that be sufficient?"

Chris's headlight was aimed at Bones's face, but unlike me, he didn't blink under its harsh glare.

"It's enough, but underground like this, cramped quarters, no electricity . . . it'll take me a month at least to build the trap. Of course, the real problem is what'll happen if the owner of this cave finds out what we're doing."

"No worries. I'm the owner, and it's wired for electricity in places," Bones replied.

Chris's response reverberated across my mind. *These people get stranger by the minute.* "Great," was what he said out loud. "Then in a few weeks, you'll have—"

"Two," Bones interrupted with a pleasant smile. The screech of protest in Chris's head was silenced when Bones added, "Unless you're not interested in a thirty percent bonus for each of you?"

Money might not be his primary motivator in being here, but Chris was interested in that bonus, and so were his crew. Over half of them were back at their headquarters examining the data from the sanitarium, but the four Chris felt were the most experienced were here. Lexie, Fred, Graham, and Nancy nudged each other, mentally and verbally running down different ways they could improve their efficiency.

"I think we could manage that," Chris replied after a quick huddle with them.

"Splendid. You doubtless guessed that this work is strictly confidential, but here's your reminder. No photos, video, or maps of the cave, and no mention of this to any of your mates." The barest flash of green glinted in Bones's eyes. "In fact, you are never to speak of this job to anyone once you're finished. Understood?"

A subdued chorus of affirmatives followed. I had no doubt that in addition to mesmerizing this promise out of them, Bones would also manage to erase the records of our transactions with N.I.P.D. once they were finished. They'd all probably end up thinking they won their money due to office quick-pick lotto tickets or something.

For once, I didn't think Bones was going over-board. This cave had been used as an ambush against me in the past when some vampires found out about it. I'd killed them, so the cave's significance—and location—had slid back into obscurity. Now we were forced to reveal it to Chris's team because it was made of limestone and had an underground river; two out of the four requirements for a ghost trap. Throw in the quartz and moissanite Bones was having delivered via trusted vampire courier, and we had all the necessary ingredients. Just any old cave wouldn't do. We had to make sure the place that would—hopefully—serve as Kramer's eternal prison was private and secure. Couldn't stick a homicidal ghost in a cave where in-nocent spelunkers could free Kramer if they knocked over the wrong rock.

"Right, then." Bones cracked his knuckles. "Let's look for a section that will work best for the trap. Can't have you wandering through here without us. You'd get lost."

And with the cave's dampness and internal tem-perature being a brisk fifty degrees, anyone lost would soon develop hypothermia. Since they'd be working here for two weeks, we'd have to bring in space heat-ers for the crew. Those had done the trick for me when I was half-human and spent many nights here with Bones.

"Are you sure you can see all right without a light?" Chris asked, doubt clear in his tone.

I had to bite my lip to stuff back my laugh. Bones's teeth shone in pearly brilliance as he flashed Chris a grin.

"Quite sure."

I lifted my leg out of the hot, soapy water, giving my foot a critical evaluation. After a nice soak in the tub, no more hints of dirt underneath my toenails, good. Helping the crew set up the trap in a shallow part of the underground river so it would be surrounded on all sides with running water meant that my feet had spent hours in finely ground silt during the past week. Bones did the heavy lifting—literally—with hauling the rocky debris in and out to make a solid platform for the trap. Chris and the other members of N.I.P.D. no longer questioned why I could stand in icy water for hours without showing any ill effects, or why Bones could pull large boulders off their perches with nary a busted hernia to show for it. A few flashes of green from our gaze took care of their curiosity on those issues.

With Bones and me helping the group lay the foundations of the trap, which was the hardest part, Chris said we were ahead of schedule. That was music to my ears. The sooner things were finished here, the sooner we could test the trap to see if it worked. Already Fabian had mentioned that the new, large quantities of quartz and moissanite made going in and out of the cave feel like traveling through a thick spider's web, and they weren't even positioned yet. Chris must know what he was talking about.

Bones appeared in the bathroom doorway, letting his gaze slide over me twice before he spoke. I had the shower curtain open, so his view was uninterrupted.

"Going out for a bit, luv."

I didn't ask what for. Bones might double as my all-you-can-eat buffet, but my blood didn't have enough life in it to sustain him. Only human blood did, and he didn't want to weaken any of N.I.P.D.'s crew by feeding off them.

Plus, that would strike me as, well, rude.

"See you when you get back," I said, lifting my leg all the way out just to enjoy the heady change in his scent as I soaped it, caressing my skin a little more than necessary.

"Tease," he murmured, voice huskier than it had been moments ago.

I learned from the best, I thought, but blinked like I didn't know what he was talking about.

"Didn't you say you were leaving?"

Green began to replace the mahogany in his gaze, his scent richening even further. Almost idly, he stroked his collar, pale fingers flicking between the fabric and the luscious curve of his neck.

Shivers broke out across my skin even though I was several degrees warmer than normal from being submerged in the tub. The line where his neck met his broad shoulders was my second-favorite place to bite him. Bones shifted to lean against the frame, as if he were positioning himself more comfortably, but what it did was send ripples along his muscles that even the dark pullover he wore couldn't hide. One leg casually crossing over the other drew my attention down his body, noting how the fabric briefly clung to a rock-hard thigh before loosening and concealing the defined shape beneath.

Need flared in me, causing my nipples to harden and strands of exquisite sensation to tighten in my loins. And all of this was before I noticed that his hips were slightly tilted, allowing for a better view of the growing bulge in the front of his pants.

"Tell me, Kitten." That deep, smooth voice brushed over me like a physical caress. "Shall I leave now, or wait until later?"

His eyes glowed pure emerald, half smile letting me know how much he enjoyed this game. I did, too. If I admitted that I couldn't wait for him to feed, he'd join me in the tub, but then would draw out the foreplay until I begged him to take me. And he would, chuckling at my impatience while possessing me with hard, slow strokes. At that thought, more nerve endings tightened in silent demand.

But if I told him to feed first, his own lust would build while he was forced to wait and seek out a nice vein to secretly suck on. By the time he came back, he'd be almost ruthless in his passion—and Bones in a primal state was truly something to experience.

At that thought, heat swept through my body like the water had suddenly turned into flames. I licked my lips and cleared my throat, but my voice still came out as a gravelly purr.

"Go now." *So all that lovely lust can build until it rips away your control.*

Bolts of power unleashed from his aura, filling the air to land on my skin like velvet-lined whips. His mouth opened, fangs dragging across his lower lip until they drew glittering drops of blood. My gaze latched there, and it was all I could do to keep from charging out of the tub to catch those drops before they rolled off his lip.

"Are you sure?"

Merciless tease! Drinking Bones's blood while he was inside me was the most incredible thing ever—and he knew it. A creaking noise warned me that I gripped the edge of the tub so hard, it was about to shatter under my hand.

"Go." No purr, all growl now. Bones wouldn't be the only one burning with unrequited desire until he got back.

I vowed erotic retribution for the knowing smile he gave me before he disappeared from the doorframe. A soft click was our hotel room door shutting behind him moments later. I leaned back, blowing out a sigh of sheer willpower. I would not call out for him to come back even though I knew he'd be lingering close by to see if I did. I'd show him that I could tease him with the same sensual resolve that he'd so often shown me.

And my reward for patience now would be a lover who was single-minded in his domination of my body later. More tremors of anticipation rippled through me. I smoothed my hands over my nipples and down my thighs, tempted to reach lower and release a little of that simmering tension before he got back, but decided not to. Some things were worth the wait, and Bones was definitely one of those things.

I'd drained the tub and was busy rinsing conditioner from my hair when my cat let out an extended yowl that was loud enough to be heard over the shower. In the next room, Dexter barked sharply, ending on a piercing whine. I tensed. Helsing might be temperamental for no reason, but I'd only heard the dog bark that way when—

Something slammed against the back of my head with enough force to send my face crashing into the wall in front of me. I spun around, blinking to get the tiny tile shards out of my eyes thanks to the new head-sized hole in the wall, but even though I couldn't see, I knew who'd attacked me. *Kramer.* How had the ghost managed to sneak up on me without any of my inner warning bells going off?

"*Hexe,*" the heavily accented voice of the Inquisitor hissed.

I ripped the iron shower rod off the wall, whipping it like a sword toward the source of that voice before realizing the futility in the gesture.

"Oh, if you had flesh, I'd beat the *ass* off you!" I swore, throwing the rod aside.

My vision cleared enough for me to see the tunic-clad figure about six feet away. The exposed cistern and chunks of ruined ceramic at my feet showed that Kramer had used the toilet tank lid to bash the back of my head. Fucker had slid that off quiet as a mouse, hadn't he? I braced to dodge whatever other bathroom items he might try to bludgeon me with next, but after a disgusted moment, I saw that Kramer's attention was focused on the apex of my wide-legged fighter's stance.

A towel was within reach, but I fought my urge to snatch it up because one, I didn't want to give him the satisfaction of acting ashamed, and two, my cold-blooded practicality recognized that distraction was a weapon.

Luckily, it wasn't the only weapon I had.

I shoved my hand into the hole my face had formed in the wall, bloodying it on the ragged tile edges. "Sic him and don't let him leave," I snarled, willing forth the Remnants with all the energy I had.

Kramer's eyes widened right before he rapidly began to fade. But aside from the cool blast of air I felt, covering my skin with gooseflesh from head to toe, nothing else happened.

"I said, sic him!" I repeated, slicing my hand so hard that the tile crumpled beneath my force.

Nothing. The only thing filling the room was my growing alarm. What was the problem? I had blood running down my fingers, my skin felt as though it crawled with icy ants, and I wanted the Remnants here like damn, but my fiendishly lethal, wrath-of-the-grave buddies were nowhere to be seen.

Kramer must have heard or sensed that I wasn't able to summon help, because he rematerialized into such clarity that I could see the white stubble on his chin and the different places where his tunic was rent from age. But despite cutting my hand repeatedly and concentrating hard enough to make my jaw grind, he was still the only apparition in the bathroom.

Eleven

THE WORST FEELING OF DÉJÀ VU WASHED over me. I'd counted on borrowed abilities once before in a fight only to discover they were no longer in working order. I should've never made that same mistake again. *Fool me twice, shame on me!*

The Inquisitor bared his teeth in something too cruel to be called a smile. "You see? God strikes down your powers of witchcraft in my defense!"

"Boy, are you wrong about who's got your back," I spat, trying to regroup. Okay, so I could no longer summon Remnants to my aid, but there must be *some*thing I could do aside from cringe and duck.

"My instructions are from on high, for 'thou shall not suffer a witch to live,'" Kramer thundered.

"'You are not under the law, but grace. Judge not lest ye be judged. He that is without sin among you, let him cast the first stone,'" I shot back. "How come you didn't pay attention to *those* instructions from on high, you filthy hypocrite?"

Surprise flickered across Kramer's features, but my childhood had been spent in a household where church attendance and Bible reading were the norm, so I could trade Scripture quotes with him all day long. Then that surprise faded, and Kramer's expression returned to its normal mask of vindictiveness.

Despite my determination to find a way to kick the Inquisitor's ass, dread still slivered up my spine. I was stark naked in a small room with a powerful, pissed-off ghost who'd already brained me with a toilet fixture, and my only effective weapon against him was out of order. For the first time in my long history of life-and-death standoffs, I had no idea what to do next. All the battle training I'd worked so hard to master would do me no good under these circumstances. I couldn't hurt what I couldn't touch, and Kramer was no more solid than a dreaded memory. As if he could sense my uncertainty, the Inquisitor's smile widened.

Hearing our hotel room door crash open almost made me sag in relief. Bones must have come back. Even though he couldn't land a physical blow against Kramer, either, two against one odds would buy us some time to come up with a plan—

"You messed with the *wrong* white girl, motherfucker!" Tyler shouted.

I don't know who was more shocked, me or Kramer. The formerly timid medium appeared in the doorway, holding a smoking trash can with what looked like burning vines stuffed inside it. His gaze darted around the bathroom, seeking out the assailant he couldn't see yet.

I had no idea what Tyler intended, but I was willing to help. "There!" I said, pointing at Kramer.

The ghost stared at Tyler, his head cocked, almost as if he were curious to see what the medium was up to. Tyler dug out a handful of those burning vines, cursing as they singed his fingers, and threw them in the direction I'd indicated.

Kramer screamed as soon as the first ones sailed through the space he occupied. His form dissolved, but a huge chunk of the countertop smashed off and hurtled toward Tyler. The medium ducked with a quickness I hadn't expected of him, and the makeshift missile landed in the bathroom wall instead.

I didn't know what was in that trash can. It wasn't garlic and weed from the smell of it, but anything that hurt Kramer was something I wanted to utilize. I lunged forward, grabbing the smoldering vines off the bathroom floor, and threw them after the hazy outline of the ghost.

Kramer shrieked again as the vines passed through him. Whatever the stuff was, I *loved* it.

"Over here," I urged Tyler, snatching up another handful. Tyler and I threw our burning bundles at the ghost like a couple of synchronized baseball pitchers. The edges of the smoking plants brushed Kramer before he could make himself poof out of the way. With a final, pained scream, the Inquisitor vanished from sight completely.

"Run, fucker, run!" I shouted, so relieved we had something else to use as a weapon that I could've hugged Tyler until his ribs creaked. I didn't do that, but I did give him a brief squeeze that nevertheless elicited an oof.

"Personal space," Tyler chided, when I let him go. "And, you know, a towel would be the least you could put on."

I burst out laughing. For years, I'd been discomfited by the blasé attitude most vampires had about nudity, and yet here I was, hugging someone I'd known less than two weeks while wearing nothing but some stray suds.

I covered myself with the closest item at hand, Bones's leather jacket, which stuck to my wet skin. "Sorry. Kramer kind of interrupted my shower . . ."

My voice trailed off because Bones suddenly appeared in the room, silver knives in each hand and dark gaze raking over us.

"I heard you scream. What happened?"

Tyler still held the trash can, its smoldering contents filling the room with a slight haze. As if on cue, the fire alarm began blaring, and water shot out from the sprinklers on the wall. In the next room, Dexter started to whine in time with the whooping of the alarm.

"What happened is my borrowed powers are kaput, and Tyler's really a badass in disguise," I replied, nudging the medium. "Look at you, busting through that door to lay the smackdown on Kramer."

Bones's gaze raked over Tyler with a new appreciation. "Well done, mate." Then he switched his knives to one hand and ran the other one over my neck. "You've blood on you. Are you all right?"

He knew that any wounds a vampire sustained would heal almost instantly, but his hand still traveled over me as if searching for injuries. Emotions tangled along my subconscious, flaring through his shields with their intensity. Concern, rage at my attack, and guilt that he hadn't been here when it happened.

"Don't," I said, taking his hand. "How could we have known Kramer would find us here, or that Marie's abilities would finally run their course?"

A little inner voice said I should have suspected that my borrowed powers were wearing off. For the past week, no new ghosts had found their way to me, but I'd figured all the time I spent in the cave around the limestone, quartz, and flowing water trap had possibly dulled my signal to the other side.

"Makes me wonder how he found us now," Bones said, his brows drawing together.

I shrugged. "Ohio's a haven for the supernatural, and we've been traipsing back and forth in public for over a week. Maybe one of Kramer's ghost buddies saw us and tipped him off. Maybe he happened to be in the area because he was drawn here like countless other ghosts."

"Or perhaps Kramer followed Elisabeth here after one of her failed tailing attempts," Bones said darkly.

That was also a possibility, and I'd be sure to tell the ghost to be extra careful in the future.

"Just what we need," I muttered, as a flustered hotel employee appeared in our doorway. Whatever he'd been about to say died on his lips as he took in Tyler, still holding the smoking trash can, and Bones and me ignoring the water spraying down on us.

"Small mishap concerning a dropped cigarette in the trash, but it's all sorted out now," Bones stated while flashing an emerald glare at the employee. "Go back and tell them to shut off the alarm and sprinklers."

The employee turned around without another word. I waited until he was out of sight before speaking again.

"We need to check on Chris and the others. What if I wasn't the first person Kramer attacked?"

Bones nodded, muttering, "Stay here," to Tyler.

"No, he needs to come, too." It was safer to be in a group in case Kramer lurked nearby, waiting to pick off any stragglers. "Besides, he might have more of whatever it is that scared Kramer off."

"It's sage," Tyler replied, squaring his shoulders. "Would've used it on Kramer that day at my shop, but I was too busy almost dying. I have more of it in my room. Besides, I'm not going anywhere without Dexter."

I dropped to my knees beside the bed, Helsing's rapid heartbeat letting me know where he was. Smart feline had run for cover once the porcelain started flying. How I'd fight a ghost while clutching a panicked cat was anyone's guess, but I, too, wasn't going to risk leaving him alone in the room if Kramer came back looking for round two.

"Come on, kitty," I murmured. "We're outta here."

I dropped my suitcase inside the small bedroom that had been mine from birth to age twenty-two. A fine layer of dust covered the windowsills and furniture, but I didn't have time to start cleaning. First things first, and that was prepping the house for way more guests than there was room for.

"Set up the EMF meters in the kitchen and family room," I heard Chris direct. "Then I want infrared and RK2s in place in the other rooms. Nothing spectral comes through these walls without our knowing it, people."

"You do that. I'm sticking close to Dexter. He'll know if a ghost is coming before any of your machines do," Tyler muttered, coming up the stairs.

Given the dog's track record, I tended to agree. Even Helsing had proven that he could sense Kramer's approach, but if the equipment Chris set up could provide an additional warning, who was I to scorn helpful technology? Dexter and Helsing had to sleep sometimes.

The good news was no one else had been visited by Kramer at the hotel. The bad news was that it wouldn't take Kramer long to correct that oversight if we stayed, so we'd needed a new place that was still within reasonable driving distance of the cave. Plus, the fewer innocent bystanders near us, the better if Kramer did find us again. He hadn't proven to be considerate of others.

That made my former childhood home our best option for the next few days until the trap was completed. My mother had sold it after my grandparents died and we relocated with my new secret government job, but I'd bought it back after a nice couple had been murdered here by vampires trying to draw me out. Since then, most people thought the place was empty. Normally, it was. I kept the electric and water on, since Bones and I occasionally stayed here when we visited Ohio. The orchard surrounding this house hadn't been harvested in years. My frugal grandfather must be turning over in his grave at the waste of so many perfectly good cherry trees. Still, the acres of overgrown orchard acted as a natural privacy barrier, hiding any lights or activity in the house from our closest neighbors.

Bones came into the bedroom, lining the windows and furniture tops with a heavy layer of minced garlic and marijuana. The former had been procured after a quick stop at an all-night grocery store, but the latter required green-eyeing a local drug dealer into giving up his entire stock. I wish I could say it had been hard to find someone peddling weed in my hometown, but it had only taken a few minutes driving through a derelict neighborhood to detect the distinctive smell and follow it to its source.

Now I could add robbing a drug dealer to my list of crimes, but what was I supposed to do? Reimburse him? That somehow seemed equally wrong, not to mention going against the "crime doesn't pay" message, but I had to admit I still felt guilty stealing the weed even though what I was doing with it was arguably more noble. Burning sage might work as a sort of supernatural flamethrower against Kramer, but the real goal was to not let him find us again. Not until we had that trap ready, anyway.

I pulled some extra blankets out of the closet and handed them to Tyler, who came in as Bones was leaving to spread more of the stinky mixture around the house.

"Pass these out downstairs," I told Tyler. "I'll get more from the other room."

There might not be enough for everyone to get their own blanket, but thank God the heater worked, and I could get more blankets tomorrow. And air mattresses. The house only had two bedrooms, and there were eight of us, but safety concerns had to overrule comforts and conveniences.

Tyler took the blankets and I foraged through the guest room for more, grabbing a couple long tablecloths from the linen closet as well. Still not enough. I went back into my old room and stripped the bed, netting me two more blankets and a set of sheets. Bones and I could sleep with our jackets covering us. As vampires, we were in no danger of catching cold.

"Do you have anything to drink here?" I heard Graham ask, dismay in his voice.

"Just tap water, sorry," I replied, coming down the stairs with my big bundle. "I'll get some food and beverages tomorrow."

Graham sighed. "No problem." Yet his thoughts belied his words.

I sure hope this bitch isn't making all this up as a desperate ploy for attention. We've been on this job over a week, and we still only have her word that this phantom exists, let alone is a threat to anyone. She could just be off her meds or on the rag—

"Hey!" Graham suddenly yelped, his hand flying to his cheek. "Something just *hit* me!"

I tensed. Red streaks marred Graham's cheek like the imprint from an invisible hand, and the air was indeed prickled with a new, angry energy, skipping across my skin like sandpaper. I glanced at Dexter, but the dog was silent, and though I didn't see where Helsing was, no distinctive feline growl split the sudden silence after Graham's pronouncement.

"Check the EMFs, the infrared, and the temperature gauges," Chris ordered, his gaze darting around. "We might not be the only ones here anymore."

Lexie, Fred, and Nancy hurried to comply. But then I found the source of that pulsating, seething energy, and my jaw dropped.

Bones stood in the hallway, fists slowly clenching and emerald blazing from his gaze as he stared at Graham.

"Don't *ever* disrespect my wife that way again."

Each word was a low, furious growl that caused all activity in the room to screech to a halt. Every head swung in Bones's direction, then mine wasn't the only sagging jaw as the crew took in his fangs and glowing green eyes. Only Tyler kept his cool, but then again, he hadn't just discovered a shocking new truth like the rest of us had.

For Chris, Lexie, Fred, Graham, and Nancy, it was the discovery that vampires existed. For me, it was the realization that *Bones* had been the one to strike Graham, and he'd done it without moving from his spot across the room.

TWELVE

CHRIS FOUND HIS VOICE BEFORE I DID.
"What the hell is going on here?"

Sounds upset, but not hysterical. Good for him, I
thought, still in a daze from the knowledge that Bones
had slapped Graham using only the power from his
mind. Up until now, only one other vampire in the
world could do the same thing, and that vampire was
over four thousand years old. Bones hadn't even hit
his bicentennial birthday yet.

But that former pharaoh, Mencheres, was Bones's
co-ruler, and he'd shared some of his staggering power
with Bones when they merged lines a while back. Immediately upon receiving that supernatural transfu-
sion, Bones's strength had tripled, and he'd gained
the ability to read human minds. I'd often wondered
if any other abilities might crop up as time went on.
Guess I should wonder no more.

But why didn't he tell me before this? Like, *Oh,*

by the by, Kitten, I'm telekinetic now. Fancy that, hmm?

"So that was you?" Tyler relaxed as he figured out that Bones's words combined with his furious glare meant that Kramer wasn't the one who'd hit Graham.

Bones looked at me, some of the tightness leaving his features.

"It would seem so."

My initial spurt of irritation melted away. Good God, this ability was news to him, too?

"You didn't know?" I asked softly.

His mouth twisted. "Wasn't sure until now."

"I will walk out of here right now if someone doesn't start making a lot of sense," Chris swore. He wasn't the only one who'd started to edge toward the front door, I noticed.

"Ghosts aren't the only freaky things that exist," Tyler summed up before I could phrase a more gentle reply. The medium waved at me and Bones. "Meet the vampires."

Lexie let out a nervous laugh. Graham looked like he wanted to throw up. From their thoughts, Fred and Nancy were each contemplating dialing 911. Chris's mind tilted between denial and an odd sense of triumph, like he'd suspected there was more to the supernatural world but hadn't known what it was.

"There's no need to worry," I said while wondering if I'd have to stop some of them from calling the police. "We don't kill people—well, not people who don't *deserve* it, that is, and—"

Graham screamed, trying to run for the door.

Bones had him dangling by the front of his shirt in the next blink, throwing me a sardonic look.

"Best not to mention any killing in a reveal speech, luv."

"Right." I sighed, catching Lexie and Fred as they also made a break for it. "Don't worry," I ordered, turning the brights on in my gaze. "We're not going to hurt you!"

They relaxed like I'd shot them each with a dart full of Valium. Bones whispered something I didn't catch to Graham, but he, too, soon had a glazed and compliant expression. Chris watched everything in silence and complete stillness, his mental somersaulting the only indication that he was far less calm than he looked.

"The way you move . . . both of you are only a blur," he said at last.

I shrugged. "The myths got some things right. Superspeed is one of them."

"What did the myths get wrong?" he asked at once.

"Uncontrollable need to kill, wooden stakes, exploding in sunlight, cringing at crosses, lack of reflection, and, oh, the stiff-collared capes. I mean, honestly, *who* would go out in public wearing one of those?"

"Fashion tragedy," Tyler agreed.

Chris continued to stare. "You forgot mind control."

"Saw that for yourself, didn't you?" Bones replied. His tone was light, but his gaze didn't waver from Chris's. "You and your crew won't remember any of this once the trap is completed, but until then, I want you to know what you're dealing with. Then perhaps one of you won't again tempt me to violence with his thoughts."

Despite the maelstrom in his mind, Chris's bearded chin thrust out.

"Don't threaten my crew."

Bones's brow ticked up. "Or you'll do what?" he asked mildly.

Chris swallowed hard. "I won't finish the trap you're so interested in," he replied. If I hadn't heard his mental prayer that these wouldn't turn out to be his last words, I'd have sworn he had balls of steel.

Bones clapped Chris on the shoulder in a friendly way that still caused the other man to flinch. "I could trance you into doing the same, but you've got bravery and loyalty, both of which I value. Keep your crew in line, and you'll have no worries."

"They can't help their thoughts, Bones," I pointed out. Sure, I'd been annoyed at Graham's crude musings, but clearly not as pissed as Bones if they'd triggered a telekinetic response he didn't know he was capable of.

Then again, anger had usually been the trigger with my borrowed abilities, and that was before I'd known I had them, too. Maybe anger was just the normal way new abilities manifested themselves. How was I supposed to know?

"Now they're warned that their thoughts aren't private, so they have only themselves to blame if they don't keep a leash on them," was his unrelenting reply. "They should be focused on the task at hand, not on insolently pondering whether you fabricated tales of a ghost because you neglected your medication, were desperate for attention, or crazed from your monthlies."

"Jesus, Graham," Chris muttered.

"Figures. Every time something happens with a woman, you guys always bring up her period," Lexie said, to an accompanying snort of agreement from Nancy.

Graham flushed. "I didn't say it out loud."

"And now you know that doesn't matter," Bones stated curtly, green flashing in his eyes again.

I cleared my throat to defuse the tension. "Okay, everyone relax and remember we just have to get through completing the trap. Then you'll go on with your lives with a nice fat bonus, and there'll be one less murdering creep floating around. I think we can all agree that's a goal worth working toward."

Cautious murmurs of assent sounded, but I hadn't been looking for a fervent chorus of "whoo hoo's!" so that was good enough for me.

"Bones." I gave a weary glance out the window where the sun was starting to creep up over the horizon. "Let's get some sleep. We have a lot to do later."

I'd just finished putting away the groceries when my cell phone rang, its musical cadence shattering the quiet. It was just Bones and I in the house at the moment. We'd dropped the others off at the cave while we gathered enough odds and ends to keep half a dozen humans comfortable during their stay here.

I expected to see Tyler or Chris's cell number when I grabbed my phone, but instead the word BLOCKED appeared. *Telemarketer,* I thought in annoyance, and was about to hit IGNORE when I paused. What if it was someone calling on Fabian's behalf? The ghost had to rely on others to make a call for him since he lacked the ability to physically dial, and his voice came through only as static over the phone. Fabian might have shown up at the hotel last night only to find all of us checked out and no information on where we'd gone to. Even if he'd thought to try the cave and heard from Tyler where we were staying now, with all the garlic and weed I was sporting in my clothes, not to mention what was set up around the house, Fabian might not be able to reach me.

Just in case it was a solicitor, though, I answered the phone with an unfriendly-sounding hello.

"Crawfield?" an equally abrupt voice asked.

No telemarketer would have my correct name since this number was listed under one of my many aliases. But though that voice was vaguely familiar, I couldn't place a name to it.

"Who's this?"

"Jason Madigan."

Ah, the team's infamous new operations consultant. From his tone, Madigan's sourpuss mood hadn't improved since our first meeting.

"To what do I owe this honor?" I asked dryly.

"You owe it to a complete lack of discretion about supernaturally sensitive information," was his cold, measured reply.

I needed his attitude like I needed an extra pair of tits on my ass. "I don't know what you're talking about. Care to start making sense?" *Or is that too much to ask, Mr. Brass Tacks?* I mentally added.

"From where your cell is transmitting, I'm guessing you're at your former childhood residence," he stated, pissing me off more that he must've started tracking my signal as soon as I picked up. "A chopper will be there to pick you up in thirty minutes."

"Sorry, but you'll just have to tell me what's up over the phone. I have other plans for tonight," I said, waving Bones over and mouthing *Madigan* while pointing at my cell.

"If you refuse to come, your visitation privileges at the compound will be permanently revoked."

A distinct click punctuated that sentence. Good thing, too, since I'd taken a deep breath so I could tell the consultant in explicit terms where he could shove his ultimatum, and that wouldn't have been smart. He probably could revoke my visitation privileges if he tattled on me to the higher-ups for cursing him out the way I was about to.

"What does he want, Kitten?"

"Death by fang if he keeps this up," I spat, my temper leaking out despite my efforts to rein it in. "I don't know," I amended with a tight sigh. "But now I know how frustrated Chris felt when you pointed out that he couldn't stop you if you decided to do something he didn't like. Karma's a bitch, right?"

Both dark brows arched. "Going to elaborate on what you mean?"

"If I don't drop everything and let myself be whisked away to the compound, so Madigan can chew me out for God-knows-what, then I only get to see my mother and the guys when they're off base. Which, as you know, isn't that often."

Bones didn't react with instant anger as I'd done. Instead, he tapped his chin thoughtfully. "Good way to find out if your uncle's discovered anything of import on the bloke, so let him feel like he's won this round. It'll only be to our benefit."

Of course. If I didn't let Madigan push my buttons so effectively, I'd have come to the same conclusion. Don also didn't know that he couldn't zip to my side whenever he wanted to anymore. Aside from seeing if he'd come up with any dirt on Madigan, it was also important to let my uncle know about my change in supernatural status.

"You'll have to stay here, Bones. Otherwise, we wouldn't be back in time to pick everyone up from the cave."

It wouldn't be right to ask Chris's team to wait in a damp, chilly cave most of the night, especially since they'd had to bunk on the floor without food last night. But I'd be damned if I'd ask our helicopter escort to pick up the gang first before flying us back to the house. Madigan might know about my old childhood home, but I wasn't about to give up the cave's location to him, too.

Bones's scent and the scrape of his emotions across mine let me know how much he didn't like the idea of my going alone, but at last, he nodded.

"You'll take sage in case Kramer manages to locate you again."

Right, because I couldn't show up to see Madigan

covered in weed and garlic. Even if *that* wouldn't be cause for a lot of questions, which it would, that mixture would keep Don away from me, defeating half the purpose of going.

"I'll call you when I'm on my way back," I said, brushing his sculpted cheekbones with the tips of my fingers. "You keep some sage close by, too, and if Helsing starts to screech, light it."

"Oh, don't fret about me." Bones smiled, but something cold flashed across his face. "I'm looking forward to making that spook's acquaintance again."

He might be relishing the chance to avenge Kramer's shower attack on me, but if I had my way, neither one of us would see the Inquisitor until we were slamming the door of the trap shut on him.

"I love you," I said, because it was a better use of words than endless repetitions for him to be careful. Logic might know that Bones was more than capable of handling himself if Kramer came after him, but the thought of his being attacked while I was away still made me sick to my stomach.

"I love you, too, Kitten."

His voice changed, becoming the warm, knowing one that made me melt a little each time I heard it. Then his lips brushed across my forehead, so feathery soft and light it was more a tease than a kiss.

"Don't let that tosser Madigan get a rise out of you, he'll only enjoy it," he murmured against my skin. "Your will is stronger than his. Show him that."

I trailed my fingers from his face down to his shoulders, pulling him closer until the hard planes of his body pressed along mine. Madigan had hung up on me ten minutes ago. That meant the chopper wouldn't arrive for another twenty minutes.

I let my hands glide from his shoulders down to the tight valley of his stomach, then dipped one inside the front of his pants.

"Why don't you help put me in a calmer mood?" I whispered.

I was on the floor, Bones's mouth crushing mine, before the last word left my lips.

Thirteen

MADIGAN GLARED AT ME AS I WALKED INTO what used to be my uncle's office. I glared right back, willpower alone keeping my gaze from glowing green and fangs from jutting out of my teeth. Not only had Madigan ignored my previous remarks about the uselessness of an ID check on the roof; he'd also installed a full-body scanner that broadcast such explicit imagery of my body onto a screen, TSA officials everywhere would weep with envy. I'd then had every bit of metal on me confiscated except my wedding ring, and had to argue for ten minutes before the new guards would let me bring in my packet of sage. As it was, they'd taken my box of matches, because of course *those* were potentially deadly weapons.

Idiots. I was a vampire, as they well knew. I could kill someone ten times quicker with my teeth or my hands. It was a good thing Bones hadn't come with me, or he might've slaughtered one of the guards just to prove a point about the whole stupid, insulting process. Finding out that Madigan had also commandeered Don's office, plus hearing his repeated mental renditions of the same car insurance jingle, had been the cherry on the sundae wreckage of my formerly good mood.

From my uncle's deep frown as he floated behind Madigan, he was in a foul mood, too.

"*So* sorry there wasn't a body cavity search," I said in lieu of a hello. "My ego might never recover."

Madigan's pale blue eyes narrowed. "Lax security might have been acceptable during my predecessor's term, but it's not under mine."

"You mean *Tate's* predecessor's term," I corrected at once, not responding to the slap against Don because I was trying to cool my temper instead of inflame it. My uncle already knew the many reasons why Madigan's new security measures were pointless when it came to vampires. All Madigan was doing with his fancy new scanner was wasting taxpayer money in an attempt to look competent to unknowing government superiors.

My uncle tugged his eyebrow, muttering, "You're not going to believe this," even as Madigan smiled.

"Effective immediately, the head of Homeland Security upgraded my position from operations consultant to acting supervisor of this operation."

Shock froze me in the process of taking a seat. "Bullshit," I breathed. "They can't yank Tate's job out from under him without even giving him a *chance* to succeed at it!"

Oh yes they can, Madigan thought, interrupting

his repeated mental mantra of the damned slogan that had blocked out the rest of his thoughts. He didn't answer out loud, though, continuing to stare at me with that triumphant little smile. *Fifteen minutes can save you fifteen percent. Fifteen minutes . . .*

It was Don who said, in a very heavy voice, "They did exactly that, Cat."

I felt like I'd been sucker punched by a sledge-hammer. It wasn't shocking that the few, top-ranking government officials who knew about this department could make such a stupid decision; I'd seen government stupidity in action before. But I was stunned that they'd do it in such a short amount of time. *That's completely unfair!* rang through my mind, and though it might sound childish, it was still true.

"Congratulations," was what I bit out, acid penetrating each syllable. "Does Tate still work here, or did you fire him in your first official act as boss?"

Some part of me hoped that Madigan had fired every nonhuman on the team. That would make Cooper and the other veteran human team members quit in disgust. Then all of us could all sit back and count down the days until the Powers That Be learned the folly of trying to fight the undead with only regular soldiers. When the human casualties piled up, the same witless politicians that promoted him would throw Madigan out on his well-dressed ass, begging Tate, Juan, Dave, and the others to come back. Hell, they'd beg my mother to come back, and she hadn't even been out on her first mission yet, but she was still tougher than ninety-nine percent of their best human soldiers.

"Tate's been demoted to junior officer," Don replied, beating out Madigan's intentionally vague response of, "Of course he's still employed here."

Junior officer. My nails dug into my palms until the scent of blood made me stop. Despite my promise to Bones not to let Madigan rile me, it was all I could do not to start screaming at him. After all the times Tate had risked his life for this operation, not to mention all the lives he'd *saved* during his tenure, he did not deserve a demotion just because Madigan was a power-hungry schmuck who had issues with the undead.

"Cat," Don began.

"Not now," I said, my attention so focused on the injustice of it all that I answered him out loud. *Oops!* "Uh, not later, but now you want to tell me why I'm here?" I stammered to cover my slip.

Fortunately, Madigan didn't seem to pick up on it. He clicked a small device, and a flat screen dropped down from a slot in the ceiling. *Really love your little gadgets, don't you?* I thought sardonically.

The screen flashed a serial number and the word "confidential" before it focused in on an image of Chris, of all people, broadcasting in what looked like night vision. His eyes shone unnaturally bright.

"Who are you talking to?" he was asking, looking around a basement that I recognized with a sinking feeling. My own voice flowed out in reply.

"One of Waverly's former residents. Can you do me a favor, Herbert? Fly through the bearded man's left arm . . ."

I said nothing as the entire exchange played out,

complete with several close-ups of my face as I directed an unseen ghost to dive bomb Chris's body. Son of a bitch! A member of N.I.P.D. must have rigged a camera down there during their setup period, but how had Madigan gotten ahold of the footage? It was barely more than a week old!

Madigan paused the video once we'd walked away from the camera's view. "Do you know where this was? On the Northeastern Investigative Paranormal Division's Web site, where anyone with a computer could see a former top secret operative blabbering on about how the supernatural really exists!"

I wanted to thump my head against the desk but didn't because it would only give Madigan the satisfaction of knowing how much he'd scored a hit—though to do it, he'd revealed an important bit of information. If Madigan had indeed found this only because N.I.P.D. put the clip on their Web site, then he had my picture plugged into a specialized facial recognition database that was normally used for the world's most wanted terrorists and criminals. *Why was he so fixated on me?*

"You see a former operative humoring a gullible investigator in order to get him to agree to take a job for a friend's paranoid client. I had no idea it was being filmed," I improvised, praying that my conversation about Kramer had taken place where no cameras were stationed.

"Really?" Madigan's gaze was blue steel. "So you weren't, in actuality, communicating with ghosts and directing their actions?"

I forced myself not to glance at Don, who hovered

behind Madigan's chair close enough to be a barber about to give him a haircut. I hadn't mentioned ghosts in any of my reports while I worked here. Back then, my experience with them had been very limited, so there was no need. If Madigan learned that some ghosts were as intelligent as any other person and could infiltrate places most covert operatives couldn't, plus could be controlled by certain people . . . I suppressed a shudder imagining how he'd exploit such information.

"To my knowledge, ghosts are incapable of communication. All the ones I've seen are just vague impressions of leftover energy, no more sentient or able to interact than a house plant."

"There goes your Christmas present," Don murmured with a flash of humor.

"Really?" Madigan slid his glasses down an inch on his nose to give me the full effect of that drill sergeant stare, but I didn't flinch. Either he was toying with me because he'd seen footage of me talking about Kramer to Chris, or he didn't know I was lying, and I could hope to brazen this out. If it was the former, I was already so screwed that getting busted lying wouldn't make much difference.

"I've had experts go over this video, and they see faint hazy distortions in the same places where you stated that a ghost had initiated contact with the subject." Madigan leaned forward. "Explain *that*."

"They also said the distortions could've been faked," Don supplied rapidly. "Without the original film, it's impossible to tell."

I'd have Chris make sure that original film was destroyed *tonight*. I sat down for the first time, flouncing a little as if exasperated.

"Come on, Madigan. If you're running a paranormal investigation company, are you going to put any footage on your Web site that hasn't been doctored first? Who's going to hire ghost hunters who don't have any images of ghosts on their business page? They might be believers, but they *are* still trying to make a buck."

His smile was thin. "Plausible. But even if someone added those distortions to the video later, how did you know exactly where the subject felt the ghostly interactions at the time that they happened?"

He had me there. As if to punctuate his checkmate, the word "gotcha" drifted out between Madigan's endless blockade of mental repetitions.

And just like that, it occurred to me how I could thwart him. *Thank you, Madigan, for being the arrogant prick you are.*

"How did I know that?" I pretended to study my fingernails for a moment. "The same way I know that fifteen minutes can save you fifteen percent on car insurance."

Fourteen

Silence met my pronouncement, stretching until the room filled with a tension that was almost palpable. I had to give Madigan credit where credit was due, because whatever he was thinking remained secluded behind a now blaring rendition of the same catchphrase. Don's brows drew together in confusion.

"What does that have to do with anything?" my uncle wondered.

I spoke the next part for his benefit. "That's right, I can read minds. Handy little unexpected perk; not many vampires have the ability."

Don looked stunned. Oh, right, I hadn't told him of my ability before. It wasn't like I'd been hiding it from him, it just hadn't come up. Madigan already suspected Bones was telepathic and had been treating me with the same caution, so volunteering the information was a necessary sacrifice in order to keep him from discovering the real bombshell about ghosts.

Finally, Madigan spoke. "I could charge you with an unauthorized breach of security for attempting to glean classified information from my thoughts."

I snorted. "I'm not *trying* anything. The ability's there whether I want it or not. If someone told you unauthorized classified information, would you be guilty of a security breach for not willing yourself to go deaf so you couldn't hear it?"

Bitch, he thought, and I was sure it was no accident that this came through loud and clear over the fifteen minutes mantra.

I just shrugged. "Sticks and stones."

"Is that what this is to you?" he asked sharply. "A game? Is national security just something that *amuses* you now that you're no longer a member of the human race? Oh, I forgot." His voice vibrated with barely concealed venom. "You never really were a member of the human race, were you, half-breed?"

I was across the desk in a blink, my face so close to his that our noses would've touched if I moved a fraction more. "How much of your own blood have you shed for humanity or national security? Because I've lost *gallons* of mine trying to protect lives, or, failing that, making sure that murderers and threats to humanity got what was coming to them." I sat back in disgust. "I bet the only blood you've ever shed was after a paper cut, so don't lecture me about national security and protecting humanity unless you've even once put your life on the line for either of them."

Two new, bright spots of color on his cheeks highlighted how Madigan had paled when I first lunged at him. His scent radiated the distinct, rotten fruit smell of fear over the stench of way too much cologne, and stray thoughts leaked out between his now-deafening roar of what fifteen minutes could save on insurance.

Dangerous . . . can't let her see . . . too much at stake . . .

"Get out," he said curtly.

I strained my mind to hear past the commercial jingle that I now hated with the fire of a thousand suns. What was Madigan hiding? Something I already expected, like plans to boot out all the undead team members? Or something more sinister?

"Get *out*," he repeated, pressing a button on his phone. "I need security," he barked. "Now."

I glanced at the door. Should I risk trying to mesmerize him before they came? Someone with Madigan's mental shields might require biting before I could crack his mind, and, frankly, I'd never bitten a human. What if I did it wrong and pierced his jugular? That would leave telling splatters of blood on both of us, not to mention he could die of an embolism in seconds if any air bubbles got to his heart. Both would be hard to explain away when security arrived.

"Don't do anything, Cat," Don urged, sensing my wavering. "These guards don't know you. They're new recruits handpicked by him, and they're all armed with silver."

Being staked or shot with silver bullets by Madigan's pet soldiers was last on my list of concerns, but it was too risky for other reasons to attempt to mesmerize any secrets out of him. I'd have to let Don do the digging for me, and, thankfully, Madigan still had no idea that he was being shadowed by the very man he'd maneuvered himself into position to replace.

I rose with deliberate slowness, almost strolling to the door. "Congrats again on the promotion."

Footsteps thudded down the hall. Madigan's new security detail, running to his aid too late to help him if there had been an actual threat from me.

"You are not to return here unless I summon you," Madigan snapped. "Do you understand? You show up, and I'll have you arrested on sight."

With great effort, I restrained myself from replying with the sentences that sprang to my lips. Like, *you and what army?* Or, *I'd like to see you try it.* But Bones's admonition rang in my mind. *Let him feel like he's won this round. It'll only be to our benefit.* I hadn't managed to stop myself from rising to Madigan's taunting before, but I could let him believe he had the power to keep me away from here if I wanted to come back, and believing that only made him more vulnerable.

"I hope you spend some time in your new capacity reading up on Don's reports about me," was what I said, in such an even tone that Bones would have applauded. "He didn't trust me either at first, but then he found out that half-vampire didn't equate to bad guy. Neither does full vampire. We don't have to be at odds with each other."

The helmeted, armed entourage arrived, one of the guards roughly taking my arm.

"Move it."

I let them manhandle me out of the room with Madigan watching. Don floated after me, muttering something too low for me to catch above the staccato of thoughts from the guards and Madigan's endless barrage of *fifteen minutes . . . fifteen minutes*. The next time I saw that commercial, I'd probably open fire on my TV.

I'd just been hustled into the elevator when a shout pierced the din.

"Catherine!"

I had my hand holding open the elevator doors before the guards even realized I'd moved. "Stand down!" one of them ordered, raising his rifle at me.

"That's my mother," I snapped, refraining from breaking the barrel off by sheer force of will.

Her appearance cut off whatever the guard had been about to say. She pushed past them into the elevator none too gently, several strands of dark hair escaping from her ponytail. The sharp blue gaze that still had the power to intimidate me lasered on the group surrounding us.

"Are you going to shoot her, or push the button so we can leave?" she demanded.

I stifled a laugh at the instant consternation her words elicited. The guard who had his weapon pointed at me didn't know whether to lower it and look like he was following her orders or keep it aimed at me and look like an idiot. He chose the idiot route, and I pushed the button for the top floor, my lips twitching.

"What are you doing, Justina?" Don asked warily.

She glanced first at him, then at me. "I'm quitting,"

she stated. "I heard what he said about arresting you if you came back, and no one's going to forbid my daughter from seeing me if she wants to."

Her words hit me right in the heart. I knew how much my mother had wanted to make the team despite my strenuous objections. She'd argued that going after murderers was her chance to avenge the lives she'd been unable to save—hers and that of the man she loved. For her to give it all up because Madigan pulled a power play made me want to hug her and punch his lights out at the same time.

Since he was now three floors away, I put my arm around my mother, squeezing gently.

"Thanks," I whispered.

Pink shone in her gaze before she blinked, glancing away. "Yes, well, I'm sure your husband has missed me terribly," she replied with heavy irony.

My laughter startled the guards so much that another one of them prodded me with his gun. Again I resisted the urge to snap off the tip and bean him with it. The doors opened on our floor, and I got out, biting my lip as my arm was grasped in a hard grip once more.

"Seriously?" I muttered under my breath. My mother glared at them, green glittering in her gaze, but a low "don't" from me kept her silent. For once.

"Thanks so much for the assistance, boys," I drawled once they all but pushed me onto the roof.

The reply I received would've resulted in their instant massacre if Bones were here. Once again, I thanked God that he'd stayed back in Ohio. He might be coolly logical under most circumstances, but Bones had an irrational streak when it came to me. I couldn't point fingers about that because I was the same way with him.

"Anything interesting happen since I last saw you?" I asked, but the question wasn't directed at my mother. It was to Don, who hovered right behind her.

"Somehow Madigan knows he's being watched," my uncle replied, frustration clear in his tone. "Even at home, he doesn't let his guard down. All the computer files he accesses are the usual classified material, and if he's on the phone, he talks in code so I can't figure out what his real meaning is."

My sigh was swallowed up by the churning of the helicopter's rotor blades as the engine was started. No time was being wasted in getting me out of here, it seemed. I would've liked a chance to talk to Tate and the guys before I left, but that clearly wasn't happening. I'd have to settle for Don's relaying a message from me later.

"I don't like him at *all,* but is it possible that he's nothing more than what he appears—an arrogant, prejudiced suit who'll step on anyone to climb up the government ladder?"

That might make Madigan a dick and incompetent for this job, but it didn't make him the menace Don thought he was.

"You don't know him like I do," Don said flatly. "He's hiding something. I just need more time to find out what it is."

"The boys are going to be so upset when they find out that Madigan's not letting you come back," my mother remarked. "Morale is already low after what happened to Tate."

I had to shake my head. Hearing my mother talk about team morale was just too weird for my brain to handle.

"You need to come with me," I said to Don, with an oblique look at the various personnel waiting for me to climb into the chopper. Even if someone heard me above the noise from the craft powering up, they'd think I was talking to my mother.

Don hesitated. "But now is the best time for me to shadow Madigan," he said, backing away from me. Actually backing away. "You rattled him, Cat. I could be missing out on important information as we speak. Whatever you have to tell me, it can wait!"

Then he vanished, leaving me staring at the spot he'd just vacated with my jaw dropped open. He couldn't even take a few hours away from shadowing Madigan to be updated on what was going on? What if I'd found a way for him to skip merrily into eternity? Was that no longer a concern of his?

I had to make sure to badger him to tell me what happened in their past for Don to have such a one-track mind when it came to Madigan, but that would have to wait until the next time I saw him.

But thanks to Madigan's proving that he was every inch the suspicious bastard I'd initially pegged him as, the first thing I'd have to do would be to uproot everyone from my old house in Ohio. I didn't doubt that in the time it took to fly me here, Madigan already had a surveillance team staked out around the perimeter, ready to record any incriminating action or word. I'd have to call Bones and tell him not to bring the crew back there. So much for all the groceries and amenities we'd just bought.

"Ready, Catherine?" my mother asked, jumping into the chopper.

I shook my head at Don's behavior as I climbed in after her. Family. If one member wasn't being a pain in the ass, another one would be guaranteed to fill the slot.

FIFTEEN

TYLER DUCKED BENEATH THE LOW ENTRANCE of the cave, his eyes darting around like he expected to be attacked at any moment.

"Are there spiders in here? I hate spiders."

"In an underground cave nearly half a mile long? No, not a one."

The look Tyler threw me said he didn't appreciate the sarcasm, but what did he expect? Rats seemed to avoid vampires with the same innate aversion other scavengers showed predators higher up on the food chain; but spiders either didn't possess that sort of instinct, or they considered us to be very distant cousins. Hey, both our species survived by drinking blood, so while I wouldn't invite any arachnids over for Christmas dinner, I couldn't ignore the similarities, either.

"If one of those hairy-legged things even *touches* me, I'm outta here," Tyler muttered.

I didn't reply. His fixation on spiders was just his

way of controlling his fear over the other, far more dangerous aspect of his trip into the cave. The trap was finally ready, but with my ghostly powers being kaput, we'd need a medium to summon Kramer to it. Cue Tyler. He might be swatting imaginary spiders off his clothes and swearing, but his steps didn't falter as he followed me deeper into the darkness.

"Don't know why the others are pissed about having to wait in the RV," Tyler continued in his faux grumbling. "I'd *love* to trade places with them right now."

"You see ghosts all the time. Most of them have never laid eyes on a full-bodied apparition, and they've worked as investigators for years."

"They don't want to see this one," he countered, serious this time.

I couldn't agree more. That was why no one but Bones, Tyler, and I were going to be in the cave. Chris had argued fiercely about being present since seeing if his invention could trap and contain a powerful ghost was the culmination of a decade's worth of theorizing for him. My concerns centered on keeping everyone alive if things went south. We compromised on his waiting by the mouth of the cave, so he could dash inside as soon as we gave the all clear. The rest of the team waited in the two recreational vehicles parked by the side of the road nearly a mile away from the cave.

Now that it was almost showtime, I regretted not making Chris and the team wait even farther away. If this didn't work, we'd have a very pissed-off phantom on our hands. Hopefully, the sage we had ready to burn would be enough to send Kramer running for the nearest ley line if things went awry, but hope wasn't a guarantee. That was why Chris had sage at the ready, and some was already smoldering in little ceramic pots in each RV, plus my mother was there, ready to heal any injuries if that weren't enough.

When I told Bones that Madigan would likely be scouring hotels looking for us after we'd absconded from the house, he'd arranged for two RVs to be brought as our hotel on wheels. The RVs came from his old friend, Ted, so they weren't procured through any rental channels Madigan could track—and knowing Ted, probably not legal ones, either. I'd also kept my cell phone powered off for the last few days while all of us worked feverishly to complete the trap. Even having it on without making a call would be enough for Madigan to trace. If everything went as planned, I'd turn it back on and resurface once Kramer was locked up and we were all safely out of Ohio. Madigan would be forced to admit that he'd been tracking me in order to be able to berate me for successfully disappearing, and I didn't think his arrogance would allow that.

Or maybe he wasn't tracking me at all. Maybe Madigan hadn't given me a second thought since I'd been thrown out of the compound. Don still hadn't revealed anything significant about their past to explain why he was so convinced that Madigan was up to no good, and despite my intense dislike of him, Madigan hadn't given me anything concrete to focus on, either. He seemed very interested in finding out if there were sentient ghosts, but any former CIA agent would fixate on the idea of invisible, undetectable spies. Yes, Mad-

igan was a prejudiced prick who'd royally screwed
Tate over, but if being intolerant and screwing someone out of a well-earned promotion was a crime, this
country would need to build a lot more jails.

"I hear them, they're almost here," Bones said
from the cavern ahead. We only had one more slanted,
rocky ledge to traverse before we reached the part of
the cave where the trap was located. Tyler picked his
way carefully, muttering about me owing him a new
pair of pants when a piece of fabric tore on a protrud-
ing limestone edge.

"Serves you right. Who wears Dolce & Gabbana to
go underground?" I pointed out.

"If I'm checking out today, I'm doing it while looking *good*," was his reply.

I wanted to reassure him that he absolutely would
not die, but the words stuck in my throat. I'd do my
damnedest to protect Tyler, as he knew, but we were
dealing with a strong, vicious spectre and a trap that
might or might not work. It had successfully held
Fabian, then Elisabeth, when we tested it yesterday,
but to tell Tyler he wasn't risking his life summoning
Kramer would be a flat-out lie, and I wasn't about to
lie to someone I now counted as a friend.

"Here we are," I said, when the cavern widened
to a thirty-foot ceiling and a small, bubbling stream
along the far wall. Bones stood in the middle of it
next to the oblong limestone, quartz, and moissanite structure. Dexter and Helsing were in pet carriers on the sandy bank, Fabian and Elisabeth floating
beside them. After all she'd been through, it was only
fitting that Elisabeth was here to witness this. Fabian

wasn't about to stay behind even though entering the cave was harder for him now with his lesser power level and the abundance of limestone, quartz, and moissanite.

My gaze locked with Bones's. If he was worried, nothing in his expression or vibe gave it away. Instead, confidence exuded from his aura, and his dark eyes glittered with anticipation. With his tight long-sleeved shirt and matching ebony pants, he almost blended into the background except for the exquisite pale contrast of his face and hands. Good thing he mostly blended, too, since Kramer wasn't supposed to see him until it was too late.

"Ready, luv?" he asked.

"Almost, sugar," Tyler replied with a cheeky wink.

I rolled my eyes. Between Bones's self-assurance and Tyler's irrepressible flirting, my lingering nervousness changed into optimism. We could do this. No, scratch that—we *would* do this.

I grabbed some sage that we'd stacked by the edge of the stream and stuffed it into my backpack, Tyler following suit. I already had lighters in each pants pockets and so did he. All that was left was to break out the Ouija board, and Tyler was already pulling it out of his backpack.

Bring it on, Inquisitor. We've got a surprise waiting for you.

"Ready."

Tyler and I stood on either side of the stone-and-quartz pedestal, the Ouija board lying flat between us. This time, the planchette didn't jump when I placed my fingers on it, as if I needed reminding that my borrowed powers from Marie had faded.

Tyler's brows went up, noticing that as well. "Something you want to tell me, Cat?"

"Nope," I said, and it was the unvarnished truth. Tyler didn't know that one of the fragile cogs in the peace wheel between vampires and ghouls loosely rested on certain people still believing that I had special connections to the dead. Luckily, no one but Bones knew the average shelf life of my borrowed powers, so I should be able to stretch out the illusion that I could raise Remnants quite a while longer.

What would happen after that jig was up, I'd worry about later. One perilous problem at a time, thank you.

"All right," Tyler said, after it became clear that was all I'd ante up on the subject. He cleared his throat, darkly musing that he'd probably get something sharp lodged in it again with what he was about to do, then placed his fingers on the planchette.

"Heinrich Kramer, we summon you into our presence."

Tyler's voice echoed throughout the cave as he spoke, his voice strong and commanding even though he inwardly cursed himself for not taking a piss before starting this.

"Heed our call, Heinrich Kramer, and come to us. We summon your spirit through the veil into our presence . . ."

The planchette began to jerk around the board in crazy, ragged circles. Tyler sucked in his breath. I strained my senses, but I'd felt chilly, tingling vibrations along my skin this whole time due to Fabian and Elisabeth's close proximity, so that wasn't any help.

Suddenly, Bones plummeted down from his hiding place in one of the ceilings many crevasses. He'd been up there so he could slam the lid down on the trap if Kramer appeared, but nothing hazy or swirly interrupted the Ouija board's smooth surface. Did he see something I didn't? Couldn't be; he set the huge, multimineral cylinder next to the trap instead of over it.

"What?" I asked, gaze darting around.

"Stop the summoning," Bones ordered Tyler. His eyes were sizzling green as he looked at me.

"People are coming, I can hear them. A lot of people."

"Shit," I sighed.

We'd left every one of our silver weapons in the RV, not wanting Kramer to have any means to permanently harm us if the trap didn't work, and he started hurling nearby objects at us. Now, with potential enemies between us and the only weapons we could utilize aside from sticks and stones, what we'd done as a safety measure had turned out to be a huge liability.

Bones cracked his knuckles, that lethal aura increasing until it prickled my skin with its energy. I strained my senses but couldn't pick up on anything aside from Tyler's concern and the sounds in the cave. Bones was older and stronger, so I didn't doubt that he was right. This couldn't be a hiking expedition stumbling across the cave by accident, either—we were in the middle of nowhere. It had to be an ambush, but how the hell had anyone found us?

Then I heard it. The murmur of voices in my head, too low for me to make out specific words, too many to be Chris's thoughts.

"Fabian, Elisabeth," Bones said low. "Find out what's out there."

They disappeared in a flash. Tyler glanced around before mumbling some words, then shutting the Ouija board with a bang.

"I turned it off. No one can come through now."

"See that shadow off to the right?" Bones asked him without turning in that direction. "It leads to a small enclosure. Wait there, and try to stay quiet."

Knew this day would end badly, Tyler thought in resignation as he did what Bones said.

The seconds ticked by as we waited for the ghosts. My hands felt horribly empty without weapons, but I consoled myself with the knowledge that I'd been in fights before against undead baddies without any silver. If we were lucky, and most of the hostiles approaching were human, bare hands would be more than sufficient.

But if someone had gone to all this trouble of finding us, I bet he or she wouldn't be dumb enough to show up with an army of only humans. There might be a lot of them, from the increased volume in my head that indicated the entrance to the cave was being surrounded, but these had to be the pawns. The question was, who was the chess player?

A hazy outline zoomed up so fast; it took me a second to determine whether it was Fabian or Elisabeth.

"Soldiers!" Fabian exclaimed. "But they are all

human. Could these be members of your old team, perhaps here because they need your help?"

My instant surge of relief at hearing they were human changed to suspicion. Bones and I exchanged a look, the tension in his aura saying loud and clear that he thought something was still off.

"Well," I said at last. "Let's see who they are and what they want."

The words barely left my lips before Bones muttered, "Bloody hell." For a split second, I was confused. But then above the collage of voices in my mind, I heard a new one, chanting a single line over and over.

Fifteen minutes can save you fifteen percent . . .

Madigan was out there, too.

Sixteen

I WALKED OUT OF THE CAVE WITH BONES AT my side. Tyler brought up the rear, holding both pet carriers. The sight that greeted us was over a dozen automatic weapons pointed in our direction, Chris on his knees off to the far right side, a helmeted soldier pressing a gun to his cheek.

And I told him it would be too dangerous to wait in the cave, I thought irreverently.

After that initial glance, I didn't look at the ring of soldiers anymore. My gaze was all for the stony-faced "operations consultant," who had the agitated form of my uncle flying over him.

"Madigan found the cave by reading one of your old reports back when Dave died," Don said. "I tried to warn you that he was coming, but the cave felt like it was blocked, and something burned me whenever I tried to fly near the RV where Justina was!"

I didn't let any of my inner groan escape my lips. Of

course. The RVs had sage lit in them, Chris couldn't see Don to pass the message along, and my uncle was too new a ghost to withstand all the combined ingredients from the trap. I'd told him where I was in case of an emergency, but what I was doing prevented him from getting to me.

"What a nice surprise," I said to the group at large, fixing a false smile on my face. "Don't tell me—I forgot someone's birthday, and this is the party police come to correct my oversight, right?"

Madigan came forward, but not close enough to stand in his soldier's line of fire, I noted. Contempt curled around the fury in Bones's emotions, but I fought against a snort. For all his talk about reading extensive reports on the undead, didn't he know that many Master vampires could *fly*? Bones and I had endless miles of open space above our heads now that we were outside of the cave. Aside from looking showy, the guns pointed at us were as much of a threat as harsh language.

"Crawfield," Madigan began.

"Russell," I interrupted him, smiling sweetly. "I know you're a stickler for facts, so I wanted to remind you of that one before you got it wrong in your future report."

His features darkened with anger, but I didn't care. He was the one who'd arranged to have a barrage of weapons pointed at us for no reason whatsoever, so politeness had already gone out the window. If not for my mother and the two RVs full of people with way too much information on what we'd been doing here, I wouldn't even wait around to hear why Dickhead had come. Bones could carry Chris and Tyler. I could grab my mother, and we could fly out of here. Madigan would never know what we were doing here because it was like a maze in the cave. Even after two weeks, Chris and the others still needed Bones or me to guide them to the trap, or they'd get lost.

But we did have two RVs full of people, and I could tell from the guards' thoughts that they were staring down a line of automatic weapons right now just like we were. Flying away while carrying Chris, Dexter, Tyler, the pet carriers, and two of *those*? Bones could probably handle it, but that was a bit beyond my skill level.

"What's in the cave, *Russell*?" Madigan asked with heavy sarcasm.

I shrugged. "Rocks. Lots of 'em."

"Don't patronize me." His voice lowered to a hiss. "What *else* is in the cave?"

I looked him straight in the eye and spoke one word.

"Mud."

Madigan's thoughts erupted into a slew of curses before he regained control and barricaded them behind the car insurance jingle that had to be what hell played for elevator music.

"You don't want to do that, mate," Bones said. His tone was soft, but each word was edged in ice. "She cares about protecting everyone your toy soldiers are holding hostage enough to ignore those insults. I don't. Think anything like that at her again, and I'll kill you here and now."

Madigan's scoff was uneasy. "Any attack on me—"

"Is the same as an attack on the United States itself," Bones finished, still in that deadly calm manner. "Heard you the first time—and didn't give a shite then, either."

Madigan eyed Bones for another tense, extended moment before turning his attention back to me.

"We know you're up to something in the cave, and we know it has to do with ghosts. It'll be easier on everyone if you tell me what it is, but even if you don't, I'll find out."

Not if I can help it. "I told you the last time I saw you; I'm doing a favor for a friend's paranoid client. She thinks this cave is haunted by old Indian spirits or something. I told her I'd have professionals check it out, so here we are."

"Swears Tecumseh, Crazy Horse, and Geronimo are holed up in there. Bitch is crazy, but her checks clear," Tyler added.

Madigan looked over at Chris, who had sweat dripping down his face even though it was chilly with the early-evening breeze.

"Is that what you were doing in there?"

Chris didn't look at me or Bones, but he knew we were watching him. His thoughts raced, wondering who he should be more afraid of: the man commanding the soldier who had a gun pressed to his head or the two vampires fifty feet away.

"We were looking for ghosts, just like they said," he rasped, being vague.

Madigan moved closer to him. "And did you find any?"

This time, Chris's gaze skidded in our direction

before he spoke. "Had some interesting EMF readings and found some cold spots, but nothing like what the client described."

"Ah." Madigan took his glasses off and cleaned them almost leisurely on his jacket. "So we're back to the 'there's no such thing as intelligent ghosts' claim, hmm? What's with all the marijuana and garlic everywhere in your old house, Cat?"

I gave him a breezy smile. "Love to get my weed on, and garlic is great for the blood."

"Do you even know how to tell the truth?" Madigan asked sharply.

"You're one to talk," Don muttered.

I said nothing. Madigan continued to stare at me, his guards holding their position even though a few of them were beginning to think that if they weren't going to shoot us anytime soon, they'd like to lower their heavy guns. I didn't think it was an accident that all these men were strangers to me. For this occasion, Madigan had left all my friends from the team behind.

"Donovan," Madigan called out, with a victorious little smirk. "Take Proctor and Hamilton and sniff out the spectre trap that the folks at the RV were talking about. Then we'll see about there being no such thing as sentient ghosts."

Fuck! If the trap was successful, we'd intended to erase the team's memories to prevent them from revealing any incriminating information like this, but too late now. Still, we might be able to brazen it out. It would take these guys weeks to find the trap if they succeeded at all.

My relief at that lasted only long enough for the three soldiers to take their helmets off and come toward Bones and me, sniffing deeply. They were human, why would they do such a thing?

The reason hit me even before Madigan's smug words.

"These men have had their senses heightened by vampire blood. Now that they have your scent, they can follow its trail right to that big stone device we're told is in there."

Double fuck! Imbibing enough vampire blood would indeed give them the ability to sniff out our path to the trap, plus make them immune to mind control. By finding the cave from old mission reports and showing up with supernaturally enhanced soldiers, Madigan had proven smarter than I'd given him credit for.

Bones folded his arms, his gaze like a laser beam as he stared at Madigan.

"Whose blood are they on? Every vampire on your team owes their fealty to me, and I did *not* give them permission to turn over their blood for such purposes."

Madigan's smile was cold. "Don't worry. I didn't get it from them."

My eyes widened before I could control myself, but this news stunned me. If Madigan hadn't tapped Tate's or Juan's veins in order to juice up his select guard, then what other vampire—or vampires?—was he in collusion with?

Then I met my uncle's gaze, and another realization bolted through me. Don didn't look the least bit surprised. With all his slurs about Madigan, he hadn't *once* mentioned a connection to vampires. How could he have left something that important out?

Bones's eyes turned green, and power crackled through the air—icy, lethal, and expanding so rapidly it soon surrounded everyone in the vicinity. I tensed for what felt like an imminent explosion. Tyler must've also sensed that a switch had been flipped. He moved away, thinking, *That guy done fucked up now.*

Madigan must've sensed that, too. He took a step back, his smile faltering. "See those visors my men are wearing? Not only do they block out the effect from your eyes, they also contain recorders streaming live images to a secure location. Even if you manage to kill all of us, others in the government will know who did it. You'll be hunted for the rest of your lives."

For a second, I wondered if Bones cared. Madigan had no idea that one did *not* taunt a Master vampire with the notion that he was using other vampires against him. But while the thought of Bones's killing Madigan didn't bother me, killing his guards for no reason other than they would feel duty-bound to strike back was repellent. Plus, then our claims that vampire prejudice was unfounded would be pretty hollow if we massacred an elite government operative like Madigan *and* some of his protective guard on video.

My fingers curled around Bones's hand, his power sizzling up my arm like I'd just been electrocuted.

"No," I said quietly.

For several seconds, I didn't know if he'd listen. That dangerous power didn't abate, and the glare he had fixed on Madigan said that the operations consultant was only moments away from death.

Then something hazy zoomed out of the cave, too fast for me to make out what it was. Icy needles scraped along my skin, and Dexter's bark was swallowed up by Tyler's muttered, "This isn't good."

"You try to trap me, *Hexe*?" a familiar voice hissed.

Kramer. From his accusation, the fucker must've figured out what the large mineral cylinder was for. Tyler had sealed the Ouija board, but not before the ghost managed to slip through.

I reached for the sage in my pants only to have a dozen weapons level in my direction.

"Don't move another inch!" someone barked.

My hands froze. I didn't want to get riddled with silver bullets because I'd have to be in good shape to protect these idiots.

"Madigan," I said. "Get your men out of here. Now."

He bristled. "I'll remind you that you're in no position to give me orders."

Bones let out a harsh snort. "I won't have to kill them, Kitten. The fools are dooming themselves."

"What do you mean by that?" Madigan snapped, oblivious to the dark swirls materializing to the left of one of his soldiers.

"You'll see," Bones replied.

In the next instant, with screams splitting the air as Kramer attacked, he did see.

Seventeen

The last of the wounded were carted off by Medevac, leaving behind only the few un- injured and the bodies in the forest. Even the soldiers and occupants from the RVs were clustered around us, Madigan wanting as many people around him as pos- sible until his transport came. Sage burned in pots in the perimeter surrounding us, but that wasn't the only smell in the air. The scent of blood and death was also heavy, clinging to the clothes of the survivors as well as emanating from the lost.

"How could this happen?" Madigan muttered, looking around at the carnage.

I'd been standing next to my mother, but Madi- gan's comment had me leaving her side to march over to where he stood. Even though the fallen men were strangers who'd threatened to shoot me, they didn't deserve to die the way they had. The fact that their deaths had been preventable only angered me more.

"How could this happen? Because you didn't listen when someone told you to *get your men out of here*."

Madigan's heart rate hadn't decreased much since Kramer began slaughtering everyone he could get his noncorporeal hands on. Sadly, that list didn't include Madigan, which was due in no small part to his being a coward. When Kramer tore through the guards, who fired so wildly at their unseen attacker that I'd taken a few stray bullets just protecting Tyler, Madigan crawled behind the barricade of our crouched bodies. Bones had draped himself over Chris and my mother joined the protective huddle to offer further buffer against the ghost and the bullets. Because of that, Madigan only had a bloody furrow in the side of his leg, more's the pity.

"This is all your fault," he stated, pointing a trembling finger at me. "You said ghosts were only faint, residual imprints of leftover energy, no more interactive than a house plant. You compromised my security and the security of—"

"Oh come on," I interrupted. "I guessed you were too stupid to be trusted with this information, and I was right! You don't have to be a weatherman to figure out which way the wind blows with you, Madigan. Lying to you was in the best interests of *everyone's* security, and I wish there wasn't a pile of dead bodies around me to prove it."

His face became mottled, and I could almost hear his blood pressure shooting up.

"How dare you? You'll be lucky if you're not both found to be accessories in those men's deaths!"

Bones ignored him, grasping one of the fallen soldiers by the shoulders and staring directly into his helmet.

"You, on the other side of this video feed. You authorized the replacement of a decently intelligent bloke with quite possibly the world's biggest arsehole—and in my day, I've met more than a few arseholes, so I'm speaking from a point of authority."

Madigan all but roared, "Get away from him!"

"He's dead, he no longer cares who's touching him," Bones replied shortly. "Pity you were more interested in garnering ammunition against her than in valuing his life while he still had it. You blundered into a situation that was far over your head, then ignored warnings to leave. Today, two vampires did more to protect your men than the human leader who was responsible for them. What will your superiors on the other end of this video think of *that*, I wonder?"

Madigan opened his mouth, his face reddening even more, when all at once, he stopped. Then I heard his thoughts snaking through the wall of rage and slogans. *He's right. Must fix this.*

"This has been a terrible tragedy," Madigan said, sounding mournful instead of about to blow a gasket like he had before. "Anytime life is lost, responsibility ultimately rests on the person in charge, and that person is me. I'll request that every aspect of today's events be evaluated so something like this never happens again, even if I'm reprimanded as a result."

"You're only trying to cover your ass seven ways from Sunday," Don said in disgust. Then he turned to me. "You see why I don't trust him?"

Oh yeah. I hadn't heard so much bullshit since

the last time I drove past a used car lot and caught snatches of the salesmen's conversations. Madigan even ambled closer to the dead man as he spoke, dragging his leg far more than the shallow wound merited. He leaned down as if to brush some dirt off the fallen solider. What it did was allow the camera to pick up every nuance of his newly somber expression and the tear that somehow found its way onto his cheek. *You coldhearted, manipulating PRICK,* I thought in disbelief.

Bones let out a snort. "Right piece of work, you are."

Madigan's lips thinned, but he quickly recovered, straightening as much as he could while balancing most of his weight on one leg.

"I understand you're both still upset. I did allow my anger to color my judgment when I didn't listen to your warning. That was a mistake."

"Is that your idea of an apology?" I asked, incredulous.

"I don't owe you one," Madigan snapped before assuming that calmer, controlled tone again. "Had you come to me about this ghost first, without any subterfuge, this tragedy would have been prevented."

"We didn't need to come to you because we had it *under control,*" I gritted out. "At least, we did until you had to track me down and interrupt us at gunpoint from trapping this fucker for all eternity, and now you want to blame this on me?"

God, if I stayed here any longer listening to his twisted version of events, I was going to beat him until he bled internally.

Bones must've had enough, too, because he took

my arm. "Come on, Kitten, let's go. We're wasting our time with this sod."

"You can't leave yet," Madigan said, that edge back in his voice.

A slow smile spread across Bones's face. "Oh?"

We were in the air before Madigan could sputter out a demand for us to stay put. I could fly well enough to propel myself in the general direction I wanted to go, but I lacked the finesse Bones had while flying. So while I took off under my own power, I let him direct us to where Tyler, my mother, and the pet carriers were located. One quick snatch-and-grab later, and they were soaring far above the ground as well. Fabian and Elisabeth didn't need to be told to follow; they whooshed after us, their forms streamlining into mere blurs.

Don stayed behind with Chris and his crew, who were unharmed thanks to the sage burning in the RVs. Even if Madigan questioned them again, they couldn't tell any more damaging information about us than they already had. Plus, Madigan would make sure they didn't repeat anything they'd seen to outside sources. Vampires weren't the only ones who were experts at concealing incriminating information. The government had extensive practice when it came to that, too.

We went straight from Ohio to our best friends Spade and Denise's home in St. Louis. No, we didn't fly everyone the whole way. Since merging lines with a vampire several millennia old, Bones now had people accountable to him spread out all over the world.

All it took was one call to his co-ruler, Mencheres, saying we needed a pickup for us to be whisked away within the hour. Good thing, too, since we couldn't have rented a car. We'd left our credit cards and IDs back in one of the RVs. Silly us hadn't figured on Madigan's commandeering the RVs and greeting us at gunpoint outside the cave. If Madigan thought to trace us through those aliases or billing card addresses, he was mistaken. Bones had everything routed through so many false channels, Madigan would only end up chasing his tail. I hoped he tried it because the thought of frustrating him pleased me in a petty, vindictive way.

When we arrived at their house, I didn't even have to get out of the car to see that we weren't the only visitors. If the flashy Maserati wasn't enough to clue me in as to who else was here, the custom GR8BITR license plate was confirmation.

"Ah, Ian's here," Bones said with none of my dismay at the prospect.

"I see that," I replied, not airing any of my opinion because Ian could hear me, and it would only amuse him. Some people took exception to being considered a pain in the ass. Ian didn't only take it as a compliment, he *reveled* in it. If he wasn't Bones's sire, I might have "accidentally" staked Ian by now.

"Cat!" Denise exclaimed, flinging open the door. She almost ran to give me a hug, whispering, "Thank God you're here. He's driving me crazy!" during her welcoming squeeze.

I smothered a laugh, knowing she wasn't talking about Spade. Good to see I wasn't the only one who found Ian irritating. How Bones and Spade had put up with him these past centuries, I'd never know.

"Cat. Justina. Crispin," Spade said from behind Denise, calling Bones by his human name. "How goes it?"

"Not as well as we'd hoped, Charles," Bones replied, also addressing him by the name he'd been born with instead of the moniker of the tool Spade had been assigned as a New South Wales prisoner.

Tyler carried Dexter out of the car and set him down. The dog took one look at the open front door of the house and ran inside. My mother followed suit after exchanging a brief hello with Denise and Spade and getting directions to the nearest guest bedroom. It was almost dawn, and as a normal newer vampire, my mother was wilting on her feet. I wasn't worried about Spade's having enough room for all of us. He was a former eighteenth-century nobleman, and the spacious opulence of the several houses he owned reflected that.

Tyler sidled up next to me, eyeing Spade with open appreciation.

"Who's Mr. Tall, Dark, and Delicious?"

"Her husband," I replied, my lips twitching. "Tyler, this is Denise, and that's Spade."

Tyler let out a dramatic sigh as he shook Denise's hand. "All the good ones are either straight or married, but I won't hold it against you that he's both."

Denise laughed. "Great to meet you. Cat's told me all about you."

"And some of it's probably true," he teased.

Then his attention became fixed on someone behind Denise, his mouth dropping before his expression turned into an open, lascivious stare. Thoughts started to race through his mind that were so explicit, I wished I could take a bat to my head to block out my telekinetic abilities.

"Tyler, meet Ian," I said without bothering to turn around.

"Daddy *like*," Tyler breathed.

He straightened his shoulders, fixing his most winning smile on his face as he all but pushed me out of the way. The jostling turned me enough to get a view of the other vampire. Ian leaned against the doorframe, his auburn hair rustling in the breeze and turquoise eyes watching everything with his usual devilishness.

"I thought Bones looked like a little slice of heaven, but you're the whole cake, aren't you, sugar?" Tyler said, holding out his hand.

Ian took the praise as his due, flashing Tyler a smile that had the medium almost tripping in his approach. When he shook Tyler's hand, Tyler let out a sigh that would've done a wistful teenager proud.

That face, that body . . . and you know *he's packing, look at the angle of that dangle!* I heard before screaming *la-la-la* over and over in my mind.

"The killer ghost is still on the loose," I announced to try to distract myself from Tyler's enraptured musings over Ian.

"The trap didn't work?" Spade asked, narrowing his eyes.

"Killer ghost?" Ian perked up, gently batting Tyler aside with a "Yes, yes, I'm truly stunning, but this interests me," remark.

"Let's go inside, and I'll tell you all about it." I nodded at Fabian and Elisabeth, who hung back almost shyly by our car. "You too, guys. We're all in this together."

EIGHTEEN

ONE WEEK HAD PASSED SINCE THE FIASCO
at the cave. On the plus side, we hadn't been
visited by Kramer during that time, probably because
of the copious amounts of weed and garlic that Spade
put in and around his house. It was so profuse that
Elisabeth and Fabian chose to haunt his neighbor's
home instead of staying at Spade's with us. The neighbors were human; they wouldn't mind. They wouldn't
even know.

The bad news was it was now the eighth of October. Elisabeth rode the ley lines every day looking
for Kramer, but she'd only caught quick glimpses of
him once or twice before he vanished. So far, there
were no indications that he'd fixated on any particular
women, but if he hadn't yet, he would soon. The clock
was ticking, and we were behind on the scoreboard.
Just building another trap wouldn't work. Kramer had

seen and overheard enough to know we were after him, so even if we did find a different, equally ideal cave, he'd be expecting us to try and ensnare him.

We were heading home tomorrow, so that Don would be able to reach us if he needed to. He didn't know where Spade and Denise lived when they were in the States, but he'd know to try my house if something came up. I expected Madigan to keep a low profile while attempting to undo the damage he'd inflicted on himself with the cave incident, so we probably could've waited longer before going home; but Denise was starting to sneeze. Being branded with shapeshifting, demonic essence might have made her practically immortal, but apparently it couldn't cure her allergies to cats.

"I'm getting a slice of cake. Tyler, you want any?" Denise asked, him being the only other person here who didn't feed primarily from a liquid diet. The six of us had been relaxing in the living room after dinner, one of my first normal evenings in weeks.

Tyler gave her a droll look. "I'm begging you to tell me your secret. If I ate half as much as you, I'd lose these fierce hips in a week."

Her smile held a hint of grimness. "I'd tell you, but then I'd have to kill you."

And if she didn't, Spade would, I mentally finished. Shapeshifting, limitless healing ability, and a metabolism that burned off calories faster than Denise could consume them weren't the only effects of the demon brands. Her blood was now a literal drug to vampires, and if word of that got out, every undead scumbag looking to make a buck selling it would come crawling out of their coffins after her.

"I'll have a piece of cake," I called out. I might be a vampire, but that didn't mean I was about to let moist devil's food cake go to waste.

"But, um, I'll eat it in my room, if that's okay," I amended, getting an idea about that fudgy icing. "I'm heading to bed."

Bones rose at those words, his eyes glinting as he met my gaze. Guess he'd figured out another use for that cake, too.

"Everyone, I'll see you on the morrow," he said. Then he went into the kitchen, took the plate Denise had just put a heaping slice of cake on, and started up the stairs.

"Retiring already, Crispin? Isn't it quite early?" Ian asked with a wicked little grin.

"Piss off, mate," Bones replied, sparing me the trouble of saying something similar.

We were halfway up the stairs when Dexter let out a sharp bark. I tensed, but then Elisabeth's voice followed, letting me know which ghost had suddenly appeared in the house.

"I know where Kramer is!"

I turned toward the sound of her voice. Elisabeth stood in the foyer with Fabian at her side. Bones set the cake plate down on the steps with a sigh.

Ian laughed. "Wretched timing you have, poppet," he told Elisabeth, and I'd be lying if I didn't admit that a small, selfish part of me also wished she'd poofed up with this good news a few hours later.

Some of her smile faded. "Is something amiss?"

"Nothing," I told her while flashing Bones a rueful smile as I started back down the stairs. "Where is he?"

"Sioux City, Iowa," she replied. "I've seen him there four times now. Far too many to be mere coincidence. This must be where he'll select his victims."

"He picks *all* of his victims from the same area? I thought you said Kramer made sure never to utilize the same place twice."

"He chooses a new location every All Hallows' Eve, very far from any of the places where the previous burnings occurred. Last year, he was in Hong Kong. Often he will hide the bodies to prevent the authorities from realizing the same type of murders occur every year. But the accomplice and the three victims are always chosen from same place."

He hid the bodies? "Why would he care if the police were onto him? It's not like they could put him in handcuffs."

"Because of his accomplices," Elisabeth replied. "If they learned the pattern of the previous murderers through periodicals or modern news, they would realize that once they've concluded their usefulness, Kramer will kill them, too."

"He eliminates every tie to his crimes, even ones from whoever's assisting him?" Ian whistled. "Starting to admire this bloke's resourcefulness."

"You would," I countered.

Elisabeth said nothing, but a spasm crossed her face that I picked up on even with her being partially transparent. Fabian floated over to her, resting his hands on her shoulders.

"You must tell them."

Bones's brows went up. "Tell us what?" Denise asked, beating him or me to it.

Elisabeth closed her eyes, seeming to gather herself together. If she'd been solid, I'd have asked her to sit down, because she looked downright, well, *ghostly*.

"Kramer does not kill his accomplices merely to eliminate ties to his crimes," she said, her voice barely audible. "He always picks those who are fanatical in their belief that they are doing God's work by assisting him in the elimination of witches. But many of them, when they see what he . . . does when he is flesh, realize it is all a lie."

Bones's expression became grim. Even Ian looked like he'd swallowed something distasteful. Denise seemed as clueless as I felt over Elisabeth's oblique statement, but then her meaning hit me, and my stomach clenched in a way that made me think I was about to spew up my liquid dinner all over the coffee table.

"He rapes them," I stated, a deep loathing spreading through me.

Elisabeth's bowed head came up. She looked right at me as she spoke the next words.

"They weren't the first."

This time, I knew right away what she meant, and more of that same fury rose in me. It should come as no surprise that this wasn't a new pattern for Kramer. I'd read enough of the *Malleus Maleficarum* to know that second only to his hatred of women was Kramer's deviant obsession with female sexuality. Rape would be yet another tool he'd use in his quest to physically and emotionally destroy women before he had them killed, and in Elisabeth's time, Inquisitors were given absolute power over the accused—and unsupervised access.

Elisabeth had endured this hellish nightmare, then watched Kramer continue on in the same despicable pattern as a ghost. Yet here she was—unbroken, uncowed, and unwilling to give up her quest for justice no matter which side of eternity she had to fight for it on.

"You're amazing, you know that?" I said, awed by her strength.

That made her bow her head again. "No, but out of everyone Kramer murdered, I alone still exist. I owe it to the lost not to give up."

Silence met her statement. Out of the corner of my eye, I saw my mother swipe at her face as if chasing away tears. It brought back an awful memory: her, covered in dirt and blood, begging me to kill her because she couldn't live with what she'd done during her first few, blood-crazed days as a new vampire. All my arguments of how the vampire who'd thrown those humans in with her—*knowing* what would happen and doing it just to torment her—was the real murderer had fallen on deaf ears. Only Bones sternly telling my mother she wasn't allowed to die because it would dishonor the sacrifice Rodney made when he gave his life during her rescue had reached her.

Sometimes, continuing on in honor of the lost was all a person had.

"Sioux City, Iowa." Bones drew the words out. "We'll go there tomorrow."

I shook myself out of the sorrows of the past. To

stop Kramer, I needed to be focused on the present. That was probably what had kept Elisabeth sane and on track all these years.

"Let's get back to Kramer's pattern. If he's so concerned about covering his tracks, do you know why he picks his victims from the same city?"

Maybe his motive would be something we could use against him. Sticking to the same area was common enough if we were talking human, vampire, or ghoul serial killers, but as a ghost, Kramer could circle the entire globe in hours if he kept hopping on enough ley lines.

"Why would he limit himself that way?" I continued to wonder. "He knows you've been after him, Elisabeth, but he's making himself easier to find by sticking to one area when he hunts for his victims."

Bleakness tightened her features. "Perhaps it's because I've proven to be no real threat to him over the years."

"That's not why," Bones stated. "Kramer can flit in and out of cities in a blink, but his accomplice is flesh and blood. Much more limiting, so if the intended victims are all located within a small geographic area, they're easier for the accomplice to collect when the time comes."

Right, Kramer couldn't kidnap those women himself unless he waited until he was solid, and that only happened for one night. Must not be enough time for the bastard to do every horrible thing on his wish list before he burned them alive. But while the accomplice was Kramer's most valuable asset, he was also the Inquisitor's Achilles' heel. If we found the accomplice in time, Kramer would spend Halloween evening all fleshed up but with no one to torture or burn. The thought filled me with savage satisfaction.

"We need to kill the accomplice as soon as we find out who he is," I stated.

"No."

All heads swung toward Bones, mine included. He tapped his chin, his dark gaze measured and cold.

"If we find out who the accomplice is, we grab him. Mesmerize him into telling us exactly where Kramer intends to hold his nasty bonfire. Then on All Hallows' Eve, we go there, saving the women while capturing both sods instead of only one. Kramer will be solid then, and he can't escape as easily when he's solid, can he?"

I stared at my husband's profile, noting how his sculpted cheekbones, curving dark brows, and exquisite crystal skin only highlighted the ruthlessness of his expression.

"So we go to Sioux City and find the accomplice," I said softly.

His mouth curved into a smile that was half predator, half dream lover.

"Indeed."

Nineteen

I PICKED UP THE CHOCOLATE CAKE ON MY WAY
to the bedroom, but that was more because I didn't
want to leave it on the steps than a continued crav-
ing for it. My thoughts were more focused on justifi-
able homicide than cake eating, kinky or otherwise.
I wasn't the only one in a more somber mood. My
mother muttered that she was going for a drive and
left the house without any further comment. It could
be nothing more than her leaving to find someone to
drink from, but I didn't think hunger was her sole motivator. I probably never wanted to know how much of
Elisabeth's treatment she herself had endured during
the time she'd been kidnapped, murdered, and forcibly
changed into a vampire, all because another vampire
was trying to get back at me. Fabian and Elisabeth
also left right after her, not needing a car to get away,
of course.

Contemplating all the sickening things that Kramer
and others like him had done made me feel like I was

covered in an invisible layer of filth, causing me to go straight into the shower after entering the bedroom. I couldn't wash away Kramer's evil from the world—yet—but I could wash myself off before bed, at least.

When I came out of the bathroom twenty minutes later, Bones was seated on the edge of the bed, absently petting my cat. His shoes were off, his shirt in a pile on the floor next to them, but he hadn't undressed further than that. I paused in the middle of toweling my hair. Normally, Bones didn't do anything halfway, but he just sat there, as if he'd run out of energy to take off his pants.

"Everything okay?" I asked, coming closer.

He smiled slightly, abandoning his attention to my cat in favor of reaching out to rest his hands on my waist. "I was just remembering when I said if I were any more relaxed about our circumstances, I'd need a smoke. Spoke too soon, as it turned out."

I took another step until the thick fabric of my robe almost brushed his face. "Yeah, well. Fate has a dark sense of humor sometimes, right?"

"We need to discuss something, Kitten."

He sounded so serious that nervousness wormed its way into my gut. "What?"

"Limits," he said steadily. "I want to stop Kramer. His sort is the reason why I fell into contract killing in the first place, as I told you a long time ago. But, much as I admire her courage, I don't want to see you turn into Elisabeth."

I leaned back to look at him, brushing a dark curl behind his ear. "What do you mean by that?"

"She'll never stop hunting him. She's accepted it

as her purpose in life, but there is a very real possibility that we won't be able to trap him. We'll bloody well try, but"—Bones flicked his fingers, blowing out a breath at the same time—"he's air all but one night a year, so we're literally chasing the wind. I'm not saying we'll give up if we can't catch him this Halloween, but I am saying that one day, even if Elisabeth doesn't stop, we may have to."

"But he can't just keep getting *away* with this," I argued at once. "How can we think about quitting? You heard what he does! And he'll keep on doing it unless he's stopped."

Bones caught my hands, his dark gaze intense. "This is exactly what I meant about your turning into Elisabeth. She's given every moment of the past five hundred years over to Kramer, in one way or another, and there's been a price for that, hasn't there? She shares her life with only her plans for vengeance, and she's more than earned that vengeance, but I don't want to see you go down the same path. Sometimes, people who deserve vengeance don't get it, and people who are due punishment escape their comeuppance."

He sighed and dropped my hands, a muscle ticking in his jaw before he spoke again.

"I'm not saying we try this Halloween and then stop if we fail. I'm willing to commit years to this because I want this sod locked in a box so he can forever know the helplessness and terror he's inflicted on others, but I can accept that it might not happen. You need to accept that, too, because know this—I won't let you sacrifice yourself in a never-ending quest to defeat someone who might not be able to be caught."

My fists clenched. "You could do that? Turn your back on Elisabeth and all of Kramer's future victims, knowing what will keep happening? You would let that murdering prick win—"

"This isn't a game, Kitten," he interrupted. "It's life, and there will always be injustice no matter how frustrating that is to accept. We'll give Kramer our best shot, but if we fail, we fail. And then we move on."

I sucked in a breath to tell him what I thought of that quitter mentality, but under Bones's hard, knowing stare, I expelled it not in a rant, but in a long sigh. Kramer was such a clear-cut case of evil prowling on the loose that it felt like a betrayal of everything those women had suffered to admit that Kramer could use his ghostly state to forever evade punishment. My knee-jerk response was to shout, *Screw that, I'll catch you if it's the last thing I ever do!*

And that was how Elisabeth had let the pursuit of him fill her life until there was room for nothing else. Part of me still wanted to call Bones a cold-hearted bastard for even considering giving up the hunt on Kramer one day, but that would just be my denial talking. I wouldn't mean those ugly words, and they wouldn't be true; nonetheless they'd been frothing close to the surface. The knowledge that I'd been about to attack the man I loved because he pointed out the very obvious fact that we lived in a world where sometimes, good *didn't* defeat evil, and the good guys didn't ride off into the sunset made me realize how far down Elisabeth's road I'd already traveled.

I still admired her for her strength of will under

repeated, devastating circumstances, but now, I also pitied her. Elisabeth lived for defeating Kramer, and nothing else. How much richer would the long years of her life have been if she'd still sought a way to stop Kramer, but chosen to *live* for something else, like friendship or love?

"You're not going to lose me to this," I finally said. "Defeating Kramer is my goal, and I'll try like hell to accomplish it, but you, Bones . . . you're my life, and you always will be."

He stood, catching my hand in his. Slowly, he raised it to his lips, kissing the ring he'd first put on my finger two years ago. Then his mouth moved up my hand, dragging over my wrist before continuing on its path up my arm, his gaze never leaving mine. By the time he reached my shoulder, I was quivering with desire and other, deeper emotions. I wanted to cry for all the years I'd let circumstances keep us apart, and I wanted to tear away his pants so he could be inside me, bringing us as close together as two people could be.

A moan escaped me when his mouth caressed my neck, his lips and fangs teasing the sensitive skin. He caught my wrists when I tried to slide my hands over his back, holding them gently at my sides. Now my moan was one of mild frustration. Even though he was so close that his aura brushed over me like a warm, invisible cloud, our bodies weren't touching. The only contact we had was his mouth on my neck and his hands clasped around my wrists, and that wasn't enough. Yet when I moved forward, he took a step back, his soft chuckle muffled by my throat.

"Not yet."

Yes, *yet*. I edged closer again, but Bones side-stepped me once more. I couldn't even slide my robe off to tempt him with bare flesh because he still held my wrists in a gentle yet unyielding grip.

"Bones," I whispered. "I want to touch you."

His low growl rumbled against my throat. "And I want to touch you, Kitten. So hold still and let me try."

What did he mean, try? I was right here, attempting to bring our bodies together, and he was the one thwarting me. All he had to do was let go of my wrists, and we'd be touching every inch of each other in about two seconds flat—

I gasped, surprise and ecstasy flaring in me at the sudden tug along the sensitive tips of my nipples. They hardened in expectation of another touch, and it came, leaving them aching with the need for more. But Bones's hands hadn't left my wrists, and his mouth was still pressed to my neck, tongue and fangs grazing over the areas that made me weakest with desire.

"How?" I managed, the question ending on a groan as both tips felt like they were being slowly, sensually pinched.

His hands tightened on my wrists. "Because I want to touch you so badly, yet I'm not allowing myself. So my mind is doing it for me. Feel where I want to be touching you right now . . ."

I didn't have time to be amazed at this exercise of his new power before a long, intimate caress had me shuddering with rapture. My loins clenched, greedily demanding more. The thought that he must've been practicing his telekinetic ability on the sly in order to wield it so skillfully now flitted through my mind before another tantalizing stroke cleared out any more musings under a tide of need. Bones continued to kiss my neck, his tongue flicking out to lave away the scant drops of blood he drew when his fangs broke my skin. A sharper, rougher moan left my lips, my eyelids lowering with the erotic sensations, until my vision was narrowed to two heavy-lidded slits.

That was why it took me a second to notice the small object right behind him, but my instincts took over before my mind roused from its state of sensual bliss. I kicked Bones's legs out from under him the instant before Helsing let out loud hiss, throwing myself forward to shield Bones from the arcing path of the knife.

Fire sliced a path from my cheek down the back of my neck. Bones spun in midair, knocking away the blade that continued to rip down my body. Through the veil of red hair that swung into my face, I saw a dark, diaphanous form start to take shape in the room.

"Kramer!" I shouted.

Twenty

Bones lunged for the sage and lighters on our nightstand, but the ghost crashed it over before he could get to it. The lighter went flying across the room, the sage getting buried under the remains of the table. That knife surged toward me again, but before it landed, Bones had me in a bear hug, rolling us out of the way. Pain cresting through my subconscious told me he hadn't rolled fast enough, but I couldn't see where he'd been stabbed. I pushed at his chest, but he didn't let me go, grimly keeping his body between me and the silver knife that kept slashing at us no matter how fast we moved.

Our door crashed open. Denise's brown hair flew around her as she charged in holding a wad of sage and a lighter. Before she could connect the two, however, the bed launched across the room and slammed into her. She held on to the sage, but lighter was jolted from her hand at the impact of the frame crushing against her fingers. It skidded across the room not far from where Helsing huddled, his hair standing on end and yowling sounds coming from him.

Another crash of footsteps coming down the hall was met with the bed and all the other furniture in the room slamming over the doorway, effective blocking it. Over the booming at the blockaded door, I heard an even more chilling sound—the metallic clang of our weapons' bag being ripped open. Before I could even shout out a warning, a slew of silver came torpedoing at us.

Bones must've heard it, too, because he whipped us to the left so violently that we crashed through the dividing wall into the bathroom. An ugly chuckle reached us over the slew of curses Spade emitted at the ghost.

"Don't come in here, there's a shitload of silver!" Denise yelled.

"She's right, stay back," Bones called out when a tremendous crash sounded like Spade used his body as a battering ram against the door and all its furniture impediments. If he was thinking clearly, he'd realize he could barrel through the dry wall in the next room a lot easier, but I didn't want him in here, so I wasn't about to point that out.

"Start burning sage outside the room," Bones continued urgently. "Sod won't be able to stand it soon enough."

Then he grabbed the edge of the ornate countertop, ripping it off with enough savagery to send hunks careening around the room. "Keep this in front of you, Kitten," he ordered, handing me the makeshift marble shield. Then he tore off a smaller hunk for himself, blood from the sharp edges painting his hands red.

"You will die, woman," Kramer hissed. I thought he was talking to me, but I didn't see his cloudy, disgusting form in either the crashed-in wall or the normal entrance to the bathroom. Then a thwacking sound coincided with Denise's yelp.

"Denise!" Spade roared.

"Stay back, you know he can't kill me!" she shouted, her voice more shrill from pain.

Bones and I burst back into the bedroom, holding up our hunks of countertops to ward off the volley of knives that immediately flew our way. Multiple explosions of pain blasted through me as the silver pierced my legs and arms, but I kept my heart protected, and everything else would heal.

Denise was on the opposite end of the room, crimson soaking her hair from a head wound and several smaller cuts darkening her clothes with blood. I hesitated, fighting my urge to run in front of her. If I did, I'd only be sending more knives her way, because Kramer was after me and Bones. Denise had just dared to interfere with his plans for us.

"Denise, try to get out," I whispered.

"I'm the safest person in this room," she countered.

Kramer spun to face us, giving Bones and me just a second to raise our marble barriers before more knives came hurtling at us.

"Stop it!" Denise yelled.

The ghost ignored her. "You try to defeat me?" Kramer hissed in our direction. "I will destroy you."

Bones replied something in German. I didn't know

enough of the language to translate, but whatever he said made the ghost howl with outrage. More knives went flying, but only aimed at him this time.

"Hurry up with that sage," I called out desperately. Spade had been kind enough to supply us with a lot of weapons for our trip home, but now that meant Kramer had more ammunition against us. Plus, he would reuse the knives, flinging them as fast as they could drop or bounce off our shields.

The ghost's powers seemed even greater than before. Was it because of the closer proximity to Halloween, or because he was still really, really pissed over our attempt to trap him in the cave? We ducked under another barrage of silver, trying to make it to some sage lying on the far side of the demolished room. We couldn't afford to let our attention wander from the knives that seemed to come at us from all sides. Or the ghost who could pop up anywhere around us in a blink, bashing our bodies with what felt like painful bursts of energy. Even with how fast we moved, we didn't know which direction the next attack would come from. All Kramer needed was one lucky strike with a silver blade, and Bones or I would be shriveled.

"You need to get the fuck out of my house," Denise snarled.

I hadn't taken my attention off the hornet's nest of silver knives around us or the ghost who could somehow amass enough energy to make me feel like I was going ten rounds with an undead Mike Tyson, but then something large and dark filled my peripheral vision. I glanced over where Denise had been—and stared.

Bones yanked me down just in time to avoid a silver knife headed right for my cheek. It landed in the wall behind us instead, but I still couldn't quit glancing back at the other side of the room. Helsing let out a frightened hiss and tried harder to hide in the bed and furniture pile.

"Bones, she's . . . she's . . ."

I didn't say more, but pointed. His gaze flicked over, and then widened as even his finely honed defensive instinct couldn't cause him to look away from what was now an incredibly fast-growing mass. Almost absently, he held up his shield at the new influx of knives thrown his way.

Cracking sounds of the ceiling giving way alerted Kramer into turning around. When he did, the knives he'd levitated for imminent attack fell to the ground, and the ghost froze like he'd magically been welded to the spot.

"*Drache,*" he managed to croak.

The bottom half of a huge creature now took up the majority of the once-spacious room, part of its neck and all of its head disappeared into the hole it had made of the ceiling. Curved scales that looked tougher than crocodile skin formed a green-and-black design over the creature's body, darkening in color as they reached its quad-runner-sized legs. A tail wider than my torso whipped out, knocking over the broken bits of furniture scattered about the room before settling in front of me and Bones like a living, flexible barricade. Two thick, horned humps unfurled from the creature's back, revealing dark green wings that took up what was left of the room even though they were only half extended. Their spiked, clubbed ends stabbed holes in the carpet as the creature appeared to use them to balance its great body. Then more wood and plaster rained down, and a new, larger hole appeared, quickly being filled by a massive, elongated head punching through the ceiling. Its jaws were as big as the bed, saucer-sized crimson eyes glaring right at the transfixed ghost while scales like a headdress flared out behind it.

"Denise, you have out*done* yourself," Bones murmured in astonishment.

I still couldn't form words yet. Yes, I'd seen Denise shapeshift before, once into a cat and once into an exact replica of me when she acted as my decoy. But I had no idea that she could manifest something of this *magnitude*. Not ten feet in front of me was what could only be described as a large dragon. One that looked straight out of the movie *Reign of Fire*—only slightly smaller, because this dragon seemed to be only about two stories tall and I think the one from the film was double that size.

If she manages to breathe fire, I thought in numbing awe, *I might actually pass out.*

Kramer remained frozen where he stood, almost as if he thought staying still would render him invisible. He seemed to have forgotten that he had the ability to poof away, because from his expression, he didn't want to be anywhere near the enormous dragon glaring down at him with rows of teeth gleaming from a snarling mouth. Yet, with the creature's tremendous girth, Kramer was practically in the dragon's lap.

Glass exploded outward as a piece of porch furniture hurtled through the bedroom window. It didn't go far, bouncing off the dragon's hind leg and almost flattening my cat, who huddled in terror behind the remains of the bed.

"Room service!" Ian sang out, appearing in the smashed-open window. He had lit sage overflowing both hands, but when he saw the dragon, he froze just like Kramer had, his fanged mouth dropping open.

"Bugger me blind and *bow*legged!"

"Don't just stand there, throw the sage," Bones ground out.

Ian shook his head as if to clear it, then he threw the sage at the ghost, who howled as he finally tried to whoosh out of the way.

More plaster and wood showered the room in the next instant. Then Spade appeared in the huge hole he'd made in the wall by the blocked-off bedroom door. I scrambled to protect my cat just in time, grabbing Helsing before the bed-and-furniture barricade collapsed on top of him. Spade, too, was packing sage, and between the huge snapping dragon that Kramer didn't seem to want to poltergeist through, and the two vampires throwing lighted greenery his way, Kramer couldn't dodge the flying plant missiles fast enough. With a spate of harsh-sounding German, he disappeared.

"What in the holy hell is *that*?"

Tyler peeked around Spade's bulk, more smoldering sage in his hands, to gape in disbelief at the dragon. His thoughts careened from disbelief, to fear, to fascination as the dragon's form wavered, began to shrink, then finally culminated in Denise wearing nothing but a few spatters of blood.

Ian appeared to have recovered from his surprise. He gave Spade an almost accusatory look.

"You're shagging a woman who can turn into a *dragon*? Blast you, Charles, I am *sick* with envy!"

"Not now," Spade muttered, pulling off his shirt and placing it over Denise. I tried to yank the blanket off the remains of the bed, but it was too tightly wedged in with the other furniture, and I only ended up tearing off a long piece.

"Kitten, this first," Bones said. Then he began to pull the knives out of me where Kramer's blades had found their mark. I winced at each sharp, efficient tug, the silver feeling like it tried to take hunks of my flesh along with it.

"Tyler, grab a blanket from the next room?" I suggested, turning my attention to the silver still embedded in Bones's body. His mouth tightened as I began to pull multiples blades out of him, but he made no sound even though I knew it hurt him as much as what he did pained me.

Tyler went to get the blanket, mumbling under his breath that this was the craziest shit he'd ever seen. Spade cradled Denise, who looked a little woozier than normal after a shift. Maybe it was the blood loss from her wounds, though they'd already healed. Or maybe it was her body taking a minute to recover after briefly becoming a thousand-pound mythical creature that looked so intimidating, it had even scared the pants off a homicidal ghost.

Tyler coughed as he came back in and passed a blanket to Denise. Smoke filled the room from the many lit plants, combined with the carpet starting to smolder from the burning piles of sage thrown onto it.

"Fire," I noted, brushing off Bones's attempts to get the last of the silver out of me. I was already done desilvering him, he apparently being able to dodge the blades more efficiently than I. I ran into the bathroom, quickly soaked several towels under the shower, then threw them over the worst of the burning spots. Bones, Spade, Denise, and Ian were stamping out the smaller places. Soon all the fire was out, leaving only some sage burning on nonflammable surfaces, like twisted metal segments of the bed frame and the hunks of the bathroom countertop that had served as my and Bones's temporary shields.

I looked around at the destroyed furniture, broken glass, holes in the ceiling, wall, and bathroom, multiple silver knives strewn about or embedded where they'd landed, and the charred carpet before shaking my head.

"Spade, you should never, ever let us stay with you again. This is twice now that we've ended up trashing one of your rooms."

He shrugged, seeming more concerned with making sure we had enough sage burning in safe places than in the disrepair of his house.

I heard a car pull up in the driveway. Looked like my mother was back. Sure enough, a few seconds later she was standing in the large hole in the bedroom wall, her expression a mixture of shock and concern as she took in the damage.

"Catherine, what *happened*?"

"Is everyone all right?" Fabian called out from what sounded like the yard. I went over to the ruined window, seeing him and Elisabeth floating well outside the cloud of sage smoke drifting out.

"What happened?" Bones repeated, his voice hard as he joined me at the window. He stared at the ghosts, his eyes glinting emerald. "What happened is the two of you were followed."

Twenty-one

I WRINKLED MY NOSE AS I SET THE PET CARRIER down in the small living room of the town house. The former occupants must have been smokers. A lingering scent of tobacco permeated the walls and carpet, but it was better than the garlicky ganja aroma we'd surrounded ourselves with at Spade's. Not that it had done any good. Kramer was obviously too powerful for that to be a deterrent. But, since I was supposed to be looking on the bright side, last night meant we didn't have to start looking for Italian chefs and drug dealers in order to layer up this place with a bunch of garlic and weed. How was that for a Glass-Half-Full perspective?

The first thing I did even before letting my kitty out was start lighting sage and putting it on some of the many incense burners and glass jars we'd acquired on our trip from St. Louis to Sioux City. We hadn't gotten any sleep between the drive, picking up supplies, and arranging for our accommodations here, but catching some winks at Spade's had been out of the question after Kramer's visit. Spade and Denise packed up just as quickly as the rest of us. Guilt stabbed me that they couldn't return unless we managed to capture Kramer. Otherwise, who knew if—or when—Kramer might decide to pop back in for another extremely hostile visit. After all, they couldn't burn sage in every room of their house for the rest of their lives. Or until we caught him, whichever came first.

I knew that Tyler was coming with us, and I expected my mother to tag along as well, but I was surprised when Denise and Spade insisted on coming to Sioux City, too. My question of why was met with pointed stares. Guess Kramer had made two new enemies in his raid, but I didn't know if Denise's dragon metamorphosis would work to terrify the ghost a second time. Even a dragon couldn't harm Kramer, and once he got over his initial terror at seeing one, he'd remember that.

Ian also came along with the comment that he had nothing better to do, and he wanted to see Denise do another "shapeshifter trick," as he called it. In spite of my personal dislike of him, Ian was crafty, powerful, and practically fearless in a fight. Too bad all that came wrapped up with the conscience of a barracuda, but he was loyal in his own way to Bones and Spade. Ian might claim he was here only because of boredom or the chance to see Denise shape shift into something unusual, but I knew better. The Inquisitor had fucked up when he tried to kill Bones. *That*, Ian cared about.

Absent from our group were Fabian and Elisabeth. The ghosts had taken their own form of transportation in the form of ley lines. Even though both of them swore that they were careful, and Kramer hadn't followed them back to Spade's, it seemed too big a coincidence. This was twice now that Kramer found us, and my borrowed powers were gone, so that wasn't the smoking gun. In Ohio, I'd blamed it on chance because the state was a supernatural hotspot that naturally drew a lot of ghosts, but St. Louis wasn't, and I doubted Kramer had gotten extremely lucky in the ley lines he rode last night.

Thus, we were in the Morningside section of Sioux City, but we'd rented an apartment for Fabian and Elisabeth just outside Kelly Park. It was necessary to give them their own place because we'd arranged for a new method for communicating with them, and we couldn't risk its getting stolen. The ghosts didn't need furniture or kitchen appliances, so the apartment was empty save for one very important item: a cell phone. Elisabeth could manifest into solid flesh long enough to use it, and who said you couldn't teach an old ghost new technology? After a few lessons, Elisabeth learned how to send a text since her voice would only sound like white noise if she called me. I'd programmed her phone so it would forward any text she sent to me to all of our shiny new cells. This way, Elisabeth and Fabian could follow Kramer without worrying about leading him back to us when they needed to relay information. In an emergency, they could poof up where we were staying, but unless things got dire, they'd reach us in the new old-fashioned way.

"Got your mum settled in with Ian," Bones remarked, coming into the town house.

Spade and Denise were staying together for obvious reasons, and I didn't trust Ian to fully be invested in protecting Tyler if Kramer found us and managed to brave the sage. That left Tyler with us and Ian with my mom. Bones was going to arrange for another vampire to stay at our cabin in case my uncle showed up with important news, but my mom could fill that position. The prospect of cooling her heels at the cabin shut her up . . . right until it was time to go in the rented town house with Ian, and then I'd done the most practical thing I could: I sicced Bones on her.

"I swear, that woman's got a mouth on her worse than you do," Tyler commented, following in after Bones. "Ian gave her the tiniest smack on the rear when she walked by, and she told him to—"

"Ian smacked my mother on the ass?" I cut him off. At Tyler's nod, I stopped lighting sage and grabbed a silver knife, feeling my fangs pop out of their own accord. "Wait here, I'll be right back."

Bones blocked my path to the door. "I have it sorted, luv. He won't do anything like that again, promise."

I stood there for a moment, debating whether to push past Bones so I could slice and dice Ian before stringing him up by the silver rings he had pierced through his parts, when Bones raised his brow.

"Don't you trust me?"

"I trust *you*, not him," I muttered.

He grasped my shoulders. "Then if you trust me, believe that it's sorted. If he proves me wrong, I vow I'll hold him down and let you stab him as many times as you please."

That image brought a smile to my face. Talk about looking on the bright side! Bones chuckled.

"Then it's settled. Now, I'll get us unpacked. Why don't you go back to lighting enough sage to make sure that ghostly sod gets a proper welcome if he pops up on us again?"

I'd like to believe that wouldn't happen, but there were two ways Kramer could indeed drop by for an unwelcome visit. One was if he'd returned to Spade's before we left last night and followed us all the way from St. Louis to here. We'd tried to prevent that by leaving very quickly and having Elisabeth and Fabian keep a lookout the first hundred or so miles, but if the ghost was sly, he could've managed it.

The second possibility was more likely, and it sucked on many levels.

"You realize we might need more than sage if Kramer overheard us talking last night about how we were planning to trap him," I stated.

"Aw, hell. I didn't think of that," Tyler muttered.

"I did," Bones said with a grim glance at me. His voice lowered until it would be impossible for anyone eavesdropping to overhear him. "Means we need to center our attention on his intended victims instead of the accomplice. Elisabeth said he never wavered once he picked his targets. That will work to our advantage."

My eyes widened, but I made sure to speak as quietly

as he despite my surprise. "How, unless we use those women as bait?"

"I hate it when you two whisper like that," Tyler muttered. "Makes me antsy."

"That's precisely what we'll do," Bones replied, holding up a finger to Tyler in the universal gesture for *wait*. "If Kramer expects us to concentrate on finding and mesmerizing his accomplice, he'll either be extremely zealous in concealing that bloke's identity, and we'll never discover who he is. Or he'll lie to the accomplice about where he's intending to hold the bonfire, sending us on a wild-goose chase while he's off somewhere else having his spot of gruesome fun. Either way, he avoids our trap."

"But if we have the women," I mused, "then Mr. No One Else Will Do would come to us to try and get them. Or he'd send his accomplice for the same purpose."

Bones nodded. "And then, either way, we'd get our chance to nab Kramer or the accomplice. In any event, the women would be safer with us than on their own."

Safer, but not safe. I heaved a mental sigh. Nothing I could do about that. Once they'd been targeted by Kramer, they wouldn't be truly safe until the Inquisitor was rotting in a trap somewhere. We might be able to protect them this Halloween, but the ghost had proven to be more than deadly in his noncorporeal form, too. Even if we returned those women safe and sound to their homes on November 1, with strict instructions to keep sage burning at all times, they had to leave sometime. And when they did, Kramer could poof up and poltergeist them to kingdom come.

If we didn't find a way to trap Kramer—which would be damn hard even if he did come right to our door—we could be saving these women on Halloween only to have them murdered in a different way later, and the same pattern would repeat the year, and the next, and the next . . .

I heaved an actual sigh this time, fixing Bones with a tired, jaded look. "We might need to see Marie."

Bones's face became as hard as granite. "No."

"Who's Marie?" Tyler wondered. I'd said that last part loud enough for him to catch it.

I mimed "wait" at him and lowered my voice again, trying to convince Bones that an audience with a woman who'd been both ally and adversary in the past was worth trying.

"Probably no one in the world knows more about ghosts and the afterlife than the ghoul queen of New Orleans. What if there's a spell that could boot Kramer right off this plane of existence?"

"Then Marie would want too much in return for it, not to mention practicing black magic is against vampire law," was his immediate reply.

"Since when did you worry about being law-abiding?" I scoffed.

His dark gaze was steady. "Since I fell in love with you and assumed Mastership of a line. If it was proven that we practiced black magic—and I don't trust Marie not to mention it—the Law Guardians could sentence us to death. That's a chance I'm not willing to take, Kitten."

I disagreed that Marie would tattle on us, but I remembered all too well how lethally efficient Law

Guardians were when it came to death sentences. I'd briefly been under one of those, and only some quick thinking combined with misdirection had prevented my head from parting company with my shoulders less than five minutes after a Law Guardian pronounced that sentence.

The only other way Marie could help us would be to give me another wineglass full of her blood, but for me to admit that my Remnant-summoning powers had run their course held its own set of unacceptable consequences.

Damn. Back to square one: trying to catch someone who was made of air and for all intents and purposes, immortal. *You don't have a chance in hell,* an insidious inner voice whispered.

Fuck you; pessimism never helped anyone, I told it.

"All right," I said, forcing a smile. "We concentrate on finding the women and let Kramer or his accomplice come to us once we do."

And if they do, that relentless inner voice continued to taunt, *you're going to need a helluva lot more than burning sage to save the day.*

Yeah, I knew that, too. But I'd resolved to believe that things would work out, and that was what I was going to do.

†wenty-two

On October 14, while all of us were in the family room watching a movie to break up the monotony of more fruitless waiting, my new cell phone finally vibrated with a text. I almost leapt up from the couch to read it, praying it wouldn't be a wrong number, then let out a whoop.

"Elisabeth sent over an address! Let's move."

Bones was already on his feet, Spade and Denise following suit, but Ian shot me a piqued look.

"You don't mean all of us, do you? The movie's not over."

"You've *seen* this one before," I replied in disbelief.

He shrugged. "Watching Snape make fun of Harry is my favorite part."

"Let him stay," Bones stated. "He can watch over Tyler while we're gone. You can rouse yourself to do that if need be, right, mate?"

Ian's mouth curled at the heavy irony in Bones's voice. "Probably."

"I'm not going?" Tyler sounded disappointed, but his thoughts indicated otherwise. *Ian, watching over me? Finally, this situation's looking up!*

I rolled my eyes. "Yeah, Tyler, you're staying here with Ian. Try not to let it upset you too much."

It won't, he thought, but said, "I'll manage," so mildly that Bones let out a snort.

I went to the refrigerator and grabbed multiple packets of sage, handing them out to Spade, Denise, and Bones. It felt weird to be loading up on plants instead of silver before a potentially dangerous situation.

My mother marched over, holding out her hand with a challenging glint in her eye. "You're not expecting *me* to stay behind, too, are you?"

"Um . . ." I hedged.

Actually, I had, thinking that Tyler would do better with my mom here to protect him if by chance Kramer showed up. Hell, if the ghost attacked during the climactic scene with Snape, Harry, and Dumbledore, Ian might not even stop watching the movie to heal any mortal injuries the medium received.

"Tyler would feel safer with both of you," I began.

"The hell I would," Tyler cut me off, glaring. *Cockblocker!* rang across my mind.

If I'd still been human, my cheeks would've been flaming. I'd been called a lot of names in my day, but never that one before.

"Fine," I gritted out, hoping Tyler's horniness wouldn't end up being the death of him. "Mom, you're coming. Here's some sage."

She took it almost in surprise, like she'd been expecting me to argue. I wanted to, but between Tyler's mental berating and the fact that I didn't want to leave my mother with only Ian to protect her if Kramer showed up, kept me quiet.

Next I passed out lighters until everyone had several. Then I went to get the final protection against a possible spectral attack: Helsing, who gave me a baleful look when I hustled him into his carrier.

Sage, lighters, and a pissed-off kitty might not look like the most conventional ghost-busting arsenal, but so far, they'd proven to be the most effective.

Elisabeth and Fabian flew into our car even before Bones had it in park.

"You must hurry, he just left!" she said, her accent even thicker with her agitation.

"Which apartment?" I asked.

She pointed at the left-hand corner of the building. "One of the top ones."

Bones's brows went up. "You don't know the number?"

"It's difficult to get such details while trying to remain unseen," Fabian replied, rallying to Elisabeth's defense.

"How many can there be?" I asked Bones, with a philosophical shrug.

He got out of the car. "Appears we're going to find out. Charles," he said, as Spade pulled up alongside us, "stay here and keep some sage burning. With luck, we'll be right back. Fabian, Elisabeth, keep a lookout for Kramer in case the sod returns while we're here."

"What about me?" my mother asked from the backseat.

"You're staying with the car," I told her as I got out, hefting the pet carrier along with me. "No offense, Mom, but your people skills suck."

She huffed in indignation. Bones flashed me an appreciative grin that she couldn't see.

"Keep it running, Justina. We may need you to fetch us in a hurry," he said, his tone very bland.

That explanation mollified her until she thought it through, which didn't happen until we were already up the second flight of stairs of the apartment building.

"You can run faster than that!" I heard her shout from across the parking lot.

Spade's reply was swallowed up by sounds from the occupants in the building, but I caught the hint of his laughter, which meant he'd belted it out without restraint.

"She's got to be steaming," I noted in amusement.

Bones's smile was shameless. "How regrettable."

We climbed the last flight of stairs to the third floor. Several apartments were clustered in the general area Elisabeth had indicated. Because it was right around dinnertime, it sounded like all of them were occupied, too. No narrowing it down that way.

"Well, how do you want to do this?" I asked. "Pretend to be Neighborhood Watch members reporting a rash of car vandalisms, or a sweepstakes clearinghouse with a big check?" That would at least get fewer doors slammed in our faces. Maybe.

"Give me a moment," Bones murmured. He closed his eyes and his aura flared, filling the air with invisible currents. After several seconds, he pointed at the two doors in the far corner without opening his eyes.

"She's in one of those units."

"And you know that because you can somehow use the Force now?" I asked, trying to limit the dubiousness in my tone.

He opened his eyes, tapping the side of his head. "By listening. You're probably tuning everyone's thoughts out, but I'm focusing in on them. A very traumatized woman is behind one of those doors, and I'll wager it's because Kramer just left."

That was what I got for doubting him. Bones was right that I'd pulled my mental shields up high and tight against the barrage of thoughts coming from the apartments, but in doing so, I'd neglected an important tool in finding our target.

"Good thing you're here. That's far too practical to have occurred to me," I added wryly.

He stilled my hand as I was about to knock on the door labeled "B."

"Don't berate yourself. I did the same thing when I first acquired this power, but I've had it much longer, so my response to it has changed. You're not used to it yet, but you will be, then accessing it will be second nature to you also."

Maybe, but it wasn't even my power to begin with. If I stopped drinking from him, that mind-reading ability, like every other borrowed power, would soon be gone. Bleakness briefly threaded through me. In many ways, I was an imposter, my significant strength and skills just the product of a supernatural dietary quirk. Without the capacity to siphon powers through feeding, I probably wouldn't be any more bad-ass than my mother. *Would the real Red Reaper please stand up?*

Then I pushed those thoughts aside and rapped on the door. I could have my personal identity crisis later, when someone else's life wasn't on the line. If anyone deserved a pity party, it was the woman we were here to collect, and from the muffled sob on the other side of this door, it seemed I was about to meet her.

"Who is it?" a strained voice called out. *Can't handle dealing with anyone right now* followed on the heels of that, discernible even through my mental barrier.

"We just moved in," I said, trying to sound friendly. "I found this cat wandering around, and I was wondering if you'd recognize who his owner is."

Seemed more plausible than my other ideas considering I was standing here with a cat carrier. The door cracked open, security chain still engaged. Cautious, good for her, but no dead bolt or chain could keep out what was after her. I caught a glimpse of matted blond hair framing a tear-stained face before I held up the carrier, showing her a glimpse of my kitty.

"Wait a second," she mumbled. The door's closing coincided with the slide of the chain being removed. She opened it more fully this time, peering at Helsing.

"Haven't seen him here before," she began.

Emerald blazed forth from Bones's eyes, bright as a traffic light. As quick as she could gasp, she was caught in their depths, mutely stepping back when Bones told her to let us inside.

I closed the door behind us, wincing when I saw

the destruction in her apartment. Her couch was over-turned, lamps and tables smashed, kitchen cabinets half-torn from their hinges, and multiple pieces of broken dishes littered the floor. Either this was Kramer's work, or she had real issues with her temper.

"Who did this?" Bones asked, still holding her gaze.

Anguish skipped across her expression. "I don't know his name. I can't even see him unless he wants me to."

That was enough confirmation for me, but Bones asked her one more question. "How long has he been coming to you?"

"Over three weeks," she whispered.

I exchanged a grim glance with Bones. That was earlier than we'd expected. If Kramer had started ter-rorizing his intended victims at the end of September, it made sense that he'd already picked out his accom-plice. It only stood to benefit Kramer if his dirty little helper was familiar with where he'd be kidnapping the women from, after all. And if Kramer was cover-ing his tracks well enough that it had taken Elisabeth over five weeks to find the first of the three women, would she be able to find the other two in just seven-teen days?

"Don't be afraid, but you need to come with us," I told her.

A single tear slipped down her cheek, but she made no protest when I started leading her toward the door. Bones stopped me, gesturing toward what I assumed was her bedroom.

"Let her collect a few things, and make sure she takes what's most precious to her. Those will help her feel more comfortable later. I'll get some sage burning just in case."

Leave it to Bones to know how to make a girl feel better, even under the most stressful circumstances.

"Come on, we're going to pack real quick," I told her, making sure I said it with the brights on in my gaze. "Don't forget to take whatever has the most sentimental value to you."

"I can't," she said, another tear trickling down her cheek.

"Sure you can," I murmured encouragingly. Then, after another glance at the carpet, I picked her up. Otherwise, her bare feet would be shredded with all the broken glass. From the coppery scent wafting off her, she had some cuts on her feet from letting us in. Why hadn't she put on shoes before answering the door?

Once we were in her bedroom, which was as trashed as the rest of the apartment, I had my answer.

"Bastard," I whispered with a fresh surge of loathing.

From the looks of her closet, Kramer had destroyed all her clothing. Suits, dresses, blouses, pants . . . you couldn't tell them apart from the piles of shredded fabric. Dresser drawers were overturned, more haphazard pieces of fabric spilled out of them. He'd even split apart her shoes.

"I don't have anything left that matters to me. He broke it all," she said, the words more heartrending because of the acceptance in her tone.

Anger made my hands tremble. Since he died, Kramer no longer had the ability to rip women from their homes, taking them away to a pitiless prison. So to make up for that, he turned their homes into their prisons. This woman—and I still didn't know her name—wouldn't even be able to leave her apartment unless she wore that robe as an outfit.

"Don't worry, we're taking you to a safe place," I promised her, picking her up again.

I'd cleared the bedroom door when Helsing let out an extended snarl.

Twenty-three

BONES WAS IN FRONT OF ME IN A BLINK, holding two fistfuls of burning sage. I held the woman with one arm and tried to reach for my own sage stash with the other, but then something heavy slammed into the back of my head hard enough to make me lose my balance. Bones whirled, grabbing us both and backing us into the wall, his body and that barrier a protective shield from any additional attacks.

"Door," I muttered, seeing over his shoulder what I'd been brained with this time. "Fucker hit me with the bedroom door!"

"Get out," an enraged voice hissed.

Blood wet my hair before the wound closed on itself, but that initial flash of dizziness was gone, leaving me good and mad. That only increased when all the broken dishes became airborne and thudded into Bones's body like glass knives.

The woman didn't scream, but she made a horrible

keening noise, squeezing her eyes shut. "No, no, no," she began to chant.

I managed to free my arms from the tight wedge Bones had us in enough to pull out some sage and light it. In the time it took me to do that, Kramer had blasted the couch into Bones. I felt his pain flaring along my subconscious as the impact drove those glass shards farther into his back, but Bones just braced himself, absorbing the blow without shifting his weight even an inch. Then he shot the unseen ghost a feral grin.

"Is that all you've got?"

Kramer howled in fury, outing his position even though he hadn't manifested in appearance yet. I took aim and threw, using enough force that the sage went all the way across the room. Another howl sounded, pained this time, making me smile with vicious satisfaction. I pelted another handful in that direction, but Kramer must have moved, because the only sounds that followed were rattling from the cabinet doors he ripped off and began to chuck at us. One of them hit Helsing's carrier, making my cat screech, but it was made of sturdy material and protected him from the impact.

"Kitty," I urged Bones, still pinned too tightly to the wall to get him myself.

Bones didn't move, but he stared at the carrier, his aura sparking like he'd just set off invisible fireworks. The carrier slid across the wall, pushing past the wood and glass in its path, until it was close enough for Bones to hook his foot around it and tuck it under the shelter of our legs.

I didn't have time to admire the use of his power

before pounding began on the apartment door, followed by a woman's voice yelling, "This is too much, Francine. I'm calling the police this time!" Then Elisabeth burst through one of the walls, Fabian following closely behind her.

"Kramer," she shouted. "Where are you, *schmutz*?"

Air swirled in tight circles near the kitchen, growing darker, until the tall, thin form of the Inquisitor appeared.

"Here, *hure*," he hissed at her.

I was shocked when Elisabeth flew toward Kramer and started swinging. Unlike what happened when Bones or I attempted that, her blows didn't harmlessly go through him. The Inquisitor's head snapped to the side at the haymaker punch she landed. Then he was almost brought to his knees by the merciless kick she smashed into his groin. Kramer couldn't be harmed by anyone with flesh, but clearly that same rule didn't apply when it came to another noncorporeal being whaling on him.

Throughout all this, the woman—Francine?— seemed to be lost in her own private hell, murmuring, "No, no, no," in an endless, ragged litany. Over Bones's shoulder, I saw that Kramer had started to turn the tables on Elisabeth. He landed a vicious kick to her midsection that made her double over. Fabian jumped on the Inquisitor's back, kicking and punching, but Kramer grabbed him and flung him off so effortlessly, Fabian disappeared through the apartment wall. Guess ghosts were similar to vampires, with age accounting for greater strength. Elisabeth and Kramer were nearly the same in spectral years; but

Fabian was much younger, and from the looks of it, not nearly a match for the Inquisitor.

"We need to leave," Bones said low. "Now, while he's distracted."

Then Bones turned his head, shouting, "Charles, to the house!" loud enough to make my eardrums vibrate.

But seeing Elisabeth getting the crap kicked out of her made me hesitate when Bones tightened his arms around us with obvious intent. Elisabeth's gaze locked with mine for a split second. Then she threw her arms around Kramer, bear-hugging him despite the brutal pounding she received to her midsection in return. Fabian flitted around, desperately trying to intervene, only to be swatted aside like a fly.

I got her message, grabbing Helsing's carrier and whispering, "Now!" to Bones.

The front door opened the instant we reached it, allowing us to exit without ripping a hole in the wall. I hadn't opened it. I had one arm around his neck and the other gripping the cat carrier. Bones's hands were likewise full, supporting me and the woman while he blasted us away faster than I could've flown. We must have been only a dark blur to the neighbor in the outdoor hallway, on her cell phone describing the noises in the woman's apartment to the police, it sounded like.

Then we were well past the building, giving me only a moment to note that Spade's car and the one we'd driven in were no longer in the parking lot before we were too high for me to make out the different vehicles. Now there was even less chance for Kramer to follow us. From how Bones seemed to have loaded up his jets, we only needed another minute or two more before the ghost wouldn't be able to discern in which direction we'd flown away.

The downside was that this had shaken the woman out of her trancelike state. She screamed as fast as she could draw breath, but with her eyes squeezed tightly shut, I couldn't green-eye her into a more calm state of mind.

"You're okay, you're okay!" I shouted to no effect. Either she didn't hear me above the whooshing of wind from Bones's speed, or she strongly disagreed. With everything that had happened to her, I couldn't blame her. When we got back to the apartment, I promised myself, I'd give her a tall glass of whatever liquor she wanted. On second thought, make that the whole bottle.

Yet even then, it wouldn't be enough to couch the devastating news I'd have to deliver: that the nightmare she'd experienced wasn't going to end unless we caught Kramer, and she'd be part of the lure we would use to attempt that.

Francine sat on the couch, a glass candle filled with smoldering sage in one hand and a mostly empty bottle of red wine in the other. The bottle had been full when I began to explain about Kramer, the other women who were even now going through what she'd experienced, and the part about Bones and me being vampires. Flying Francine out of her apartment kinda let on that we weren't human, so there was no sense in trying to keep that secret while telling her everything else. Spade, Denise, and my mother got here about an hour after we did, but so Francine didn't feel like she was being ganged up on, only Bones, I, and Tyler were with her at first. Everyone else was in their respective town houses.

I didn't know if it was the alcohol or the suggestion Bones had planted earlier in her mind that she could trust us, but Francine was a lot calmer than I expected her to be at these revelations. It was possible she was in shock, and most of what I said didn't register to her, but her thoughts weren't in line with that. She had a few token moments of "vampires don't exist" and "this can't be happening," but overall she seemed to accept that what we were telling her was true. Three weeks of being tormented by an invisible entity had evidently disabused her of the idea that the paranormal didn't exist.

"I knew I wasn't crazy," was what she said when I finished speaking. "No one believed me when I told them what was happening. For a little while, I tried to pretend they were right. That I was doing all these things to myself through multiple personality disorder or whatever other psychosis applied, but I knew better."

Francine glanced down at the wine bottle and let out a jagged laugh. "This is my first drink since all this started. My friends already thought I'd just snapped because of—of other events. I didn't want them to add alcoholism into their rationalization that what I described couldn't really be happening to me."

"What other events?" Bones asked at once.

She balked, and I hastened to add, "We don't mean

to pry, but it might help us find the other two women before it's too late."

Francine let out a long sigh, scratching her hand through her sunshine-colored hair before she spoke.

"My mom died about six months ago. Dad passed on when I was really little, so she was all I had growing up. It really messed me up, which was way too much drama for my boyfriend, so he moved on to greener pastures. Then right before *he* started showing up, someone broke into my apartment and killed my cat. I mean, what kind of sicko does that? They didn't even steal anything, just killed her and left!"

"That's *awful*," Tyler breathed. He hugged Dexter as he spoke, the dog in his usual spot on Tyler's lap.

"So sorry for everything," I murmured. I meant it, but the clinical part of me analyzed this against what I knew about serial killers in general and Kramer in particular. Francine and Elisabeth didn't really look alike aside from both being Caucasians in their later twenties, so that wasn't a trail to follow, and aside from the cat murder, everything else Francine related was, sadly, what I would expect. Francine didn't have many close ties left, making her more appealing to a stalker like Kramer. It was harder to isolate and terrorize someone who had a strong support network around her.

"Looking back, do you think Kramer might have been the actual culprit behind your cat's death?" Bones asked, zeroing in on the same oddity that bothered me.

Francine rubbed her forehead wearily. "I don't think so. The person broke the lock on my front door to get in. Did it while I was at work, and most people in my building are gone during the day, too, so no one saw it happen. Kramer never broke anything to get in. He just . . . showed up." Watery smile. "And then broke everything inside, but never the locks."

"Destruction of the witch's familiar," Bones murmured. His mouth twisted. "Animals as familiars were one of the precepts set forth in many witch trials, and cats were commonly associated as a familiar. This could be nothing more than coincidence . . . or perhaps it's the accomplice's first test of loyalty."

Breaking and entering, plus murdering something innocent for no reason other than warped superstition? Yep, sounded like just the warm-up Kramer might use for his human apprentice. Furthermore, Kramer had to know that animals could sense his presence. He'd tried to kill Dexter the first time Tyler summoned him. Poor dog still had that cast on his back leg, and Helsing would have been in worse shape if not for some lucky breaks. Getting rid of any pets his targets owned meant those pets could never warn their owners of Kramer's presence before he wanted it to be known.

Prick.

Francine blinked back tears. "So it's because of me that my cat was killed?"

"You're not responsible for *any* of this," I told her firmly. "Kramer is. Him, and whoever the shit is that's helping him."

"But you're going to stop them, right?"

I had to glance away from the poignant hope in

Francine's face before I promised all sorts of things I wasn't sure I could deliver on.

"We're sure going to try," I said, meeting Bones's steady dark gaze, "and you just gave us a new lead to start on."

Twenty-four

"This is the place," I said, shielding my eyes from the morning sunlight.

I might have lost access to the Homeland Security's database thanks to Madigan's new position as boss, but a lot of the information that led us here was all a matter of public record if you were willing to pay a fee. A little hacking into the Sioux City Police Department database provided the rest. In the past two months, approximately 106 households in the Sioux City metro area had reported burglaries. That was a big number if we were doing door-to-door searches, but out of those, only thirty-eight were reported by women living alone. Filter that further by women between the ages of eighteen and forty-five living alone where the burglary resulted in the injury or death to a pet, and that number dropped to one.

If we were right about the connection between dead pets and Kramer, we'd found one of the remaining two women less than six hours after Francine told us her story. Maybe this new woman could give us information that could lead to Kramer's final intended victim. Then we could start the really hard part: building another trap for Kramer that we could lure the ghost into. We had all the materials. We just needed a new place with a freshwater stream to set them up in.

But we had to do all this without Madigan finding us and screwing everything up again. On the principle that I'd vowed to stay optimistic, I wasn't about to calculate our odds.

One thing was already in our favor: Someone with a heartbeat was in Lisa Velasquez's home. I glanced at the clock in the car—10:17 A.M., miserably early for vampires but past the time most people had to be at work. Maybe Lisa had taken the day off. Maybe she worked second shift.

Or maybe she was being so tormented by a ghost that she'd gotten fired from her job for bizarre behavior and frequent absences, just like Francine had.

"We should've brought the cat," Bones muttered, eyeing the one-story house where Lisa lived. If we were right, Kramer could be lurking in there, just waiting for us to cross the threshold.

"Helsing's almost been killed a couple times. I'm not risking it, especially when we're pretty sure those past attempts were deliberate, and we only get a two-second warning hiss before Kramer whales on me anyway."

"His attacking you first the past three out of four times is what concerns me," Bones replied, an edge to his tone.

"What can I say?" Wry smile. "I'm irresistible."

Bones shot me a look that said my humor was wasted on this subject, handing me two glasses full of already smoldering sage. Then he took two more for himself, leaving the other two lit containers in the car. Both of us had more sage in our coats, plus the prerequisite lighters, but this time, we weren't waiting to flame up. Sure, we'd look a little strange to whoever opened the door, but that was the least of our concerns.

"Hear anything interesting?" I murmured, as we walked to the door. I had my mental shields lowered as much as possible without the voices overwhelming me, but I wasn't as good at filtering through unfamiliar ones yet, and Lisa lived in a subdivision bordering a busy business district.

He closed his eyes, his power flaring for an instant. "Whoever's in there is asleep," he stated.

That made this easier. I glanced around, didn't notice any neighbors watching us, then marched up to the closest window, peering inside. No such luck, the drapes were drawn. I tried the next window. Same thing. Bones picked up on my intention and circled around the back of the house.

"Here," he called out after a moment.

From his tone, he'd struck pay dirt. In the few seconds it took me to get to where he was, Bones had the sliding glass door open. Either he'd used his mind to unlock it or leaned in and pulled up at the right angle; either would've taken about the same amount of time.

I followed him inside, mouth tightening at the destruction inside that Lisa had tried to conceal with her tightly drawn drapes. Bones followed the steady sounds of a heartbeat to Lisa's bedroom, which again looked so similar to what Kramer had done at Francine's that we didn't need to wake Lisa and question her to get our confirmation. Besides, speed was of the essence.

Bones put down the burning sage to place his hand over the sleeping woman's mouth, stifling her instant scream as that jolted her into awareness. I felt guilty about the sudden frantic race of her pulse and the terror that spiked across her mind, but by the time Bones finished telling her we were taking her somewhere safe, and we wouldn't hurt her, her heart rate had slowed to almost a normal rhythm, and her thoughts mirrored the suggestions he'd implanted with his gaze.

When he picked her up and the covers fell back, I saw she was wearing a nightgown that was so ripped, more flesh was revealed than covered. *Bastard,* I silently swore at Kramer, shrugging off my coat.

"No," Bones said, voice low but sharp. "She can wear mine, but you're keeping that sage close."

Arguing with him would only take more time, and Kramer could show up at any moment. Bones doffed his coat, handing it to Lisa. She put it on, still mechanically obedient thanks to the power in his gaze. I hated the necessity of highjacking her will, but at that moment, her immediate compliance was in her very best interest.

I handed Bones a few extra packets of sage and a couple lighters that he put into his pants pockets before picking up the lit containers again.

"Straight to the car, Lisa," he instructed her, gaze warily flicking around as we walked from her bedroom to the front door. I was braced the whole way, expecting one of the broken pieces of furniture or dishes suddenly to levitate and slam into us, but nothing happened.

We opened the front door and all my muscles tightened again, waiting for it to fling back and bash into us, yet only the bright sunlight waited on the other side. The car looked untouched, twin lanterns of sage still burning in the front cup holders and filling the interior with a light veil of smoke.

I got into the backseat with Lisa, rolling down the window enough that she wouldn't choke from the haze but not too much that all the ghost-repelling smoke escaped. Then Bones peeled out of the neighborhood fast enough to cause a couple homeowners to peer after us as we sped by, and still, no sign of Kramer.

My relief was mixed with suspicion. "Do you think he's off somewhere else at the moment? Or that he's letting us get away unscathed because he wants us to lead him right to Francine?"

"Doesn't matter," Bones said, glancing back at me. "We're not driving straight back to the town house."

"No?" That was news to me.

His mouth quirked. "No, which is why you're going to turn the brights on in your gaze and tell her to remain *really* calm, else in another ten minutes, she'll scream our bloody ears off."

We left the car at the end of a cornfield, and Bones flew us the rest of the way with the explanation that

ghosts couldn't follow after about the half-mile height
marker. Now that he mentioned it, I realized Fabian
and every other ghost I'd seen had always kept pretty
close to buildings or the ground when they traveled,
unless they were hitchhiking on an airplane or something similar. Bones had us as high as Lisa could take
without it being too cold or oxygen depleted. At that
height, it would be harder to spot us against the clear
morning sky, but Bones had packed a light blue sheet
that we wrapped around us for even better camou-
flage. Maybe when I got more used to flying, I'd treat
it with the same thoroughness he did, but for now, I
was still doing well if I didn't crash when I landed.

Once we got Lisa settled and explained all about
Kramer, her story turned out to be eerily similar to
Francine's. She was divorced, no siblings, and while
her father was still alive, he was in poor health in a
nursing home. She'd also had a recent string of bad
luck, like losing her well-paying job several months
ago because of company downsizing and her house
going into the early stages of foreclosure. Working
two part-time jobs hadn't been enough to pay her
mortgage, and working at all cut off her unemploy-
ment. Add in a botched robbery where her cat was
killed, and Lisa's friends thought her claims of something invisible attacking her at home were a clear case
of stress manifesting in the form of paranoid delu-
sions.

Lisa seemed glad to meet Francine even though
she was sickened to hear that the apparition who'd
tormented her was doing the same thing to other
women. Still, I understood why it was a relief for Lisa

to meet someone who not only believed her but who knew exactly what she'd been through.

The same went for Francine. All the empathy Bones and I could give wasn't the same as what Francine got when she spoke to Lisa. They were survivors of a battle that we could try to imagine but hadn't lived through like they had, so our understanding was limited.

After we'd answered all her questions, Bones went next door to update the rest of our group, and I escorted Lisa upstairs to Francine's room, where there was another bed and a clean outfit waiting for her. Later, I'd order both of them some new clothes, but for now, I left them alone. Francine had only slept a few hours, and Lisa looked like she needed a nice long rest, too. I didn't imagine either of them had had a decent sleep since Kramer targeted them, but with sage burning on their nightstands, two pets capable of sounding a warning, and two vampires here to protect them—plus two more nearby—they were as safe as they were going to get.

Tyler wandered into the kitchen, wearing a pair of sweatpants and a sleeveless shirt. From the faint creases on his cheek, he'd just rolled out of bed. Since staying with us the past few weeks, Tyler's schedule of when he was awake and when he slept had drastically altered.

"M'n," he mumbled, though it was after two o'clock in the afternoon. "Want some coffee?"

I drank it with him to be sociable, but I'd never liked the stuff even before Bones's blood became my beverage of choice.

"Not this time. We haven't been to bed since yesterday morning, so we're about to catch a few hours' sleep. Oh, and we have a new guest."

A wide grin slid across his face. "You found another of the women already?"

Tyler had fallen asleep before we got Lisa's information, and instead of waking him when we left, we'd just had my mother come to watch over him and Francine. I grinned back, feeling more lighthearted than I had in a while.

"Her name is Lisa, and she's upstairs with Francine."

Tyler stuck his fist out, and I touched it with mine. "Nice work, kitty cat."

"I didn't do it alone," I protested, but I was pleased by the compliment.

At last, we were making headway. Elisabeth and Fabian were still trying to track Kramer to determine who the final target was, but in the meantime, we didn't have to sit on our hands and watch the days ominously count down on the calendar. Police reports weren't the only way we could search for the last woman. We could check recent burials in pet cemeteries, veterinary offices, animal cremation companies, hell, even county records of rabies vaccinations to help narrow down our list. Somewhere in that mix had to be a trail leading to her.

Upstairs, Dexter let out a half whine, half bark. From somewhere else in the town house, Helsing meowed. Tyler and I both tensed. I yanked some sage from my pants pockets and had it lit before Bones came bursting back into the town house.

"Where is he?" he demanded, holding a handful of burning sage aloft.

"I don't know," I whispered, charging up the stairs to Francine and Lisa's room. God, what if Kramer was in there now, hurting those women after I'd just told them they were finally safe!

"Cat!" a male voice called from outside the town house.

I froze in the act of flinging open their bedroom door. I knew that voice, and while it belonged to a ghost, it wasn't any of the ones I'd expected.

A door's banging open only punctuated the effect of Spade's words. "Cat, your uncle's in the yard."

Twenty-five

I muttered an apology to Francine and Lisa for barging into their room and ran back down the stairs almost as fast as I'd climbed up them.

"Charles, wait inside with the women," Bones muttered, brushing by Spade to go outside. I did the same, dropping my sage into the nearest candle on the way out.

Don floated above a set of bushes, rubbing his arms like he was trying to erase something from them. "Can you get that stuff away from me?" he said to Bones, who still held two fistfuls of sage. "It burns. Couldn't even go inside the house because of it."

"How did you get here?" I asked, incredulous. We'd arranged for a vampire to house-sit at our Blue Ridge home in case Don stopped by looking for us, but that was only so he could call us and relay any messages Don had. To my knowledge, the vampire hadn't known we were in Iowa, let alone staying in Sioux City.

"How do you think I got here? By mailing myself?" Don said grumpily. "Now's not the time for your trademark witticisms, Cat—"

"Answer the bloody question," Bones interrupted, still not dropping the sage but not coming any closer to Don, either.

Don huffed out what sounded like an aggravated sigh. "By *focusing* before I jumped on one of those crazy energy roadways Fabian talked about. It wasn't nearly as easy as he said it would be, by the way. You wouldn't believe the places I ended up before I found you—"

"When did Fabian say this?" Bones demanded. I just stared at my uncle, feeling like my body was filling up with ice.

Don shot Bones an annoyed look. "Would you stop interrupting me? And you know when Fabian said this. You were there."

"You found me without anyone telling you where I was?"

But my borrowed powers from Marie were gone! That had been proven when I failed to raise Remnants, and no other ghosts had randomly found their way to me, not to mention my inability to control a ghost's actions anymore.

"Yes, Cat," Don replied, an edge to his tone. "You told me I could do that after I first died, remember? Now you're shocked that it worked?"

Yeah, I was. Shocked speechless, in fact. Bones turned around and went inside without another word. Once there, I heard him mutter something low to

Spade but couldn't make out the exact sentences. Spade left to go back to his town house right after.

My uncle didn't care about what the other vampires were doing. He stared at me, tugging on a nonexistent eyebrow.

"Madigan's fake repentance period is over, and he's implemented a slew of new security measures against guess what? *Ghosts.* He's duplicated everything you did at the cave, and your old house, smothering the compound in marijuana, garlic, and lit sage, not to mention infrared cameras and recorders. It's prevented me from following him, let alone from speaking to Tate—"

"Can you feel anything special about me right now?" I cut him off, still reeling over the implications of his finding me on his own.

"Is it too much to finish a sentence without someone interrupting me?" Don snapped.

I marched over to him, my shock giving way to dread. "This is important, so answer the question!"

My uncle let out another of those exasperated noises but then ran his hand briefly through my arm.

"You . . . vibrate. I don't know what else to call it. Other people don't do that, whether they're human, vampire, or ghoul." Then Don frowned, running his hand through me again. "But it's softer now. It was much stronger the last time I saw you."

"Sparks but no fire," I whispered, understanding at last.

He frowned. "Come again?"

"Just like before, when my hands sparked, but I'd

lost enough of the pyrokinetic power from Vlad's blood to turn those sparks into big streams of flame." I whirled around and began to stride to the door, stopped when I realized Don couldn't follow me, and swung back again. "The other places you ended up when you were trying to find me, was one of them New Orleans?"

His frown deepened. "Yes. I went straight to this large, antebellum-looking house, but I couldn't go inside because it had a barrier around it like this place does."

Marie's protection against unwanted ghostly visitors, I mentally filled in. Don didn't know that he'd just done a flyby on the ghoul queen of New Orleans, drawn by the original source of the power of which I only had traces left in me now.

But those traces, while not enough to summon Remnants or bend ghosts to my will, were obviously enough for a determined phantom to find me, as evidenced by Don's appearance. And if he'd been able to follow that remaining, albeit weak thread of power, then so would another ghost who'd be really keen to know where I was, considering I'd made off with two of his intended victims.

"You tried to enter the house, then flew back because the sage burned you?" I asked, looking around the brightly lit backyard.

Don nodded almost warily. "Yes."

Both pets had reacted to a ghost trying to come into the house, but now that my uncle was fifty feet away in the yard, Helsing and Dexter were quiet. I edged closer to the front door, realizing there was a chance that Don wasn't the only ghost within the perimeter.

Elisabeth and Fabian had been telling the truth, I thought grimly. They hadn't been followed either time by Kramer. No, the Inquisitor found us at Spade's house the same way he must've found us at that hotel in Ohio—by following the supernatural trail that led from Marie Laveau back to me. Poor Fabian probably didn't even realize that connection was still active because he hadn't needed to look for me. He and Elisabeth had known where I was the whole time.

Power sliding along my back was Bones appearing in the doorway behind me. I glanced over, mutely noting the two large handfuls of smoking sage he held out to me. Tyler stood close by, Dexter clenched in his grip and my cat in a carrier by his feet. Bones had either overheard my conversation with Don or figured it out for himself.

"They all need to get out of here," I said.

Bones's mouth brushed my ear as he bent down to whisper his reply. "They'll be gone soon, Kitten."

Good. They needed to be far away from me, or I'd lead their tormenter right to them, if I hadn't already.

"I'll be right back," I murmured, then walked over to Don, wary of every noise or flicker of movement around me. He was only twenty yards from the front door, but that distance seemed to stretch with every step I took.

"I need you to leave now," I said once I was close enough to touch him. "Find me again tomorrow." Then I whispered where, trying to keep my voice low enough that only he could hear me.

"What's going on?" Don asked, as soon as I was finished.

"Listen to your niece and leave," Bones stated brusquely.

Don opened his mouth like he was going to argue, but Ian's "Here we are, Crispin!" distracted him. The auburn-haired vampire strolled down the sidewalk like he hadn't a care in the world. My mother followed behind him, her pajamas suggesting she'd just woken up. Spade and Denise brought up the rear, both of them giving the yard the same cautious looks I did. I was tempted to run back into the house, but I waited, not wanting to draw suspicion if someone other than they were watching.

Bones stepped aside from the doorway, letting all of them enter. Less than ten seconds later, Francine, my mother, and Ian came out. My mom had her arms around Francine as if hugging her from behind. Ian flashed us a grin, then grasped my mother with both arms, vaulting straight up into the sky with a burst of nosferatu speed.

Don's "Where are they going?" barely left his lips before the bushes across the yard exploded with movement, like a large, invisible force had smashed through them.

No need to play it cool anymore! I ran toward the house, a cloud of smoke flooding out from the front door to envelop me before I got there. It was so thick it wafted out into the yard. My uncle jumped back like he'd been scalded when some of it touched him.

"Told you to leave, old chap," Bones muttered. Then he pulled me inside, whatever else Don said lost in the howl of German that erupted from the yard.

Tyler was in the family room, a pile of burning sage on the tile and a fan aiming that smoke like a Gatling gun at the doorway. With Bones slamming the front door shut, Tyler turned off the fan, coughing a little at the grayish haze that started to build up in the room.

Something like a percussion boom sounded right before the windows exploded. I had Tyler flat on his back, my body shielding his, before the glass finished falling. Upstairs, Lisa screamed, quickly followed by what sounded like something heavy beating against the walls of the town house.

"Charles," Bones said warningly, stuffing cushions in front of the blasted open windows. I was torn, wanting to help him contain the smoke in the room and being afraid that if I moved off Tyler, Kramer would rush in and kill him.

"Hold on tightly now," I heard Spade mutter, then another boom reverberated through the house. Lisa screamed again, but this time, the tail of it faded, growing fainter, as if coming from a much greater distance.

Fly, Spade, fly! I thought, knowing he'd be carrying Denise to safety, too.

More furious German came from outside the house, the banging increasing until the walls trembled. Listening to it made me savagely happy, because it proved that Kramer couldn't follow them by air. If he could, he wouldn't be outside trying to huff and puff to blow the house down.

"Bones, you have to get Tyler and Dexter out of

here, too," I whispered. He could fly much faster than I could, not to mention I had the whole "here I am!" transmitter thing still going on.

"Not leaving," Tyler gritted out. "But get off . . . my fucking kidney."

I moved my knee away from his lower back. Hadn't meant to jam that into his side, but I'd kind of been in a hurry to cover him before.

"You have to leave. He'll find me wherever I go for at least the next month or so," I hissed back, remembering how long it took for my hands to stop sparking. "You want to get killed?"

"No. That's why I'm not leaving," Tyler replied more emphatically, yet so soft if I wasn't on top of him I might not have caught it with the racket outside. "If you're gonna trap him, you'll need me, and I *need* you to trap him," he finished. *Dumb-ass,* flashed across his mind, but he didn't end his sentence with that last part out loud.

Despite a ghost's beating in the walls and Dexter barking loud enough to make my eardrums hurt while cowering under a nearby table, I couldn't help my snort of laughter. Dumb-ass? Tyler was the one refusing to go to safety. Talk about the proverbial pot and kettle.

Bones came over, glass crunching under his feet with every step. "Neighbors are calling the coppers. Stay with him. I'll gather what we need, then we have to go."

We'd rented the entire trio of town houses to make sure no units were attached to ours, but even that hadn't been enough of a low profile with the fit Kramer was throwing.

"Looks like you're leaving after all," I noted to Tyler.

He grunted. "I hate flying with you guys, have I told you that?"

I cast a quick look outside, where it sounded like Kramer was now ripping up the lawn in his rage.

"Sorry. A lot of vampire tricks take getting used to."

Twenty-six

Bones and I waited next to the Cathedral of the Epiphany, one of its tall steeples casting the shadow of a cross over where we stood. I told myself that was a good omen even though I couldn't shake my tenseness. At eight in the evening, the area wasn't as busy, but enough people were around that I worried about more than Tyler's safety if Kramer showed up. Earlier today, we'd checked Dexter and Helsing into a kennel. It wasn't a long-term solution, but it was the best choice until Spade could arrange to pick them up. The pets, like Francine and Lisa, would be safer away from me.

Toward that end, we'd spent last night in an abandoned meatpacking facility in the Stockyards, keeping sage burning on the cold cement floor all evening. Even though it was miserable, and none of us slept, we couldn't justify getting a hotel room and endangering anyone unlucky enough to be in the rooms next to

ours. Bones made some calls, and tonight we'd be in
a rented house without any close neighbors, but not
until we spoke to my uncle. There were some important questions that only Don could answer. *He better
show up,* I thought, glancing at the clock on my cell
phone. I wouldn't put it past my uncle to stand me
up if an opportunity arose for him to follow Madigan
without being detected.

My concerns were laid to rest when I spotted a
ghostly figure floating over the park's rolling hills,
wearing a business suit instead of an old, mended
tunic. I didn't know what made certain clothes appear
on ghosts—Don hadn't died in a business suit, after
all—but that wasn't what I was burning to find out.
He'd barely gotten within earshot before I started in
on him.

"How long did it take from the time you started
looking for me to when you popped up on our lawn
yesterday?"

"Hello to you, too, Cat," my uncle replied with a
faint shake of his head. Tyler sidled over, squinting
in the direction I faced. Must've figured out from my
question that a ghost was here even though he couldn't
see him yet.

"Lives depend on your answer," Bones told my
uncle crisply.

Don gave his eyebrow a few thoughtful tugs. "It
was around five in the morning, Tennessee time,
when I began to concentrate on you like you told me
to. What time was it when you saw me?"

"A little after two in the afternoon." With the time
change, that was about ten hours. Far, far longer than

when I first had Marie's blood and Fabian attempted to find me. That took him anywhere from minutes to less than an hour to zoom to my side, depending on how far away I was.

Bones gave Don a speculative look before turning his attention to me. "He's not used to navigating by ley lines and he's not nearly as powerful as Kramer. Best to assume it would take the Inquisitor half that time."

Five hours. God, that wasn't enough time to get anything significant done before the ghost found us.

"We were at the meatpacking plant longer than that last night," I pointed out, hoping Bones was wrong.

"And he could've been there, waiting to see if Spade and the others joined up with us," he replied.

Good point. Why would Kramer tip his hand if it wouldn't net him anything he wanted? Bones and I weren't his main targets; those women were. Kramer certainly hadn't let on that he'd found the town house until Ian blasted away with Francine. No wonder nothing had happened when Bones and I took Lisa from her house. Kramer already knew where we were headed. The fucker was probably laughing the whole time he watched us, thinking we were making it easier on him by keeping both women under the same roof.

Well, at least he wouldn't be laughing now. If Kramer had been watching us all last night, he'd know the others hadn't met up with us, and it wouldn't take him long to figure out that they weren't going to. When that happened, I expected him to express his displeasure in his usual way—trying to murder all of us.

"Oh, there he is," Tyler remarked. "You're the old guy from the cave in Ohio. Howya doin'?"

"I'm dead, how do you think I'm doing?" my uncle replied sourly before floating closer to me. "What happened yesterday, Cat?"

I let out a short laugh. "The same ghost from that day at the cave dropped by, and as you can tell, his mood was the same, too."

The suspicious look Don gave me was one I remembered well from the early days when I worked for him, and I didn't know about our family ties. "What did you do to make him so angry?"

"What did I *do*?" I sputtered, so outraged by the question that I couldn't even begin to formulate an answer.

"I don't have the patience for this today," Bones growled, running a hand through his hair. "All you need to know, Williams, is that we'll be surrounding ourselves with burning sage until we catch this sod again or you can't locate her by concentrating, whichever comes first."

Even if my reaction hadn't been enough, the edge to Bones's tone should've told Don to tread lightly because we were both on our last nerves, but my uncle seemed oblivious to the warning.

"That won't work," he stated. "Cat knows I need a way to get to her if something comes up at the compound. How am I supposed to do that if every place you're staying at is smoked out like a Christmas ham?"

Did he not notice what happened at the town house yesterday? I wondered in disbelief. "We don't have a

choice. If Madigan pulls any new shit, Tate and the
guys will have to handle it on their own. If there's a
life-or-death emergency, go to our cabin. A vampire's
there who can get a message to us."

That was the best I could do. I didn't expect Madigan to make a lethal move against the guys, but if he
did, I'd act. In the meantime, Don would just have to
accept that he couldn't drop in on me until the last of
Marie's power was out of my system, and we didn't
need to burn sage twenty-four hours a day anymore.

My uncle stared at me like I'd grown two heads.
"It's really that easy for you to shuck me off? I might
not be solid, but I *thought* you still considered me to
be your family."

I sucked in a gasp, feeling like he'd just punched
me in the gut. Before I could release that breath in my
defense, Bones's voice lashed out.

"Don't you dare attack her. If you'd been forth-
coming with what you knew about Madigan, it's very
likely we'd have no need to keep sage lit around us
because that ghost would be locked in a trap."

Don bristled. "Now wait a minute—"

"No, I won't," Bones said, his anger blazing forth.
"It's obvious that you knew Madigan had connections
with other vampires, and yet you didn't inform us. If
you'd been honest, we could've anticipated his actions
instead of being caught off guard at the cave. But no,
you chose to keep silent about that."

"You don't understand. I . . . can't tell you everything about him. Not yet," Don said roughly.

Bones stabbed his finger through my uncle's chest.
"Keep all the secrets you fancy about things that don't

endanger her life, but it's clear Madigan has an interest in her and an agenda beyond climbing the corporate ladder. Either tell us everything you know about him now or stay away from your niece."

Don backed up at the vehemence in Bones's tone. So did Tyler. I admit to flinching because his aura crackled with enough power to make it feel like I was standing in a sandstorm. I'd only seen Bones more upset one time, and that incident was still burned on my memory.

Bones turned to me then, his gaze dark and steady.

"I'm sorry for how that will hurt you, but I can't have him near when he's withholding information that might get us killed. What if Madigan had showed up at the cave with his vampire associates instead of juiced-up humans? What if he had informed our enemies where we were? We had no idea the sod had connections to our world beyond the team members I sired, yet Don knew, and he kept it to himself."

Back at the cave, I'd also noticed that Don hadn't looked surprised when Madigan proved to have soldiers hyped up on vampire blood that didn't come from Tate or Juan. In the midst of everything that had happened, I hadn't had a chance to question him about it to see if I was right, but now there was no need. My uncle's guilty yet defiant expression confirmed it all.

"You need to spill what you know before anyone else gets hurt, or worse," I said, drilling him with my gaze.

"If I tell you everything, *he'll* just kill Madigan because that's all he knows," Don snapped with an accusing wave at Bones. "But killing him before I find out what I need to know might end up costing innocent lives. You want that kind of blood on your hands?"

Bones's laughter cut the air like a whip. "Know whose blood I care about? Hers. And those women the ghost is after, I care about their blood, too. So you're right that I'll kill Madigan if he's a threat to them. In truth, if we weren't so busy, I'd be tempted to kill the sod so he couldn't interrupt us the next time we attempt to trap that ghost."

Don's expression was wary now, as those flatly delivered words clued him in to how serious Bones was. "You can't do that. Cat, promise me you won't let him do that."

I thought about the years I'd known Don. He had some truly noble qualities, and I knew he loved me, but he'd always been secretive and somewhat Machiavellian in his actions. I'd been okay with that back when I worked for him, but I wasn't okay with it now, considering how it had endangered me and Bones in this latest incident.

Bones was right—Madigan's unknown vampire ties meant he could've brought a far more dangerous entourage with him to the cave. Plus, if we'd known that Madigan was more than a puffed-up suit, we would've picked a place that had no ties to my former team. I thought of everything I'd read in the *Malleus Maleficarum* about what Kramer did to those who were at his mercy. About Elisabeth's face as she described her rape, torture, and death, and Francine and Lisa being the latest in a long line of women Kramer had marked for the same horrific fate.

My mouth hardened. "Either you come clean with us about Madigan, or Bones is right. You need to go."

"How can you say that?"

I hated the betrayal in Don's voice. I loved him like the father I'd never had, so it struck me right in the heart, as did the repelled look he gave me.

"Every Halloween, three women are kidnapped, raped, tortured, and burned alive by the ghost that Madigan's interruption prevented us from trapping," I replied, meeting the gray gaze that was identical to my own. "Bones and I might not get another chance to trap that ghost, and if we don't, many more women will die." I drew in a breath for courage. "I love you, Don, but you can't keep treating me like an employee on a need-to-know basis. Even if you don't trust Bones to react rationally to whatever you know about Madigan—and I disagree with that—after all we've been through, you should at least trust *me*. I've more than earned it."

Bones slid his arm around me, his aura changing from dangerous spikes of anger into strength, pride, and compassion. Those emotions flowed over me and through me, seeping into the very fiber of my being until it felt like we'd melded into the same person.

Don's expression hardened into a stubborn mask that I well recognized, and I knew with deep sorrow that my words had fallen on deaf ears.

"I can tell you this—Madigan doesn't have ties to the undead world like you're thinking. Any vampires he's getting blood from are his captives, not his allies, and no, I don't know who they are or where they are."

He didn't say anything else. He just dissipated with

that mixture of stubbornness and how-could-you still stamped on his features. I blew out a long, slow sigh, leaning in closer to Bones's embrace.

"Looks like that's another problem we need to deal with," I said. If these captive vampires were random Masterless murderers, then Madigan could keep them and tap their veins like tree trunks for all I cared. But if they were innocent vampires snatched up while minding their own business, or they belonged to a powerful Master who might take revenge on their capture by wiping out my entire former team, we needed to act.

Right after we found a way to lock up a homicidal ghost, that was.

"Indeed. Madigan's playing on dangerous ground, and so is your uncle," Bones said, his tone still edged in anger.

Tyler patted his shoulder in a comforting way. "Family. Aren't they a motherfucker sometimes?"

That summed it up so well, there really was nothing else left to say.

Twenty-seven

A THICK CLOUD OF SMOKE HUNG IN THE AIR, its acridness stinging my eyes. The cellar had no windows, and the single door that opened into the farmhouse pantry was always closed when Bones and I were down here. If I were human, I'd have passed out within the hour, but of course oxygen wasn't an issue for me. Neither was the darkness. The only light came from the orange halos around the sage as the flames curled the plants into blackened, smoking remains, but Bones and I had no trouble seeing as we pieced together hunks of limestone, quartz, and moissanite into another trap. We'd spent the majority of the past five days down here, working toward that single goal. Good thing we'd helped Chris and the team make the last trap so we knew what we were doing, and if we spent the next week down here, we'd have it done in time.

Then we had to worry about finding a way to force

Kramer into it. No matter how I turned the problem around in my mind, it always came back to our best chance being when he was solid. I couldn't force vapor into the trap. Neither could Bones, even considering that he worked on expanding his telekinetic powers almost as much as on this trap, but those were useless against a disembodied form. Yet waiting until Kramer was solid meant waiting until Halloween night, and we hadn't found the third woman yet, so her life was at risk. Plus, the Inquisitor might only show up if we used Francine and Lisa as bait to draw him out. All the different things that could go wrong haunted me whenever I considered that option, no pun intended.

A knock sounded on the cellar door. "He's back," Tyler called out.

Bones rose, but I waved him back before wiping aside a chunk of hair that had come loose from my ponytail.

"You went the last two times. My turn."

His lips tightened, yet he made no comment, knowing it would lead to an argument that I'd win. I wasn't about to let him bear all of Kramer's loathsome personality, and the ghost only got more pissed when he was ignored. Considering the damage he'd already done to this house, we had to buy it by the time this was over.

I went up the stairs, noting that the wooden steps vibrated from the multiple thuds reverberating through the house. *What's he using now?* I wondered. Kramer couldn't come inside, not with all the sage we kept burning in every room, but he made good use of everything in the near perimeter. The car we'd driven here had been impressively destroyed, its windows and tires not lasting the first night, the rest of it bashed and battered over subsequent days. The old farmhouse lost its windows on that first night, too, plus a section of the front porch. We'd nailed wood over where the glass used to be, which proved far more durable, and spent a few hours watching TV until Kramer ripped off the satellite dish and chucked it through the car windshield.

Thank God there were no neighbors nearby to hear the unbelievable racket, but that was why we'd chosen this property. The surrounding land had once been a soybean field but clearly hadn't been planted or harvested in a while. I didn't know what circumstances had led the former owners to leave and, failing the sale of the house, choose to rent it, but it was the perfect place for Bones and me to build the trap without Kramer's prying eyes seeing what we were doing. All the materials had been delivered and put in the cellar before I got here, so Kramer hadn't been able to follow us to this place until after they were safely out of sight. I had no doubt the ghost knew Bones and I were busy with something, but he could only guess at what.

Tyler sat in the pantry, my iPad next to him and an open can of SpaghettiOs to the right of that. We'd stocked the refrigerator when we came here, but then Kramer ripped out the electrical lines leading to the house, and that meant no power to keep things fresh. He'd zapped himself in the process, all that electricity coursing through him rendering him solid for about ten minutes, but beating his ass while he was channeling high voltage would have only resulted in Bones or me getting electrocuted, too. Pity the trap wasn't ready yet. That would have made getting the bejesus shocked out of us worth it.

Tyler had been eating canned goods ever since the food spoiled, and his baleful expression said loud and clear that he hadn't developed a taste for them in the process. I didn't remind him that Bones could fly him to Spade's, where there would be plenty of better food to eat. Tyler was determined to help us catch the ghost, and any mention of his leaving was met with flat refusal.

"Want a bite?" Tyler said, holding up a speared forkful of noodles and meat medley.

I managed not to grimace out of sheer force of will. "Ah, no thanks."

"Me neither," he said, coughing a little before he went on. "Have I told you about all the steaks you're going to buy me when this is over?"

"Kobe, filets, prime ribs, you name it," I promised him. "Any luck on your research?"

While Bones and I were in the cellar cutting various rocks and minerals to piece together the trap, Tyler had been scouring the Internet for any authentic-sounding reference to a weapon against ghosts. It burned through a new backup battery a day, damn that lack of electricity, but as the time drew nearer, I was more anxious to find something that might help us prod Kramer into the trap. Yes, we had burning sage, but that made Kramer poof away—helpful when we wanted him gone, but not so much if we wanted to force him into a ghost jail. So far, Tyler hadn't come up with anything that we could test on Fabian or Elisabeth, but he was determined that the information existed and just had to be found.

"What do you think of this?" Tyler asked, turning the iPad around so I could see the screen.

I stared at the page displayed, wondering why Tyler was showing it to me. He must be starting his Christmas list early because this item had nothing to do with the supernatural. Then I looked at it more closely, thought it through . . . and started to smile.

"I *love* it," I said, careful in my reply because I knew Kramer was listening. "I want ten. No, make that two dozen. Bones has his credit card numbers memorized, get them from him later. We'll ship them to where Spade's staying."

Tyler grinned. "Sure will. Say hi to ol' Michael Myers for me."

"Huh? Oh, because Kramer's a Halloween serial killer, I get it. Sure, but you make sure to stay in here and don't come out."

He rolled his eyes. "Girlfriend, *you* might be dead, but I don't want to be yet. Bet your ass I'm staying in here."

Another crash sounded near the front of the house, louder than the other ones. My cue that Kramer was getting impatient. I'd love to leave him out there stewing in his own ectoplasm, but we had to keep the house standing for the next week, so we could finish the trap. Getting it out of here without the ghost seeing was going to be tricky enough. We didn't need to add to that trouble by having to move the trap to a new location just to finish it.

I left the pantry, passing through the kitchen with its bare, open cabinets—those doors made for great window coverings—and the family room where mattresses were the only furniture. When I got to the main entrance of the house, I picked up one of the glass jars filled with burning sage and ducked out of habit as soon as I opened the door.

Sure enough, a hunk of tree branch went whistling over me, followed immediately by two side mirrors from the car. They clanged into the family room, one landing on the mattresses, the others resting by the rest of the items Kramer had chucked at Bones earlier. I made a mental note to carry them out later and reappeared in the doorway.

"*Guten Tag,*" I said, hefting the sage jar in salute. "Stay where I can see you, or I go back inside."

I knew he'd comply because, for some twisted reason, Kramer liked to do his cursing and threats to our faces. Grumbles in German came from the side of the porch that had the worst damage to it. If Kramer kept ripping out porch boards and flinging them at the house, there wouldn't be any more of it left in the next couple days. But the sage that had Tyler continually coughing kept Kramer from entering the house. All he could do was poltergeist things at it while cursing us in a mixture of German and English, with possibly some Latin thrown in for good measure.

Dark swirls appeared next to the porch, then the familiar white hair sticking out like a stack of bleached hay topped the ghost's tall, thin frame. I waited, not saying anything, tapping the side of the glass in mute warning.

"*Hexe*," Kramer hissed once he was fully manifested.

"Uh-huh," I replied, recognizing the German word for witch and wondering how long he would ramble on this time. "I'm a woman, so that's how you see me. Watching the feminist movement these past several decades must've really burned your toast."

The Inquisitor didn't respond with a slew of curses like normal. He just smiled wide enough to reveal teeth that were best kept unseen. *Eww* didn't begin to cover my revulsion at those scraggly brown stumps.

"Toast? No, that is not what I burn," he replied, his expression showing that he savored each word.

If I hadn't known that Bones was in the cellar working on this murdering prick's trap as we spoke, I'd have turned around and gone right back inside. But that would only mean more damage to the house that we'd have to take time away from the trap to repair; plus it would let Kramer know that he'd gotten to me. My biggest motivator for staying, however, was simple: Every second that Kramer was out here pissing me off meant he wasn't tormenting the last woman he'd picked out. Elisabeth still hadn't found her, and our research efforts hadn't turned her up yet, either. I wasn't alone, with no one believing me about the torment the ghost dished out, like she was. I could stand here and deal with him because it was all I could do for that woman until we found out who she was and brought her to Spade and Denise.

"You're going to have a lonely Halloween this year, what with Francine and Lisa being out of reach," I noted coolly. "And what *will* you do when we find the last woman—and we will, my snaggle-toothed friend. Then the only things you'll be toasting with your temporarily fleshy paws are marshmallows."

That got me the curses I'd expected earlier. Some of it was in English, some in German, but I was getting pretty well versed at recognizing certain words, so I got the gist of it.

"Blah blah blah, I'm a slutty witch, and the fires of hell await me, blah. You really need some new material. My mother can curse me out better than that."

A porch board went sailing at me. I knocked it aside with one hand, the other still wrapped around the sage jar. Kramer wouldn't dare to attempt one of those energy punches at me as long as I had that close by, and those punches hurt a lot more than random objects if he got lucky and the next one he threw landed on me.

"I've been thinking of what I'm going to wear this Halloween," I said, as if a board being chucked at me wasn't worth interrupting my train of thought. "I haven't dressed up for it in ages, but you've inspired me. I think I'll go as Elphaba from *Wicked*. She was a misunderstood witch who had a mob after her, but she tricked them and won in the end. Heartwarming, right?"

More curses, this time insulting not only me, but the womb that bore me and the dark lord who fathered me. That part, at least, Kramer got right. My father was a Class A asshole. He and Kramer had that in common. They'd have everything in common soon if I got my way. My dad was currently serving a life sentence consisting of truly cruel and unusual punishments, from what I'd heard.

"I just love our talks," I went on, avoiding the three new boards that he hurtled at me. "I'm not really sure what *you* get out of them, but they're good for me. Why, last night, I took some curtain scraps and a few slivers of board pieces and made a little Kramer doll. Then I ripped its arms and legs off before driving a nail up its ass. I mean, if you hadn't come by yesterday, I wouldn't have thought to do that—"

"You will die in flames!" Kramer roared, zooming up so close to me that the smoke from my jar of sage brushed him before he caught himself and pulled back. I didn't move, not wanting to give Kramer the satisfaction of even a flinch. His gaze bored into mine with cruelty too deep to be madness, and when he bared those repellant teeth at me, I couldn't help but think that when he was alive, his breath would've stunk enough for me to smell it from a dozen feet away.

"I don't think so."

My voice was steady, and I didn't blink as I stared back at him. "I'm a vampire, so it's possible for me to die by fire if it's big enough, and I can't get away, but I'm guessing I'll die one day at the hands of some Master vampire who's stronger, faster, and just plain luckier with a silver knife. You, on the other hand, won't ever die, will you? You'll stay stuck in that air cloud you call a body, watching the world pass you by while you can't do anything except rage at it, and most of the time, no one in it can hear you. Me? I'd rather be dead than that."

Kramer didn't move, but I felt his fury in the coldness that rolled across my skin, as if the air had dipped ten degrees in the past few seconds. Then, a ripple flowed across his body like a rock skipped across a pond, making him hazy for the barest moment before he flared into full living color. His tunic wasn't brown, it was gray with mud splatters all over it, and his eyes were deeper green than the pale color they'd looked before. He had pockmarks in his skin that the haziness and his stubbly white beard had concealed, and his silvery hair still held faint streaks of blond.

Without reaching out my hand, I knew he was now as solid as I was. Elisabeth had looked much more vivid when she'd been flesh, and so did her murderer.

"Is that mud from the old misguided idea that putrefied flesh equated to holiness, or from you landing in a big puddle when Elisabeth incited your horse to throw you and break your neck?" I asked softly. "I wonder how long you can hold on to that flesh before it's gone. Two minutes, maybe three?"

As I asked the question, I silently dared him to make a move. *Please, oh please, try to hit me. I so want to show you what I can do against an opponent who isn't made of air!*

Kramer smiled. Those teeth were more vivid, too, and that wasn't a good thing.

"What you should wonder is how many more witches I must burn before I am powerful enough to wear flesh every day instead of merely one," he drew out, each word falling like a drop of poison. "I think not many."

"You think burning women alive will turn you back into a real boy?" God, was he a sick bastard!

That nauseating smile widened. "Fear strengthens me just as blood feeds your miserable kind. I drew strength from sighted mortals until I was able to appear to whomever I chose. It took centuries of that before I could wear flesh again, and it lasted only minutes. Yet after I burned my first trio of witches on Samhain, I was whole for an hour. Now each witch I send to the flames provides me with such a feast of terror that it strengthens me like nothing you could imagine. In time, I will not be limited to walking the earth only on Samhain but will reside in flesh whenever I choose."

Even though I knew that Bones would chew me out for leaving the smoke-filled safety of the house behind me, I couldn't resist lunging forward and whipping my fist across Kramer's jaw as hard and fast as I could. It connected with a crunch that was so satisfying, I'd swung another one before I could think, breaking the sage jar across his face because I still had it gripped in my other hand.

Kramer disappeared before the glass shards fell to the porch. Pain blasted in my gut, though, letting me know he hadn't gone far. I backed up, hitting the doorframe in my haste, grabbing a handful of the smoking sage before Kramer could go in for another blow. Or before the porch caught fire, which would be even worse.

"If you're done playing with that sod, care to move away from the door? Or will you make me knock you over?" an English voice drawled.

I'd been so concentrated on Kramer, waiting for a glimpse of those telltale dark swirls or—even better—another chance to connect a blow to his temporarily solid flesh, that I'd let my other senses become lax. Ian strolled across the remains of the bean field, one hand grasped tight on my mother's upper arm and the other holding a large wad of smoldering sage. He must've flown them both in. Good thing, because if he'd driven, Kramer would have another car to trash before the night was through.

"Kramer's out here," I warned them, glancing around but still not seeing where the ghost had gone off to.

Ian snorted. "That's why I said you need to move." Then he picked my mother up, flying toward the door like they'd been fired out of a gun. I moved out of the way just in time to avoid being barreled over.

"Take your hands off me," my mother snapped once she was vertical instead of horizontal.

"Now that we're here, I will," Ian replied, letting her go. She stepped back several paces, but Ian just brushed off some lint from his clothes as if he couldn't care less. Then he looked around at what used to be the family room but now looked more like a junkyard from the mattresses, boards, tree limbs, and car parts haphazardly littering the floor.

"I say, Reaper, this place looks almost as dreadful as the one I grew up in. Is all this from that pesky ghost?"

"The very same," I said dryly. Kramer started up a whole new batch of curses at this interruption, revealing that he was still on the porch, but Ian and

my mother weren't here because they'd missed us, so
something must be going on. "Let's go into the cellar
where the three of us can have a little more . . . privacy."

The grin Ian flashed me made me relieved to see
white, even teeth again, but I should've noticed that it
was steeped in wickedness.

"I've had mothers and daughters at the same time
before, but you're Crispin's wife, so I must regretfully
decline."

"You are such a *pig*!" my mother exclaimed, saving
me the trouble of saying it.

Another spate of English and German came from
the porch. Looked like Kramer thought Ian was a pig,
too. In this one and only one thing, we were in agreement.

"Buh-bye, asshole," I told the ghost. Then I shut
the front door, Kramer still bitching on the other side
of it, and swept out a hand to Ian. "Follow me. Once
we're downstairs, you can tell me and Bones the real
reason you're here, aside from amusing yourself with
sleazy remarks."

"Oh, I'll tell you right now," he replied smoothly.
"Your dear mum tried to eat one of the women you're
attempting to save."

Twenty-Eight

The cellar seemed much smaller with the four of us in it. Tyler sat at the top of the stairs, the door cracked so he could get enough clean air to breathe, but not open all the way because we didn't want a certain nosy ghost to overhear our conversation.

I didn't need to ask my mother if Ian was correct. The instant guilt that flashed across her face when he made his unbelievable statement was answer enough for me. What I waited to ask until all of us were underground was one simple question.

"What the hell *happened,* Mom?"

"It was an accident," she muttered, looking at the plain wooden wall instead of me. "It wouldn't happen again."

"Yes it would, and if you bit Denise the next time, Charles would kill you no matter whose mother you were," Ian stated.

I rubbed my forehead against the mental image

Ian described. If my mother bit Denise and tasted her demonically-altered, drugging blood, Spade *would* kill her. He'd do it even though it would cause a huge rift between him and Bones because of me, not to mention how it would horrify Denise. But the lengths a vampire would go to in order to protect his spouse superseded all other bonds.

"You did the right thing bringing her here," Bones said to Ian, and I had to agree. I'd thought keeping her with Spade and Denise would be safer, but not if she was still struggling with her hunger enough to attempt feeding from people who were off the menu.

"What triggered this, Mom? Do you know, so we can prevent it from happening again?"

"Ah, and here's the richest part," Ian said, elbowing my mother.

She smacked at his arm, still not making eye contact with anyone in the room. "I've got it under control now."

Ian laughed out loud at that. "No vampire can stop feeding and be under any control for long, my pretty little imbecile."

I was so stunned by his statement that I didn't react to the insult. "You haven't been feeding? But all those times you went out saying you were going to—"

"Lies, lies, lies," Ian said cheerfully. "I'm the last person to judge for that, but she actually thought she could sustain herself by sucking the blood out of raw meat packages—and while that's funny in a dozen different ways, it's not practical in the least."

Bones had his emotions tamped down, a sign that whatever he was feeling toward her right now wasn't something he wanted to share with me. If it was any-thing like my emotions, he wanted to shake her while screaming, *Are you out of your fucking mind? With everything going on, you have to decide that you're going to be the world's only vegetarian vampire? Did it ever occur to you what would happen if your bril-liant plan didn't WORK?*

But I said none of those things, partly because it was clear Ian had already given her his unedited opinion on her ill-fated scheme, and also because she looked like she was about to cry. I could count on one hand the times I'd seen my mother cry, and it wasn't something I wanted to see again, let alone cause.

"Okay," I said, taking in a deep breath to quell the part of me that still wanted to go with the shake-and-scream approach. "How long have you been attempt-ing to live off meat package blood?"

"Since I quit the team," she mumbled. "Tate used to give me bagged plasma, but once I left, I knew that wouldn't happen anymore, so I tried to find an alter-native."

My eyes bugged as I calculated the time. Bones still said nothing, his face carefully expressionless and his aura closed off like a vault. Tyler wasn't nearly as locked down in his reaction. *Bitch, you are SO lucky you didn't try to eat my dog*, rang across my mind.

"Okay." My voice was almost a squeak with my incre-dulity. "That didn't work, so, uh, who'd you try to eat?"

She said nothing, worrying her lower lip between teeth that were harmlessly flat at the moment.

"Francine got frightened by a noise and cut herself after squeezing a sage glass too hard," Ian supplied.

"Your mum pounced on her and started sucking away. Would've been arousing if not for all the screaming."

"Ian," Bones drew out warningly.

He grinned. "You're right. I was aroused anyway."

I punched him in the chest without even thinking about it. My mother's bottom lip quivered.

"I didn't mean to. I just couldn't stop myself."

"Of course you couldn't. You're a *vampire*."

The exasperated statement came not from me, though I'd been thinking it, or from the other two vampires in the room. It came from Tyler, who climbed down the stairs even though the increased smoke made him cough.

"You know: fangs, flashy green eyes, and super-speed? All that caught your attention already?" At her scoff, he added, "So why'd you think you could opt out of the 'drinking human blood' part?"

"I refuse to tear into someone's flesh, holding them down and stealing their blood . . ." Something dark flashed across her expression before her features twisted in pain. "I won't do that again. Ever."

Her tone hardened at that last word, and I knew she was remembering her first days as a vampire when the prick who sired her threw in humans with her. It took the last of my anger from me, though a bucketload of frustration still remained.

"There's no need to harm anyone when you feed, Justina," Bones said. "But as you've discovered, you can't wish away your need for blood, and animal blood will not suffice for long."

"Maybe I just need more of it. There wasn't a lot in those meat packages," she insisted.

A mental image of my mother sneaking around at night to suck on cattle or goats crossed my mind. What if that was the real source of the Chupacabra legend, and they were actually vampires in denial like she was? Nothing would surprise me right now.

"You could drink a slaughterhouse dry, and you'd still lust over the first human you chanced upon," Ian replied pitilessly. "Be easier on our kind if we didn't need human blood, but we do, and you're no exception."

"Even if I wouldn't hurt them, I refuse to force anyone to give me their blood by ripping away their willpower," my mother said. "So unless I start stealing from blood banks, I don't see another solution."

"Drink me."

My head swung in Tyler's direction with almost the same amount of disbelief my mother showed. Tyler shrugged.

"None of her concerns apply with me because I'm offering, so she won't be ripping away my willpower, and she damn sure won't be holding me down and tearing open my anything."

"Are you sure?" I'd hate for him to feel pressured because he was the only person here with a pulse. We could make other arrangements. Lots of vampires had willing donors. A few phone calls, and we could have a donor here although that person would have to leave right away because of Kramer and his whole *kill first, say hello later* tendency.

"I'd rather have her drink a little from me now with someone here to control her than sit around waiting for her to lose it again." Then Tyler's stare turned pointed as he looked at my mother. "And you *will* lose it again. You're already looking at me like I'm a big juicy steak. Can't kick you out, either. Cat would just worry herself sick about you and every other fool near enough for you to bite."

Then he turned to Bones, folding his arms. *This offer ain't free, but we'll talk price when Mama's not here, and so you know? I don't come cheap,* he thought at him in a clear, concise way.

I had no qualms about paying him. That seemed a far better trade than Tyler's offering out of guilt or compulsion. The barest smile touched Bones's mouth. He nodded once, and Tyler rolled up his sleeve, holding his bare arm out.

"I didn't say I would do this," my mother argued, but her gaze welded onto the veins throbbing beneath his coffee-colored skin.

Ian snorted. "I've never heard a less convincing protest."

"You're doing this, and you're doing it now," I told her sternly. "Tyler's right. You're a danger to him and every other human until you get your hunger under control, and I know you don't want to hurt anyone by accident."

I didn't say *again,* but the word hung unspoken in the air. My mother tore her gaze away from Tyler's flesh to look first at me, then Bones. She squirmed.

"I can't do it with you two watching me," she finally stated.

"What?" I sputtered.

She waved an impatient hand. "It's too weird. You're my daughter, and he"—she looked at Bones, who flashed her an impudent grin—"he's too arrogant," she finished.

"No one's more arrogant than Ian," I said under my breath.

He winked at me. "Thank you, Reaper."

Bones rested his hand on my back. "Come on, Kitten, let's leave them to it. Ian, I charge you with their safety. We'll be back later."

I looked at Tyler, but instead of any concern about Bones and me leaving, his thoughts were busy contemplating things about Ian that I didn't need to hear. "Are you okay with only them?" I asked anyway.

"Fine. Shoo," he said, flicking his fingers for emphasis.

"Okay, we'll see you soon."

Bones propelled me up the stairs, his mood seeming to lighten with every step.

"I'm certain it won't be that soon," Ian called out.

I wasn't a hundred percent sure, but I thought I caught Bones muttering, "Right you are, mate."

TWENTY-NINE

THE LIGHTS FROM SIOUX CITY GLITTERED IN the distance like diamonds flung on the ground. Below us stretched mile upon mile of farmland, interrupted every so often by houses, roads, and factories. I wasn't worried about being spotted. For one, it was night, and with our black clothes at this height, we'd be practically invisible. For another, we were outside the city limits in the rural counties, where agriculture far outnumbered people.

"This was a good idea," I murmured.

I'd thought we were just going to wait in the demolished family room until Ian announced the all clear, but Bones took me in his arms and blasted us away before Kramer could even poltergeist up some boards to fling after us. Now we were miles away from the house, high enough that I had no one's thoughts in my head but my own, and it was just the two of us. Finally, for the first time in weeks, we were alone, no one right outside our door or floating threateningly around the house.

Bones tightened his hand on mine. We were spread out like two birds—arms extended, legs straight, the wind rushing around us like an invisible waterfall. This was the first time I'd flown when we didn't have some pressing agenda to accomplish, and though it was cold up here, I didn't mind. I felt wonderfully free. The chill in the air was such a small price to pay for that.

"Before we met, I'd fly for hours to clear my head," Bones said, his voice reaching me even over the rush of wind. "It was the closest I came to finding peace, but though several of my mates could fly, I always went alone. I never wanted to share this with anyone until you."

I looked over at him, struck by more than the perfection of his features or how the wind made his clothes cling to him like a second skin. His mouth curved in the type of smile I hadn't seen on him in a long time—carefree, and the emotions rubbing my subconscious were edged with a joy that made me want to move heaven and earth so he could feel it all the time.

"I'm so glad to be here with you like this," I whispered. It had taken years filled with more trials and pain than I thought I could endure to bring me to the point where I could soar by his side, but I'd do it all again, a thousand times over, to share this moment with him.

He smiled. "Speak up a bit, luv. Can't hear you with this wind."

I rolled myself beneath his outstretched arm instead, not stopping until I'd maneuvered myself under his body. He folded his arms around me, our bodies still streamlining across the midnight-colored sky. Bones was dressed the same way I was, in a black, long-sleeved shirt with matching pants and boots, but his neck was bare. I pressed my mouth there, savoring his moan as my tongue crept out to taste his skin.

"You remember the first time I did that?" I murmured, slipping my arms around him.

"We were dancing." His voice was richer with the desire I felt rising in him. "And you were taunting me with how much I wanted you."

I smiled against his skin, tracing another sensitive spot with my tongue and enjoying his resulting shudder.

"I didn't know that then. I just thought you were easy."

His laugh rumbled out, hard arms tightening around me. "I was, but I still wanted you more than I believed possible. You don't know how mad you drove me those first several weeks. It tormented me seeing you every day and being unable to touch you because you hated me."

"I hated myself more." Another whisper, but this one he heard. "You showed me how to accept myself, and I loved you long before I could admit it to you."

His head dipped, cool lips covering my own. I opened my mouth, seeking his taste, moaning at the velvety softness of his tongue and the two sharp fangs that now protruded from his teeth. Mine slid out as well, grazing his when our kiss deepened, and he slanted his mouth over mine.

His power enveloped me, brushing along my senses with a depth that went well beyond lust. Our tongues twined together, that intimate dance sending waves of sensation through my nerve endings. I slid my leg around his hips, rubbing against him in silent, hungry invitation. His hand moved lower, clasping me closer, and the friction when he arched his hips made starbursts go off in my loins. His body was so hard, so sleek, so filled with pulsating energy, and the cradle of wind against us only aroused me more. This wouldn't be like those stolen moments in the cellar with Tyler in the pantry at the top of the stairs and an angry ghost hurling threats and curses outside. This moment was ours, and we had as far as we could fly in the wide-open expanse of sky to savor it.

Unless, of course, this sort of thing couldn't be done while flying. From the thick length pressing against me combined with the devastating way Bones rocked his hips, he wasn't teasing. He had more than enough power to keep us aloft, but flying also required concentration. I didn't think I was supporting myself in the air any longer. I was too focused on the sensual way his tongue tangled with mine and the bursts of pleasure that unfurled every time that bulge rubbed my clitoris. I'd probably have tumbled right out of the sky if not for his arms around me.

Even if he could keep us in the air the whole time, that had its own set of complications. Bashing into some small private aircraft because Bones's attention was focused on the radar below his waist instead of what was around us would be tragic for everyone. Maybe seeking out a spot in one of the fields below

was the best idea. Yet there was something electrifying about touching each other while soaring through
the air that made me want to stay up here.

"Is it possible . . . up here?" I asked, tearing my
mouth away from his.

"Yes." A fervent hiss that spiked my desire.

I pulled his head down again, everything in me
tensing with expectation when he reached inside
my jeans, his other arm still supporting me. Then a
moan tore from my throat at his fingers seeking out
all the spots that made me burn. I arched against him,
gasps spilling out between our kisses, reaching down
to grab that lusciously hard flesh beneath his zipper.
It overflowed my hand, too thick to close my fingers
around, pulsing with his power and the blood Bones
directed there. I rubbed him in time to the same
rhythmic strokes he used, his mouth absorbing my
wordless cries.

That sweet inner ache became more intense with
every penetrating stroke of his fingers. I wanted him
inside me, but the more I opened my legs, the higher
it made my jeans ride up.

"I want you now, Kitten," he growled, biting my
lower lip and sucking the twin drops of blood his
fangs drew. Then he raked his tongue across his fangs
before closing his mouth over mine, flavoring our kiss
with the ambrosia of his blood.

In a smooth motion, Bones flipped me over. His
arm crossed between my breasts to support my upper
body, and he hooked his feet around my ankles to
keep my legs from dangling. Then he brushed my
wildly whipping hair back to kiss my throat, using

his free hand to tug my jeans and panties down to my thighs. The blast of frigid air on my most sensitive parts was forgotten when I felt the probe of hard flesh behind me. Bones reached down, guiding that long, thick length to my center. I gasped, arching back against him, mentally cursing the bunched material around my thighs that prevented me from opening myself wider to him.

His mouth sealed over the spot on my neck that would be madly jumping with my pulse if I still had one. I rocked back again, trying to encase him inside me, frustration and rapture building when he only teased me with the head of his cock.

"Open your eyes," he urged me, the words vibrating against my throat.

I didn't know how he knew I'd closed them—I was facing the other way—but I opened them as asked. Between the red whips of my hair, I saw vast cornfields spread out beneath us, darker and less distinct from our height, but noticeably swaying in the breeze. They were more stunning viewed from above because the distance hid the sight of drying husks and cracked stalks, making them look like miles of an undulating, golden ocean. Seeing those gently swaying fields filled me with a form of peace I hadn't felt in a while. My roots came from the country, not from concrete or asphalt jungles, and up here, there were no ghosts chasing us, literally or metaphorically.

The sheer splendor of the sight made my chest tighten and tears sting my eyes. All the darkness lately made it easy to forget the world contained more than people trying to hurt other people. It had beauty, too, if you knew where to look—and remembered to open your eyes. Bones's mouth continued to caress my neck, making me shiver with a longing both passionate and poignant. I could feel his hunger in more than the hard length of flesh intimately pressed against me. His aura surrounded me, passion and need combining to scorch my senses, but he'd waited to take me until I saw something that he knew, somehow, would heal a piece of me I hadn't known was broken.

There were words for what he meant to me, but if I studied every language ever spoken for the next thousand years, I still wouldn't find enough of them to describe it.

I reached down, clasping my hands around his and squeezing, wishing he could still read my mind so he'd know even a portion of what I couldn't put into sentences. His lips moved against my throat in what felt like a smile.

"I love you, Kitten," he whispered.

I was about to reply in kind, but only a gasp came out because he sank his fangs into my neck while thrusting deeply at the same time. The double impact ignited my senses, setting my nerve endings ablaze. The grip I had on his hands tightened, more ragged noises escaping me as he pulled out very, very slowly—and then thrust forward hard enough to wring a shout from me.

Vampire body heat didn't rise, and the cold air around us probably meant I'd clock in under room temperature; nonetheless, I felt like I grew warmer. Another tantalizingly slow withdrawal built that sensation of heat, and when it was followed by a swift, deep thrust, I felt like my skin would start to spark. The puddle of material around my thighs kept my legs together, but that meant I could grip him tighter, and I did. The extra swell of pleasure cresting over my emotions let me know how much he liked that, so I kept doing it, squeezing him with every muscle I had when his flesh slid out inch by achingly unhurried inch.

"Don't. Stop," he growled.

I tried to keep my eyes open, to look at the stunning canvas we were soaring above, but the mounting ecstasy kept dragging them shut. It built, drawing from the slightest movement of his body as well as those fierce, rapturous thrusts, until my entire body shuddered from the intensity. His arms were like steel bands around me, molding me to him hard enough to bruise, but I wanted him to hold me even closer. Each slide of his fangs into my neck seemed to send more heat through me, each thrust coiling the pleasure tighter in my loins. I didn't want him to stop, either. I needed to feel his flesh merging into mine, tried to hold him there with every clench of my thighs and inner muscles. His groans inflamed me, but that was nothing compared to his aura raking through me, merging his feelings with mine. Through that, I knew exactly when to move faster. When to let go of his hands and grip his hips to hold him to me, then I knew nothing except shattering ecstasy when he lost control and took me over the edge with him.

For several moments afterward, I couldn't move. I could only cling to him, savoring every last tremor of his climax and the continual, tingling ripples from mine. Finally, my lids fluttered open. At some point,

I must have closed my eyes again. We were no longer over the golden, swaying cornfields, but a patchwork of roads, thankfully too high for the streetlights to present any collision issue—or embarrassing illumination.

"Do you know where we are?" I murmured, reaching up to run my hand through his hair.

He turned his head, nuzzling me through the material of my sleeve.

"Not a clue."

My laughter was breathy from afterglow. "Poor navigator you might be, but you are one hell of a pilot."

His chuckle mingled with mine. The angry blare from a horn drifted up to us, a reminder of the real world waiting to intrude, but I closed my eyes and rested my head back against him.

The real world could wait a few minutes longer.

Thirty

On October 26, not four hours after Bones and I put the finishing touches on the new limestone/quartz/moissanite trap, my cell phone beeped from a text. I was in the shower, rinsing suds from my hair and trying to ignore how the water seemed to get icier every day. No electricity meant no hot water. If the carbon monoxide exhaust wouldn't kill Tyler, I'd set up a generator in the house just to be able to take a hot shower again.

I continued rinsing my hair, not rushing to read the text because it was about the time Denise would send her daily updates, letting me know everything was okay on their end. If it were urgent, she wouldn't text. To conserve the battery in my phone, we didn't chat verbally, and to be honest, it was easier to text back "no news" than admit out loud that we still hadn't found the last woman. All of us watched the days count down on the calendar with increasing dread.

Kramer hadn't been coming around as much in the

past week. The knowledge that he was probably splitting his time between readying his accomplice for the
woman's kidnapping and escalating his torment of her
was enough to make me feel like I had a permanent
case of nausea. Unless we found her, that woman had
just over a hundred hours to live.

It was just me and Bones at the house right now.
Ian, Tyler, and my mom were at the Southern Hills
Mall. Ian prowled about seeking his own version of
food, and my mother kept watch over Tyler just in
case Kramer happened to stumble upon them. Hopefully soon, my mother would follow Ian's lead and
vary her diet. I half wondered if that was why he insisted on going out so frequently and taking them, although maybe it was just a case of boredom combined
with cabin fever.

After I got out of the shower and dried off with a
few brisk, efficient swipes, I grabbed my cell from
the countertop and read the text. My first thought was
that it was gibberish. Letters, symbols, and numbers
were run together without spaces, some repeating,
some not. Maybe Denise's phone got jiggled around
in her purse or pants pocket and my number was re-
dialed by mistake; I'd butt-dialed people by accident
before. But this wasn't coming from Denise's cell. It
was from Elisabeth's number. I looked more closely
at the message.

6THST5360#(SC5360WEST^THSC5360WEST6THSTSC

It took me another two rereads before I figured out
the pattern. "Fifty-three sixty West Sixth Street, Sioux

City," I sounded out. Then louder, excitement running through my veins like a bolt of lightning. "Fifty-three sixty West Sixth Street, Sioux City. Holy shit, she did it! Elisabeth found her!"

But why was her message such a mess? When Elisabeth texted Francine's address weeks ago, it had been neat and distinct. This looked like she'd been trying to text while juggling at the same time. What would cause her to send a message so garbled that she'd risk the chance of my not understanding it?

By the time Bones came into the bedroom, I'd figured it out, and I met his gaze with a mixture of hope and grimness.

"Elisabeth found her," I repeated. "And it looks like she texted the woman's address while trying to fight Kramer off, so Kramer knows she found her, which means he also knows that we'll be on our way."

Even with the direct air route we'd take, it would still be a good twenty minutes until we got to Prospect Hill, the neighborhood in Sioux City where that address derived from. Bones could fly faster, but I couldn't, and if he burned through his power getting both us there quicker, that would mean he'd be running on less reserves when it was time to make our speedy exit. We already had to expend energy making sure we were high enough to avoid being spotted by commuters in the after-work, rush-hour traffic. It wouldn't be fully dark for another hour, but even though the early evening was still light enough to raise our profile, waiting wasn't an option.

It seemed like forever before we spotted the white

monument that marked the Prospect Hill area. Seeing the MapQuest overview before gave us an idea of which area to land in, but obviously people didn't have house numbers conveniently displayed on their roofs. Bones took us above where we thought her street was and zoomed downward in a straight line, landing us in the middle of some tall hedges. The ground shuddered, and our feet went ankle deep into the earth from an impact far harder than usual. I immediately crouched into a kneeling position, helping to distribute some of the force. It still hurt like hell, but with the area bordering downtown and lots of people window-shopping, seeking dinner, or otherwise strolling around, we couldn't afford to glide to an easy landing and be spotted. With almost every cell phone having recording capabilities, we'd be on the news and Internet before you could say compromised supernatural security. Then not only would we be in deep shit with the vampire Law Guardians, but Madigan, with his facial recognition software programmed to flag my image, would also know exactly where we were.

"All right, luv?" Bones asked, shaking off any injuries from the equivalent of being dropped like a bowling ball from five thousand feet faster than I could.

"Fine," I gritted out, wincing at the pain that shot through my back when I stood up. I might've saved my legs by kneeling, but my angle must've been wrong, because I heard several things pop in my spine upon standing. A few sharp tingles later, and the pain was gone. Nothing beat being a vampire when it came to healing abilities.

Bones took some sage out of his pockets and lit it. I did the same, careful not to let any of the burnt edges fall to the ground. There were dry, crinkled leaves everywhere, and starting a fire would be a great way to draw a lot of unwanted attention to us.

We came out of the hedges and started walking toward the nearest intersection as though we were a normal couple out for a stroll. From the mutters I picked up on, the people closest to the spot where we'd landed were wondering about the noise and the momentary vibration they'd felt, but thankfully hadn't connected those things with two people dropping out of the sky. With how fast we'd descended, we would have been nothing more than a brief streak even to someone who'd been looking right at that spot.

"That's Cook Street," Bones said low, nodding at the street sign in front of us. "Sixth should be coming up . . ."

His voice trailed off, tension ringing from his aura like invisible fire alarms. I followed the direction of his stare, dread creeping up my spine.

A tunic-clad man floated in the middle of the street, white hair unmoving in the breeze. Cars drove right through him, the drivers unaware that they'd just come in contact with one of history's most prolific serial killers. And even though he was too far away for me to see his eyes, I knew the Inquisitor was staring right at us.

Our arrival in the neighborhood hadn't gone unnoticed by everyone.

"Bones," I said softly, "I'll draw him off. You go get her, then meet up with me."

His lips barely moved, but I could still hear his hushed reply. "I'm not leaving you."

We only had seconds before Kramer attacked. Already the ghost was starting toward us, and I knew it wasn't to shake our hands, and say, "Howdy, neighbors!"

"You're a man; not tempting enough for him," I whispered rapidly. "But you're stronger and faster than I am, so you're that woman's best chance if she's still alive. Now quit arguing and *go*."

So saying, I handed my sage to Bones and ran right toward Kramer, making sure to wave my arms so he'd see I didn't carry any of that ghostly flamethrower anymore. Behind me, Bones ground out a curse, but I didn't turn around. I was right, and he knew it. He might not like it, but that didn't change the reality.

Now, to get Kramer to come after me instead of protecting his final target. Unless he'd killed her already, what happened with Francine should have shown him that he couldn't stop us from taking her. I hoped he decided to unleash some of his frustration over that on me instead of spending those last few moments with her.

"Hey, Casper the Ugly Ghost!" I called out when Kramer seemed more focused on what Bones was doing than on my closing in on him. "Bet I can whack that stubbly jaw before you can catch me!"

That turned the heads of the other people on the sidewalk, but my attention was all for the hazy figure in the monkish tunic. I was now close enough to see Kramer's nostrils flare at my reminding him of the two punches I'd landed during the brief time when he'd been solid. He glanced behind me again, though, as if still deciding whom to attack. *Take the bait!* I urged him, then dove to cover the last several feet between us.

"Here comes bitch slap number three!" I announced, swinging my hand through his jaw.

He wasn't solid, so my fist flew through harmlessly, but either the gesture or the words made up his mind. Kramer spat out a curse and rounded on me, his own arm shooting out.

I ducked, but not fast enough. Pain burst through the side of my head, the energy he managed to harness feeling even stronger than a punch from solid flesh would have. I caught myself before barreling into a store's front window, crashing into the wall instead. At least that only chipped off some plaster instead of shattering glass. Then I spun around to face the ghost.

"That was pathetic," I snapped. "I don't even need sage to fight you. You're pussy enough all on your own."

His face twisted with rage, and a torrent of German erupted from his mouth. I took that as my signal to run for it, darting through the throngs of people going about their business on this lovely autumn evening.

I had made it as far an outdoor sports bar when it felt like a wrecking ball crashed into my back. It sent me flying forward, completely off-balance. I managed to turn enough to avoid the family with the small children and instead crashed into a table with several young men crouched over beer pitchers and chicken wings. The table broke under my impact, foamy liquid, glasses, and orange-smeared chicken parts splattering over me. The four men who'd been

seated around it stared down at me in disbelief, two of
them still holding chicken in their hands.

"What's your *problem*, lady?" one of them gasped.

They couldn't see that a ghost had blasted me into
them, but did they really think I'd just swan dived into
their table out of boredom? From my vantage point on
the floor, I could see Kramer approaching, his form
disappearing every time he had to poltergeist through
someone in his way. I glanced back at the quartet of
young men, desperately trying to think of something
that would make them and the other patrons run away
before the ghost got here.

"I'm on the rag and desperate for attention," I improvised, remembering Graham's derisive thoughts
from that day at my old house. "So if you want to live,
get the hell away from me!"

With that, I shoved the remains of the table at them,
doing it slow enough so they could avoid it. They leapt
out of its path and started backing away. Thankfully,
they weren't the only ones. The outdoor seating area
quickly began to clear of people.

"Crazy bitch," I heard, but my attention was all for
the ghost. He was only a dozen feet away now, his
mouth opening in a snarl. I needed to get him clear of
these people before he decided to start killing some of
them just for fun.

"Come and get me, limp dick!" I yelled, vaulting
over the wall. A less-crowded section of shops was on
the other side, parked cars lining the streets but their
owners mostly elsewhere. I didn't look back to see if
Kramer had taken the bait but continued my stream of
insults while running flat out. "I know that whole bit

about witches depriving men of their virile members was just your excuse for not being able to get it up unless you could—"

Something smashed into my back, sending an explosion of pain through me. It also threw me off-balance again. I ended up skidding down the sidewalk face-first, my velocity carrying me several feet before whatever he'd done to my back healed enough for me to stagger to my feet. As soon as I did, an invisible sledgehammer landed in my gut, knocking me back to my knees.

Someone screamed. I couldn't see who because my vision was blurry and filled with red. I spat out blood, sickening crunching noises sounding with that slight movement of my jaw. My face burned like it had been set on fire, but I got up again, braced for the blow I knew would come. *Get away from the people, away from the people,* I repeated to myself. No matter what he did to me, I'd heal. They wouldn't.

I made it a few feet, barely seeing where I was going because though I could feel my face mending, I still had blood in my eyes. Then I heard an ominous metallic boom and white-hot pain exploded all through my body. Lights flashed in my vision, and my ears rang with the sound of crunching metal and shattering glass. Now I really couldn't see, but the smell of gasoline and the tremendous weight pressing on me let me diagnose what had just happened.

Motherfucking ghost upended a *car* on me!

I didn't have time to be stunned at how much stronger the proximity to Halloween had made Kramer because the acrid scent warned me that I needed to move *now*. The ghost was probably busy trying to score a lighter or make lots of sparks to ignite all that flammable liquid contained in the fuel tank on top of me. I'd had a car explode next to me once before, and it had almost killed me. Being trapped underneath one if it went off? I'd be all the way dead, no doubt about it.

I tensed every muscle in my body, ignoring the flares of pain that were multiple broken bones trying to knit back together, and heaved up with all of my strength. Agony flashed through me, making me momentarily dizzy, but the weight moved off as far as my arms and legs could stretch. Another blisteringly painful heave, and I slithered out from under it, letting it fall back down with a crash once I was clear.

Several blinks later, and I could see enough to be dismayed at the cluster of people gathered nearby, each of them displaying varying degrees of shock. I didn't see any phones held up capturing footage, though, so I had to be grateful for that. Then I caught sight of someone else staring at me. Kramer floated in the empty space along the road where the car had been parked, his green gaze locked onto me with unrelenting intensity.

I didn't know why he wasn't zooming in for another of those bone-cracking energy shots, but damned if I'd just stand here and pose for him until he got around to it. I whirled, pointing myself in the least-populated direction of the street, and started to run. More bones crunched, and my skin felt like I'd been staked on an anthill before I finished healing, but I didn't stop running, waiting for the next blast of pain that would signal Kramer's catching up with me.

I heard a whoosh, then something hard pressed into my gut. My instant defensive reaction stilled when I recognized the power flooding around me, crackling the air with hidden currents. The ground left my feet as I was yanked upward, one strong arm around my midsection, the other locked around someone screaming in a high-pitched, feminine voice.

That scream was the sweetest music I'd heard because it meant Bones had gotten to Kramer's last intended victim in time to save her.

†hirty-one

ONCE WE'D GONE HIGH AND FAR ENOUGH
away that we knew Kramer couldn't have followed, Bones texted Spade and told him to meet us
at War Eagle Park where I-29 was closest to the Mis-
souri River. It had been over an hour since we left
Kramer raging on the ground, but we still wouldn't
risk taking the woman directly to Spade's and giving
the ghost even the smallest chance to track her there
through me.

Her name was Sarah, and she hadn't settled down
much since Bones took her away from her house, not
that I blamed her. If that flight hadn't been enough
to scare her senseless, it only took five minutes talking to her to realize that Kramer had tormented Sarah
to the very edge of sanity. With Francine and Lisa
out of his reach, he'd clearly made up for lost time
with her, just as I'd feared he would. Sarah's thoughts
were a mixture of white noise, terror, and repetitions

of the same crap Kramer had spouted to me about not
suffering witches to live and his being unstoppable.
Bones and I told her she could trust us, making sure
our eyes were lit up when we said it, but she seemed
past the point of being calmed by our gazes.

Some people, for reasons of genetic anomaly,
trauma, or staunch willpower, needed to be bitten
before vampire mind control would work, but I
couldn't bring myself to bite her on top of everything
else. She didn't try to run, so maybe some of what
we told her was getting through even though the poor
woman jumped at every noise, gaze darting about as
if expecting Kramer to pop up and continue his abuse.
I could only hope that a few days of being around
Francine and Lisa would help bring Sarah back from
what seemed to be a near mental breakdown.

Of course, what would really help Sarah and the
other women would be for us to manage to stuff their
tormentor into that stone-and-mineral trap. Then
they could take all the time they needed to heal from
the emotional damage he'd inflicted on them. Anger
burned through me. Most murderers I'd encountered,
while still vile to the bone, only sought to destroy
people's bodies, but that wasn't enough for Kramer.
He had to crush their minds, hearts, and spirits, too.

Spade descended from the night's canvass, and
Sarah reared back, the scent of fear exploding out of
her pores. Guess seeing another person drop out of
the sky was too much for her right now. I held on to
her, murmuring that he was a friend, and she'd be safe
with him. Only when I told her that he'd take her to
Francine and Lisa did she calm down enough to stop

trying to pull away. I'd told her about the other two women Kramer had set his sights on, and how they were safe. Words were nice, but seeing them for herself would do more to prove to her badly wounded psyche that Kramer wasn't the all-powerful punisher he'd made himself out to be than any reassurances I could give her.

Bones walked over to his friend with a last pitying glance her way, taking Spade off to the side to warn him about her fragile mental state, I assumed. After a minute of hushed conversation, they came back. The other vampire held out a bundle to her that I gratefully recognized was a coat. Bones and I left so fast to retrieve her, we hadn't thought to grab our own coats, let alone bring an extra one for her.

"Sarah, this is my very good mate, Spade," Bones said, calling him by his chosen name instead of the one he normally used. "He'll take excellent care of you."

She took the coat but then edged closer to me. "He? Aren't you coming, too?"

Her dark topaz gaze was pleading, fragmented thoughts revealing that she didn't want to go without me. It might be because I was another woman, and that made me feel safer to her, or because Spade looked rather imposing with his great height and black coat surrounding him. Our proximity to the river even had his shoulder-length hair blowing dramatically around his face, adding to the effect, but in addition to being trustworthy, Spade also had a deep chivalrous streak.

"I can't come now, but I'll see you soon," I promised her, exchanging a glance with Bones. Real soon, considering we'd deliver the trap to Spade's in the next couple days, then wait for my inner signal to lead Kramer right to us.

Wait until Sarah found that out. Then she'd be extra, extra nervous.

Or maybe we'd be lucky, and she'd know who the accomplice was. Two out of three women had fit the same pattern before Kramer started attacking them, and I was betting Sarah wouldn't be the exception.

"Sarah, you had a cat recently, didn't you?" I asked her. "One who died? Do you happen to know how it happened, or who did it?"

Her thoughts seized with that question, making it hard to pick out the coherent ones from their less stable, scattered counterparts. I caught words like "hung" and "break in," though, confirming my belief. Francine's and Lisa's cats had been hung, too, their little bodies left on display. Step one in the beginning of Kramer's reign of torment.

"Do you know who did it?" I pressed.

She shook her head, getting so visibly upset that Bones nudged me. "Let her get settled first, Kitten," he murmured. "She'll be better able to answer questions with Denise and the others."

He was right. This was too soon, and it was a long shot that she'd know who killed her cat, anyway. I gave Sarah a quick hug goodbye, telling her again that this would all be over soon, and she'd be safe.

God, let that be true, I prayed.

Spade held out his arm to Sarah as if he were offering to escort her to a ball. "Please come with me," he said.

She looked at me. I nodded, forcing a smile. "He'll take you to the others, and I'll see you soon."

With obvious reluctance, she took Spade's arm. Spade gave a last nod to me and Bones, then swooped Sarah up and winged her away with all the flair of those old Dracula movies that the real Vlad Tepesh hated. A scream trailed after them, growing fainter, until Sarah's voice was lost to the darkness.

I turned to Bones with a slight smile. "Beam me up, Scotty."

His snort was soft with amusement. "You don't need me for that. You can beam yourself now."

"I know," I said, sliding my arms around him. "But I'd rather fly like this."

His arms circled me, strong, hard, and infinitely blissful. "So would I, Kitten."

Much later, I heard the distinct rustle of boards on the porch that said someone was out there. Had to be Kramer. I stayed seated on the family room floor with my back propped against the wall and debated ignoring him. If I moved, Bones might wake up, and he'd just fallen asleep. It was my turn to make sure all the sage stayed lit while everyone else slept. Kramer had been known to chuck branches or boards at sage jars to knock them over, trying either to burn us out or extinguish the repelling smoke. Neither was an option we wanted to explore, hence the shifts.

If left up to Bones, he'd split up the watches between himself and Ian, but that wouldn't be fair. My mother couldn't help her weariness as soon as dawn struck, but I could stay awake as well as the men could.

All of us slept in the family room, sharing the four mattresses that we'd brought in from the bedrooms. It might not be comfortable—and it sure as hell wasn't romantic—but it was safer. If by chance the watch-person *did* fall asleep and Kramer managed to sneak past the sage and get in, he wouldn't be able to single out the most vulnerable of us without waking all the rest. Not with the way we slept, clustered around each other.

Another creak of the boards sounded outside, but this time, it was followed by a whisper I couldn't make out. I frowned. That was unusual for Kramer. He normally liked to bash about while stringing curses together as loud as he could squawk. The ghost knew when we slept, too, so he frequently stopped by at dawn for maximum pain in the ass effect. But whispers? It made me curious enough to get up. It might be Fabian or Elisabeth, unable to venture inside because of the sage and trying to be considerate by not waking everyone with a loud greeting.

I crept toward the door, keeping as quiet as I could. No need for everyone to wake up and investigate the odd whisper. Bones stirred, but his eyes remained closed. My mother was dead to the world, Tyler's snores continued uninterrupted, and Ian didn't even twitch. I couldn't help shaking my head as I looked at him. Ian slept like a baby every morning—well, a baby who continually kept one hand down his pants. Guess his misdeeds didn't bother his conscience enough to cost him a moment of shut-eye.

Carefully, still trying not to wake the others, I opened the front door. To my surprise, it was Kramer

floating over the far side of the ruined porch instead
of Fabian or Elisabeth. He let go of one of the loose
boards when he saw me, beckoning me forward with
almost a friendly gesture.

Oh, sure, I'll come right over without getting any
sage first, I thought. Did he think slamming that car
on me had knocked my brains loose?

I gave him the finger, then picked up two of the
nearest jars of sage, deciding to go a few feet away
from the door only because I wanted to give everyone
else a few more moments of sleep. If Kramer kept to
his usual form, he'd be cursing and hurling boards at
the house soon enough.

The Inquisitor didn't respond to my fingered opinion. He simply waited without moving or speaking
while I walked over without making a sound on the
rickety remains of the porch. I kept the door open,
and, though I ventured away from it, I made sure to
stay within two good lunges.

"Fancy seeing you again," I said, keeping my
voice low.

That moss green gaze raked me from head to toe,
but not in the sleazy way he'd done on other occa-
sions. This time, it was the gaze of an enemy sizing
up his opponent and finding her lacking.

"Do you truly believe that you, a mere woman, can
defeat me?"

Aside from the gender insult, this was the most
rational I'd ever seen Kramer. He sounded genuinely
thoughtful and his voice was as quiet as mine—a huge
departure from his normal, trumpeted witches-will-
burn rants. I could respond to his question by listing

all the other arrogant bastards I'd taken down over the years. Or by pointing out that I'd already defeated his plans for Francine, Sarah, and Lisa by putting them out of his reach for now, but I preferred to remain underestimated. *Don't worry about widdle gurly me, big bad monster. I'm harmless.*

"Talk is meaningless. We'll know who's defeated whom when it's all over, and there's only one of us left standing," I replied.

From the faint scraping sound, someone in the house had woken up and was headed toward the door. Before he got there, I knew it was Bones from the brushes of his aura. Even whispers had disturbed his light sleep. Kramer didn't seem to notice. His attention didn't waver from me.

"Though you are a woman, you are strong," the ghost said, still in that same musing way. "You pushed the car aside as if it had no effect."

Actually, it had hurt like hell. Under other circumstances, I might have stayed under it saying things like "Ow, ow, oww!" while I waited to heal, but I didn't have the luxury at the time.

"You're not the first person who's tried to kill me with a car," was what I said, shrugging as if either time hadn't been a big deal. I could feel that Bones was in the doorway, but he didn't come out, keeping concealed from the ghost in the shadows of the doorframe.

Kramer smiled, cold and calculating. "I knew it would not kill you."

Interesting. Now that he mentioned it, he hadn't been running around trying to ignite the fuel tank while I was briefly trapped under it. Didn't it occur to him to try to blow the car up? Or was he lying about knowing the car wouldn't kill me?

Far be it for me to understand the mental workings of a maniac.

"What's with quiet chatting instead of your usual blustering?" I asked, changing the subject. "You lonely because Francine, Lisa, and Sarah are out of your reach, so you have no one to talk to?"

Please get pissed and tell me who your accomplice is, I silently urged him. *Go on, impress me with how much time you spend with whoever that prick is!*

But he didn't. He gave me another of those contemplative looks instead. "Why do you risk so much for them? They are nothing to you."

"No, they're nothing to *you*," I corrected at once, "but they mean something to me because they're in trouble and I can help. If I only put my ass on the line for people I loved, I'd be no better than half the monsters I've hunted. Even evil people risk themselves for loved ones. Just because you picked women I don't know doesn't mean I'm going to sit on the sidelines and let them die."

His smile grew, showing those brownish molars in between gaps of gums. I couldn't help but think it was poetic justice that he would keep that nasty mouth all through eternity, hopefully while locked in a homemade jail.

"You still believe you can stop me, *Hexe*, but you can't. You don't fear me, but soon, you will."

"No, I won't," I replied sharply. "You won't draw any strength from me because I've got your number,

Inquisitor. You might be harder to kill with your whole lack of a physical body, but you're no scarier than all the other assholes that are now dead while I'm still standing."

"Until Samhain," was all he said, then vanished from sight.

I stared at the spot where he'd been, a smile of my own twisting my mouth.

That's what I'm counting on, fucker.

Thirty-two

On October 30, as soon as night's con-cealing veil fell, Ian, Bones, and I flew away from the tattered farmhouse. Each of us was carrying a large, tarp-draped object. My mother and Tyler were staying behind, leaving for Spade's tomorrow after-noon via a more conventional mode of transportation: a taxicab. That way, in case my borrowed abilities had faded to where Kramer couldn't locate me by concen-trating alone, he could follow them to Spade's house. They'd take plenty of sage with them in case the ghost did more than trail them, but my money was on Kramer's trying to be sly and staying unseen. After all, they weren't the targets he'd so carefully picked out. Francine, Lisa, and Sarah were the ones Kramer really wanted, and we wanted to be sure he found his way to them.

Once we had everything in place, anyway.

That was why we didn't fly our large bundles right

to Spade's. We went to a defunct building that had formerly been a combined sewer overflow facility in Ottumwa instead. Underneath the building, a series of storm drains, tunnels, and sewers led to the Des Moines River. It wasn't as perfect a setting as our cave with its underground river—and it smelled a damn sight worse even though it hadn't been operational in years—but it would suffice. Bones had had his co-ruler, Mencheres, purchase the building and its surrounding riverside property over the past couple weeks using a dummy corporation. Couldn't risk someone else tearing this down to put a new business up and disturbing what we hoped would be Heinrich Kramer's final resting place. Now, we just had to carve a hole in the underground trunk sewer deep enough to reach the river's water table so that we could ensure the flow of fresh water around where we intended to place the trap.

It had taken Bones and me plus Chris's team a week to lay the previous trap in place. We had exactly five hours to set this one up, and we had carving up the trunk sewer to contend with, too. I didn't want to calculate how long our odds were, trying to focus instead on how powerful Bones, Spade, and Ian were. I'd do my damnedest, too, and either we would finish or we wouldn't. The only thing that was certain was there was no time for hand-wringing.

We landed outside the empty facility, and I set my heavy section of the trap down as soon as my feet hit the ground. Flying for an hour while toting that bulk made me appreciate how effortlessly Bones carried me when we flew together. Granted, I weighed less than this hunk of rock, but he'd also flown while carrying me and at least one other person, and he made it look easy even while going faster and farther.

"Brilliant landing," Ian commented, giving a pointed look at the long furrow I'd carved in the earth when I touched down. "We're trying to keep a low profile, and here you've gone and made it look like a meteorite hit."

I'd been proud of myself for not blasting through the side of the building—staying in the air was *far* easier than landing!—so I snootily lifted my nose at him.

"I'm less than two years undead, and I'm already flying. How long did it take you to find *your* wings, pretty boy?"

Bones snorted at the indignation on Ian's face. He was nothing if not competitive. "You had that coming, mate."

"Power leech," Ian replied sulkily.

He had me there, but Bones laughed. "You'd give both your stones to have that ability, not to mention she flew before turning into a vampire, so that's hers alone."

"If you're through squabbling," a smooth voice called out from the building, "perhaps we can set about securing this trap?"

Spade was already here, good. I looked at my large chunk of rock and the entrance to the building. Then I cracked my knuckles. First things first, and that would be making a new door large enough for all the pieces to fit through. I only hoped the tunnels leading to the trunk sewer were wide enough not to need their own form of remodeling.

The five-hour countdown had just begun.

Four hours and twenty-two minutes later, Ian stared at the reassembled trap secured in the bottom of the trunk sewer, water sloshing over it from the adjoining hole we'd torn through to reach the Des Moines River. A breath of laughter escaped him.

"You've made it look like a huge cauldron. That's spectacularly twisted of you, Reaper."

I wiped some of the brackish, cold water away from my face before replying. Everyone else waited in the tunnel above, but I wanted to check the bottom of the trap one more time to make sure it was steady. Yes, call me paranoid. If all went well tomorrow, once Kramer was in the trap, we could do a more thorough job of reinforcing the entrance we'd dug into the sewer wall and the base of the trap to make extra sure that time and erosion wouldn't disturb Kramer's jail cell; but for now, it looked like it would hold.

"Kramer's obsessed with witchcraft, so I wanted him to be in familiar surroundings. Never let it be said that I'm not sentimental."

Despite the flip words and feeling more exhausted than I could remember, I also wanted to whoop for joy. We'd done it! The trap was secured, river water washing over its bottom half, with time to spare. Not much time, true, but I wasn't going to quibble. I could even give Ian a big sloppy kiss for how hard and fast he'd worked. Arrogant, obnoxious pervert he might be, but damn, could he accomplish an objective when he set his mind to it. I'd never doubted Bones's or Spade's power and dedication, but Ian had surprised me.

"Let's leave before your spectre finds this place," Spade said, disappearing out of sight into the tunnel. His voice floated behind him. "Denise will be so relieved to hear we're finished."

I climbed up the sewer wall, accepting the hand Bones gave me to lift me the last few feet of the way. "You brought a car, right?" I called after Spade, hoping the answer was yes.

"Of course," his reply drifted back. "Knew none of us would fancy burning more energy to fly back, and tomorrow, we'll need everything we can muster against Kramer."

How true. Then I cast a glance at how muddied and wet we were and gave Bones a rueful look. "We're going to trash Spade's stuff again."

He grinned. "No worries, I'm sure it's a rental."

Spade drove, Ian rode shotgun, and Bones and I took the backseat. I was so glad to lean against him and just shut my eyes that I didn't even mind being wet, cold, and filthy. Spade turned the heater on, so it wasn't long before I began to feel toasty warm, too. After spending a couple weeks in a house with no electricity and the frigid night air blowing in from countless slits in the boarded-up windows, the heat felt like heaven to me. In fact, I was so relaxed I must have dozed off, because the next thing I knew, the car jerked to a stop, and the landscape around us had completely changed.

We were on a narrow gravel road leading to what

looked like a pretty, two-story white-and-blue house at the end of it. Hay fields stretched out for acres behind the property, and a horse barn stood empty off to the far right side of the house. It was wonderfully quiet, no neighbors visible in the immediate vicinity and thus no noisy intrusions from their thoughts to crowd my psyche.

"Christ, no," Spade whispered at the same time I realized that a complete lack of other people's thoughts was a very, very bad sign. I should be picking up on four minds in the house ahead. Instead, there was only ominous silence.

Spade didn't open his car door—he pushed it aside so violently that it sailed away from the vehicle with a metallic ripping sound. Then he was nothing more than a blur headed toward the house. The rest of us got out, but not as fast, Ian shoving the car into park to keep it from rolling. Dread made me feel like the blood in my veins had just been replaced with ice water. I ran toward the house, a string of denials resounding in my mind. *Not Denise. Please, no.* She was my best friend. It would be horrible enough if something happened to Lisa, Sarah, and Francine, but I couldn't stand it if Denise was . . . was . . .

Spade ripped the front door off as well, disappearing into the house. The three of us were close behind him. Sharp barks coming from upstairs made it impossible to detect any heartbeats, and the sound made Bones pause before entering, dragging me to a halt with him. Maybe Dexter was barking because of the crash the door made when Spade tore it from its hinges.

Or maybe it was because Kramer was still in the house. Had he managed to manifest flesh a day early? Bloody shoe prints showed that someone had come down the staircase and gone out the door, and I didn't smell any sage burning. Denise was immune to most kinds of death, but Spade always kept some demon bone on hand in case any hellish buddies of the one who had branded her showed up looking for vengeance. Had the bone knife that was made of the only substance that could kill Denise been used against her? *Oh God, what had Kramer done to them?*

Ian didn't wait, but went into the house with a brusque, "Get some sage lit before you follow." Upstairs, Spade cried out, a harsh sound of grief that made my knees almost give out. Tears making my gaze blurry, I grabbed a handful of the waterlogged sage I'd kept in my pants and lit it, hurrying inside and then up the staircase carrying my smoking bundle. From the sounds and smell, Bones was relighting and refilling the jars in the house, trying to form a protective barrier though it might be too late.

I didn't need to follow the bloody shoe prints that led to the first room on the right. Spade's choked voice was a heartbreaking beacon. I burst into the room, anguish ripping through me when the first sight that greeted me was a mass of blood, bone, and things I didn't even want to name splattered on the wall of the open closet. Ian stood to the side of it, Spade at the bottom of that grisly montage, cradling a blood-soaked form that didn't move. Dexter was off in the corner, growling and barking while tracking crimson paw prints on the carpet.

"I'm okay," I heard a feminine voice say beneath the barking and Spade's ragged repetitions of Denise's name.

I stuffed back the sob of relief that rocketed up my throat. Ian was more practical, pulling on Spade's shoulders.

"Let her go, Charles. You're probably holding her too tightly for her to breathe."

Spade leaned back, revealing the upper half of my friend that I hadn't seen before, and I staggered where I stood. Denise had three mangled holes in her sweater that looked like exit wounds from bullets. She'd been shot in the back enough times to kill any normal person from their tight placement near her chest, but not enough to put *her* down. She must have turned around and gone after her shooter. That was why the assailant aimed for her face next. From the wall, her still-misshapen features, and the cherry pie look under the back of her head, he'd emptied his gun into her.

The accomplice had somehow found this place and attacked when the rest of us were away trying to hammer the final nails into Kramer's coffin. *How had he gotten in?* I wondered, still shocked from the sight of Denise. She knew not to let any unfamiliar men in, and she wasn't very easy to take down, as the carnage in this room proved.

Bones appeared, grimly taking note of the blood-sprayed closet and Denise's condition. "No one else is in the house," he stated, confirming what my senses had already suspected. "I don't see any signs that Kramer's here now . . . or was here before. None of the sage jars are overturned or disturbed. They merely burned out, but not too long ago from the looks of it."

Spade brushed a matted clump of Denise's hair back, and I winced at what stuck to his hand.

"Can you tell us what happened, darling?"

From the way her gaze seemed to roll around the room, she was having trouble focusing. No shocker there; I was amazed she was even conscious. She must have been shot a couple hours ago for her to have healed to this extent, but even with her demon-blooded regenerative abilities, she was still in rough shape. I wasn't sure a vampire or ghoul could have survived all the damage she'd sustained, yet despite the fact that she looked like she'd dove headfirst into a wood chipper, she managed to mumble out a reply.

"Lisa and Francine . . . asleep. Heard . . . awful noise. Came in here . . . saw Helsing . . ."

My kitty wasn't in the room at the moment, from the two sole heartbeats I heard now that Dexter had quit barking. Helsing was probably hiding downstairs. All the recent run-ins with Kramer had taught the kitty to seek cover at the first hint of loud noises, so the gunshots would've sent him running.

Denise lifted a crimson-painted hand and vaguely pointed at the wall behind her. "Pulled him out . . . of the noose . . . then felt the gunshots."

Noose? That snapped my attention to the belt dangling from the closet rail, the bottom of it hooked into a circle. All the clothes were pushed to either side, leaving that single item in the middle, but with the bloody remains of Denise's head all over the wall, I hadn't focused on it at first glance.

Bones edged around Spade and Denise to pluck out the belt, a muscle in his jaw flexing as he sniffed it.

"How did he get in, Denise?" I asked, kneeling so we'd be more at eye level. "Can you tell us anything that could help us find out who he is?"

Her gaze rolled around again, and she blinked several times, as if she were fighting to stay conscious. It was Bones who spoke, and his voice was dryer than ashes.

"Not he, Kitten. She."

Denise managed to nod, while her eyes rolled back in her head. "Sarah," she mumbled right before passing out. "Sarah shot me."

†hirty-†hree

I DIDN'T WANT TO BELIEVE IT, BUT EVEN WITH pieces of her head not fully regenerated yet, I didn't doubt Denise's statement. The woman we thought we were protecting from Kramer's evil intentions must actually have been his *accomplice* instead.

"I'll kill the bitch," Spade snarled, emerald blazing from his eyes and fangs flashing out from his upper teeth.

From the roiling fury leaking out of Bones's aura, Spade would have to take a number and get in line.

"Get Denise cleaned up, Charles," Bones said. "She's been through enough without waking up covered in her own blood and brains again."

Spade scooped Denise up, carrying her out of the room while still muttering under his breath about all the different ways he was going to kill Sarah. I was too shell-shocked to begin plotting her death, but I knew my own murderous rage would come soon.

"Kramer hates women, why would he partner up with one?" I wondered, trying to sort through this bombshell.

"Easy. He knows what he intends to do with her once she's fulfilled her usefulness," Bones replied shortly.

She'd been useful indeed, getting her enemies to lead her right to Lisa and Francine. No wonder Kramer had been so smug the last time I'd seen him. Guilt burned its way over my emotions. We'd promised Lisa and Francine that we'd protect them. Instead, we'd helped the co-conspirator in their murders to orchestrate the worst sort of betrayal right under our noses.

"Where'd she get the gun?" Ian asked.

"We kept three of them here in anticipation of the accomplice's accompanying Kramer in his attack," Spade replied from another room in the house. "Showed each of the women where they were, how to use them . . . though Sarah already knew how to shoot, bloody slag."

She must have forced Lisa and Francine to go with her at gunpoint. After what they would've seen her do to Denise, I had no doubt the women would have been too frightened to refuse.

Bones gave me another of those unreadable looks before he spoke. "She didn't leave with Lisa and Francine on foot. Did you have another car here?"

"Yes." The bitterness in Spade's voice was clear despite the sounds of a shower turning on. "I left it for Denise in case of an emergency."

Sarah used it to cart away Francine and Lisa in-

stead, probably stuffing them in the trunk after bind-
ing and gagging them. If she really wanted to ensure
a smooth ride, she'd have bashed them in the head and
knocked them out for the trip. Just thinking about it
made me want to bash my own head in frustration.
From the looks of Denise, they'd been gone for hours,
long enough to be far away by now. Sarah probably
put her plan into action shortly after Spade left to
meet us at the facility.

Maybe she left something that would give us a
clue as to where she was taking them. I doubted it,
but just standing around was making me crazy. I left
the ruined bedroom and went downstairs, looking for
trash cans. *Please let Sarah be stupid enough to have
jotted down incriminating information on something,
then thrown it away.*

"I'm surprised you didn't hear any of her plans
from her thoughts, Crispin," I heard Ian say.

"They were scattered, unstable, and frequently in-
coherent. I thought it was because of Kramer's abuse,
not malicious intentions," was Bones's measured
reply. "Believe me, I wish I'd paid closer attention."

Me too, but the brief time we'd spent with Sarah
had been mostly while we were flying. That made her
scream mentally and verbally—not much coherency
there. Then while we waited for Spade, she'd only
shown a fear of vampires—understandable ninety-
nine percent of the time with people who had just
found out about their existence—and a desire to meet
Lisa and Francine.

Boy, had we been wrong about her motivations
behind *that*. The other sickening part of this whole sit-

uation was the knowledge that if Sarah was Kramer's accomplice, not his third intended victim, that woman was still out there. As if in pitiless reminder of how time was running out, I passed a clock on my way to the kitchen. Five minutes after three in the morning, making it officially October 31. Halloween was upon us, and we'd been the ones tricked all over the place.

"One of us should fly over the area to see if we can spot the car while the others stay here and search for clues," I stated, heading for the trash can in the corner. "Someone should go by Elisabeth's apartment, too. Kramer might have damaged her phone after she sent that last text, and there's still a third victim to be found. Maybe Elisabeth's noticed another woman who Kramer's been hanging around—"

"I know who the third woman is," Bones stated.

That stopped me in the process of pulling out wadded-up bits of food, paper, and packages from the kitchen trash can. He came down the stairs, his expression frozen into beautifully sculpted, unyielding planes.

"You do? How? Who is she?"

That dark brown gaze didn't waver despite the babble of questions I lobbed at him. "It's you, Kitten."

"Me?" I blurted in disbelief. All activity upstairs ground to a halt from the sudden silence. "It's not me. Why would you even think—"

"You're the only one who fits," he cut me off. "Who else has Kramer fixated on these past several weeks? *You.* He followed you around even before he knew we were setting a trap for him, always attacking you first except the one time I was kissing you, and he tried to kill me for it. The time frame of when he picks his victims fits because he met you right when Francine and Lisa said he started tormenting them. You've suffered recent tragedies like they have. You've been staying in the Sioux City area. He even had Sarah try to hang your cat! Why would he do that unless he considered Helsing to be your familiar as he did with Lisa's and Francine's cats?"

"He knows animals can sense him," I whispered, reeling at all the points Bones brought up.

"Sarah didn't do a thing to Dexter, did she?" he noted. "You fit Kramer's profile perfectly save for one thing—you're not single. But he has a plan to separate you from me, and I'm telling you now, I won't allow it to happen."

I scoffed to cover the realization snaking through me that everything Bones said made sense. What was the first thing I'd done when I met Kramer? Told him I had witchcraft in my veins and sicced a bunch of Remnants on him. He'd called me a witch from that day on, among other choice names, and talked about how I would burn, but I'd brushed that off as meaningless ranting. Too late, I realized that nothing Kramer did was meaningless.

I'd been so sure I'd beat him because he'd vastly underestimated me. Looked like I'd been the one to vastly underestimate him.

"Kramer knows he can't separate us," I began, then the final realization hit me, making my jaw clench shut.

Not unless I thought by going to him alone, I could save Francine and Lisa.

Bones's smile was more a twisting of his lips.

"That's right, luv, which is why I expect it won't be long until you're visited by a ghost."

Ian left the house to do a flyover of the surrounding areas on the off chance that Sarah was dumb enough to park Spade's car where it could be seen. Spade stayed upstairs with Denise, cleaning her up and accelerating her healing by giving her some of his blood. From what I could hear, she was sleeping almost normally now, her pulse no longer weak or thready. Bones was on Spade's laptop, hacking into every account of Sarah's he could find to see if she owned or rented any other properties where she might have taken Francine and Lisa. We could hope she'd been that dumb, but if she was directed by Kramer, I doubted it. The ghost had proven to be more than clever, and there were so many empty, abandoned places they could use that wouldn't leave a trail leading back to Sarah, it would be a miracle if we found anything that way.

I found Helsing hiding underneath the family room couch, flattened out to fit in the narrow space. I had to lift it for him to crawl out, then spent several minutes coaxing him onto my lap. He hissed if my hand brushed his neck when I petted him, either out of bad memories or bruising. Or both. Dexter stayed by my feet, seeking the reassurance of closeness but not daring to jump on the couch where he'd be in range of Helsing's swatting paws.

Tyler and my mother were on their way over. No need for them to wait until later anymore. Bones fitted the broken front door back over the space, using nails to hold it in place since the hinges were damaged beyond repair. Anyone coming or going would have to use the back door. Sage burned softly in every room, preventing any type of spectral commuting. Even so, Kramer's presence seemed to loom in the house, mocking us from the scent of blood permeating through the closed bedroom door where Denise had been shot to the jars of sage that we had to keep refilling and relighting. When I heard rustling outside that wasn't caused by the wind or the natural sounds of wildlife, I wasn't surprised. I eased my kitty off my lap, careful not to jostle him since he had to be sore from Sarah's rough treatment, and stood.

Bones remained on the couch, laptop in front of him, tightly coiled energy flaring past his shields for a moment.

"See if you can glean any useful information," he said, nailing me with a hard stare, "but you are *not* leaving with him."

That last part was said with an undercurrent of steel. I nodded, not arguing because I had no intention of going anywhere with the Inquisitor. At least, not yet.

I went out the back door of the house, heading toward the vacant barn where I'd heard those rustling sounds. I hadn't brought any burning sage with me, but I didn't expect that Kramer would have come here to attack me. No, my money was on his being here for two reasons: to gloat, and to make me an offer he didn't think I could refuse.

Sure enough, a tunic-clad figure hovered about a

foot off the ground near the open doors of the barn. I held out my hands to show that they were empty of sage and stopped about twenty yards from him.

"You touch me even once, and this conversation is over," were my first words.

From the way his eyes gleamed, that statement pleased the Inquisitor. "You finally fear me, *Hexe*?"

"I'm low on patience," I replied. "So playing our usual games is last on my list of things I want to do."

He came near enough that if he stretched out his arm, he would touch me, but I didn't back away. I wasn't kidding about my warning. If he laid even one energy-filled finger on me, our conversation was over, and he could rage at me while I was back inside the sage-filled house.

"My servant brought the others to me," he said, clearly relishing each word.

Though not a muscle on me twitched, the confirmation hit me like a punch to the gut. *Francine, Lisa, I am so sorry.*

"You came all the way to tell me something we figured out after seeing my friend's brains decorating the wall?" My single laugh was filled with scorn. "Come on, Kramer. Even you aren't that arrogant."

"You no longer care about their lives?" he asked, narrowing that green gaze at me.

I shrugged as if I hadn't guessed what was coming. "Nothing more I can do for them now, is there?"

The same breeze that lifted my hair around my shoulders did nothing to the ghost across from me. Not an inch of Kramer's mud-splattered tunic rustled, and his white hair continued to frame that wrinkled, angular face like bleached straw around old leather.

"You could yet save them . . . if you defeated me in battle tonight."

And there it was. Kramer knew I had to go to him willingly. He couldn't send his human accomplice to kidnap me, not with the way Sarah would get her throat torn out on sight.

I'd promised Bones that I wouldn't sacrifice my life, but neither could I turn my back because the stakes had been raised. I wasn't about to make it easy on the prick who was responsible for all this, however. My chin lifted.

"What makes you think I'd be crazy enough to leave the safety of all the sage I can surround myself with to meet you anywhere tonight?"

Kramer smiled, slow and confident. "Because, *Hexe,* you still believe you can defeat me."

Damn right I can! I wanted to snap back at him. Then I wanted to slap that arrogant smile off his face and stomp those remaining brownish teeth right down his fucking throat. But I could do none of those things because in his formless state, he had every advantage, and I had none.

But once the sun set tonight, he'd be flesh, and the rules would change.

"Even if I did think that," I said coolly, "my husband might not want me to try it. He's the protective type, as I'm sure you've realized."

It sounded like Kramer snorted. "You do not recognize any man's authority over you. Even if he did object, you would defy him."

The words "man's authority" annoyed my feminism, as he doubtless intended. But I'd learned the hard way—twice—what a mistake it was to turn my back on Bones with the mistaken idea that some challenges could only be overcome if they were faced alone versus together.

Kramer couldn't understand that because such logic was rooted in love and mutual respect, things entirely foreign to the hate-filled man floating across from me. So I'd let him believe he was right.

I lowered my voice to a whisper. "I do what needs to be done, and if someone doesn't like that, no matter who they are, that's too bad for them."

Satisfaction flitted across the ghost's face, and when he spoke, his voice was equally low. "Sarah will meet you at the entrance of Grandview Park in Sioux City. She will have instructions to take you to me, but she will not know where the other women are, so your mind manipulations will be useless on her."

I smiled slightly. "Aren't you forgetting to tell me to come alone and unarmed?"

His gaze raked over me with utter contempt. "Bring any weapon you choose, but you already know if you don't come alone, you will never get your chance to discover if you can defeat me."

"Don't touch those women until you see me again," I told him with a contemptuous rake of my own gaze. "I don't want you too exhausted to put up much of a fight before I stomp you into the other side of eternity."

His mouth curled in cruel anticipation. "If you don't come at dusk, know that those women will suffer more than all before them."

Then he vanished without waiting to see if I had a

reply to that. I didn't. Pleading with him to be merci-
ful to Francine and Lisa would only ensure that he
meted out even harsher torture. All I had was my hope
that Kramer would try to save up his energy for me—
and that he didn't trust me enough to really be gone.
I couldn't see him anymore, but that didn't mean
the ghost wasn't still close by. He might be hanging
around to make sure I didn't run inside and tell Bones
when and where I was supposed to meet Sarah. He
might wonder if Bones would physically try to prevent me from leaving.

Curiosity killed the cat; I hoped it would make a
ghost stick around. If he was here, then he wasn't bru-
talizing Francine and Lisa. I turned around and began
to walk back toward the house. Now all I needed to
do was talk my husband into setting aside his every
protective instinct plus his innate sense of vampire
territoriality. Not an easy task, but if I couldn't come
up with enough logical reasons why this was the right
decision, then maybe I shouldn't go to Kramer tonight
after all.

Thirty-four

"No," Bones said, as soon as I walked in the door. He wasn't on the couch anymore but pacing by the entrance, his eyes flashing green.

The tiniest smile tugged at my mouth. Guess Bones decided on a preemptive strike. "No what?"

"No, you're not trading yourself for them," he replied, striding up to me. "I know you too well, and while I loathe the thought of leaving Francine and Lisa to die, if it's a choice between you or them, it's you."

I didn't say anything to that, just went around the house and began to draw the drapes. Bones had his emotions locked behind an iron wall, but from the sizzle of power in the air, he was ready to fight me tooth and nail.

That was fine. I didn't expect anything less from the man I'd fallen in love with. Once all the drapes were closed against any ghostly prying eyes, I grabbed a pen from the kitchen and began writing on the nearest piece of paper I found, which was a grocery receipt.

Kramer's probably listening, keep arguing.

His laugh was short and humorless. "No trouble there, luv, because it's not happening."

"This is so like you to try and tell me what to do," I said while writing *Kramer doesn't want a trade, he's daring me to come out and fight him alone tonight.*

"You think I'd let you anywhere near that ghost when he'll have the flesh he needs for his stated intention of raping you, then burning you alive?" He snorted. "Even if I didn't love you, I wouldn't allow that to happen."

I didn't have more room on the grocery receipt, so I found a paperback book someone had left on the island in the kitchen and tore off a few of the emptier beginning and end pages.

With me, his flesh will be his weakness, not his strength.

"I can take care of myself," I said loudly, just like Kramer would expect me to. "And you don't get to order me around."

"Are you so foolish you'd rather die than listen to reason?"

Anger and frustration flowed around me from his aura, but though his words were cold, he read the page I handed to him. If he truly meant what he said, he wouldn't bother.

Go to Elisabeth's apartment. Tell her Sarah will meet me at the entrance of Grandview Park in Sioux City at dusk. She can follow us from there, then tell you where Kramer and I will be. I'll hold him off long enough for you to get there. Then we'll take him to the trap. Same plan as before, only I'll lead you to him instead of the women leading him to us.

Kramer thought I'd fall victim to my pride and thus agree to facing him alone, but with two other innocent lives at risk, I wanted backup. He wouldn't fight fair, and I had no intention of being the only one playing by the rules.

"There's too much risk, which you'd see if you weren't blinded by your own arrogance," Bones said harshly.

I didn't know if that was him acting or me failing to make a dent in my arguments, so I wrote my answer to the accusation.

Kramer didn't follow Elisabeth to Spade's. He followed my signal and found us. She's an expert at evading him. This will work.

Out loud I said, "Arrogant? You should talk since you seem to think you can make all my decisions for me! I'm not a child, Bones. You can't tell me what to do and just expect to be obeyed."

I had to let you go out alone when you were challenged to a duel, I wrote, staring at him once I was finished. *It was harder than hell, but I did it.*

He muttered a curse while running his hand through his hair. "That's not the same."

My pen flashed across the page. *Yes it is, and just like Gregor wouldn't have stopped if you refused his challenge, Kramer won't stop either. He never wavers once he picks a target, and no one can hide from the dead forever! What if he attacks me while I'm in a fight with another vampire? I'm in more danger if I DON'T go.*

"This isn't the first time I've faced death, and I don't intend for it to be the last," I said, repeating the same words he'd told me before fighting in that fateful duel. "I've chosen to live a dangerous life, but it's *who I am,* and that wouldn't change even if we'd never met."

The barest smile touched his mouth though his aura spiked with dangerous pulses of emotion-driven energy.

"Low blow, Kitten."

I held his gaze with a faint smile of my own. "Someone once taught me to take every cheap shot and every low blow in a fight."

His stare was so intense that I half wondered if he could somehow see into my mind. That would be helpful. Then he'd know this wasn't my pride talking. It was my experience. I wasn't like all the other women Kramer had singled out over the centuries. No archaic system of law was against me, I wasn't abandoned by friends and family, and I might be flesh and blood, but I wasn't human. Just like the Inquisitor hadn't been human for a long, long time. With me, Kramer would finally be picking on someone his own size.

Kramer had only seen me run before. He'd never seen me stand my ground and fight. Tonight, I'd show him why the undead world referred to me as the Red Reaper.

Bones suddenly grabbed me, his mouth slamming over mine in a kiss so fierce I tasted blood when he lifted his head. But that didn't bother me. I licked the blood off my lips with a hunger that matched the fire in his gaze, wanting to throw him to the floor and take him with enough roughness to leave cracks in the wood. *I love you,* I mouthed, pulling his head down for another blisteringly violent kiss.

He pushed my mouth down to his neck, almost forcing my fangs into his skin with the way he ground against me. I took him up on the silent demand and bit, drinking deeply when his blood came, not moaning out of bliss because I didn't know how closely Kramer might be listening. His hands ran over me in a forceful, possessive caress while I drank, absorbing strength as well as nourishment from that heady liquid. When the crimson flow slowed to a trickle despite my suction and Bones willing it out to me, I stopped, licking his neck free of any lingering traces. I felt heavy and full, my senses buzzing from the excess of my feast. I normally drank about half that much when I fed from him, but I knew why he wanted me to drain him. He could refill, but once he was gone, I couldn't.

He cupped my face when I drew back, staring into my eyes while he dropped his shields and let his aura flood over me, twining into my emotions until I couldn't tell where my feelings ended and his began. From the frustration, love, lust, and worry pouring off him, I guessed that he wanted to make love to me until neither of us could think . . . and then tie me up and pile heavy boulders on me until after the sun rose. The intensity in all those feelings told me that the absolute last thing he wanted to do was what he did next.

"I won't stand here and listen to any more of your ridiculous notions," he said, nothing but coldness in his tone. "You want to throw your life away? Fine, but you'll do it without me. I'm finished with you."

If I wasn't tied so deeply into his emotions, hearing it would have crushed me. But I smiled, squeezing his hands and feeling my heart overflow. He squeezed back before bringing them to his lips and brushing a soundless, fervent kiss onto them.

Then he let go, turned around, and walked out, slamming the back door behind him.

Ian came into the house right after Bones stormed out. Kramer must not have been the only one outside listening. He looked at me, raised a brow, then picked up one of the pages with my hastily scribbled words and read it.

"Since you and Crispin are now finished and I have a few hours to kill, how about that shag?" he asked with heavy irony.

"Bite me," I sighed, gathering up the pages.

He winked. "Of course. My second-favorite thing to do in bed."

I didn't reply to that because I knew Ian wasn't serious. He'd read enough to realize our breakup was staged, but trust Ian not to miss a chance to be a jackass. Spade came down the staircase next. His wary expression as he looked at me said he wasn't aware that what he'd overheard was faked. He'd witnessed a real breakup between me and Bones before and had to talk sense into both of us later, so he was probably thinking, *Bugger, not this again.*

I handed him the pages and gave him a thumbs-up

sign. After a few brief moments, his frown cleared, replaced by lethal intentness as he looked up at me. Then he took the pen and wrote three words in the space left on the page.

I'm going, too.

I didn't say anything. After what Sarah had done to Denise, not a single argument I made, verbally or otherwise, would talk him out of that.

THIRTY-FIVE

THE CAB DRIVER STOPPED ALONG THE STREET, and I glanced in the distance at the white outdoor theater shaped like a huge half shell.

"Here we are," he said cheerfully.

I checked the meter and pulled the appropriate amount of money out of my pocket. "Thanks, and keep the change."

"All right. Happy Halloween."

That was what I was hoping for, too. I got out, watching his taillights fade away as he drove off. Then I tightened my leather jacket around me and leaned against the welcome sign, waiting.

Fifteen minutes later, when the sky had changed from indigo to obsidian and stars replaced the last dying rays of the sun, a sleek Mercedes E class sedan pulled up, the make and model car Spade had left for Denise. Sure enough, the tinted window rolled down to reveal Sarah at the wheel, her black hair pulled back into the same sort of severe bun Elisabeth normally wore. On Elisabeth, that style highlighted features that were lovely without the slightest hint of makeup. On Sarah, it only served to make her look harsher, drawing attention to thick eyebrows that could really use a good tweezing and a mouth that was compressed into a thin, tight line.

"If you kill me, you will never find the other women," were her first words when I opened the passenger door.

Her thoughts were that same blend of fear and hatred against a larger white noise backdrop that I now recognized as a mark of the insane. When we met, I'd thought Kramer had been the one to drive her nuts. Now I realized it was probably Sarah's unstableness that had drawn the Inquisitor to her in the first place.

"Oh, I'm not going to kill you now," I told her, sliding into the seat. "You'll die tonight, make no mistake, but you'd better hope it's by someone else's hand rather than from Kramer's."

Her topaz gaze flitted to mine before she quickly glanced away. "He told me you would lie to me, but I already knew that witches were incapable of telling the truth."

My snort was grim. "I don't know what warped you, Sarah. Maybe it was a shitty upbringing, maybe it was a guy you loved ditching you for another woman, but remember, 'For with the measure you use, it will be measured to you'? You're going to find out what that means, and wow, will you wish you hadn't."

"I won't listen to any more of your lies, unclean

thing," she hissed. Then she drove about a hundred yards before pulling off and parking in a darker section off the shoulder. My brows lifted. Kramer couldn't be so dumb as to meet us here, could he?

"Is this the place, or did you forget where we're supposed to go?"

Sarah took the keys and got out, tapping them on the roof of the car in a nervous staccato rhythm. "Kramer says you will fly me to where he is."

Uh-oh. I didn't look around for the ghost I knew Bones had sent here, but that was my first instinct. If I flew, Elisabeth wouldn't be able to follow me, and that would mess up the rest of our plans.

Had Sarah seen me fly? No, Bones had snatched me off that street and flown both of us to War Eagle Park. Kramer shouldn't have seen me fly, either, because Bones had flown me when we picked up Francine, too. Maybe he was just sending Sarah on a fishing expedition.

"Not all vampires can fly. I'm too new to have that power yet," I told her, not moving from my seat.

Those keys banged harder on the roof. "You're lying again. Kramer told me he saw you fly near a cave in Ohio. You will fly me to him, witch, or he will know you betrayed him, and those other witches will pay your penalty."

My teeth ground together. That was right; I'd flown with Bones when we evacuated my mother, Tyler, and our pets from the cave in Ohio. We'd thought Kramer had left because the slaughter of Madigan's soldiers had stopped, but the sneaky little shit must've been hanging around watching us. And he obviously suspected me of having ghost allies tailing me tonight to insist that I fly to him instead of letting Sarah drive me. Maybe I was wrong, and he didn't think I was blinded by a vain desire to defeat him all by myself. That, or he was too careful to risk it.

Once I arrived, it would take several hours for Elisabeth and Fabian to locate me by concentrating on my fading power. Kramer had to know how long it took him to reach me that way, so he'd know he had a good chunk of time to work within. Goddamn ghost was covering all his bases.

I thought about how much my borrowed abilities had faded. Then I thought about all the valid dangers I'd listed if we didn't manage to defeat Kramer sooner rather than later. There had to be a way to take Kramer on without turning my back on Bones and the others.

Sarah banged again on the roof. "I'm not waiting any longer. If you don't do as he says, I'm leaving."

Oh, I wanted to take her high in the sky, all right. And then drop her so I could enjoy listening to her screams before she splatted on the ground. But if I kept Kramer waiting much longer, I was sure he'd put his new flesh to repulsive use. Frustration made me clench my fists. If only I had more of that borrowed power left in me, but no, I was stuck at the final "sparks but no fire" stage of my abilities.

Although . . . maybe my faded powers from Marie would still work if I gave them the proper accelerant.

"You're out of time," Sarah said coldly, leaning down to stare at me through the driver's side window.

I got out of the car and shrugged. "All right, I can fly." Then I flashed a toothy grin at her. "But I can't land that well, and that's the God's honest truth. So you'd better brace yourself on the way down, because it'll probably hurt."

I flew over the vast fields interspersed with houses and mostly empty roads, looking for the PumpkinTown farm Sarah told me about. Of course, I might have passed it several times already. The whole area was an agricultural mecca, with soybean, hay, and cornfields surrounding farmhouses, barns, and various storage facilities. At this height, the swaying golden cornfields reminded me of the night Bones took me flying, and regret squeezed a lump into my throat. Bones would be so worried when Elisabeth gave him the news that I'd flown to my meeting with Kramer, but if he used that infallible logic of his, he'd realize I still had the ability to cast a trail of bread crumbs leading to me. While this wasn't the plan he and I had discussed earlier, it should still turn out the same. It would just be cutting it closer than either of us preferred.

I pushed my guilt and all the softer emotions aside. I didn't need them now. I'd need them later when I was with Kramer.

More lights than normal clustered about a mile ahead. I flew toward them, noting derisively that Sarah had her eyes squeezed shut. No help there. Then I dropped lower to better see if one of those cornfields had a large maze carved into it. That would be easier to spot than looking for a sign that would be facing the street, not the sky. Sure enough, outside of the circle of trees that surrounded a picturesque house, barn, pumpkin patch, and stable was a cornfield with a distinct abstract pattern carved into the stalks. Unlike most of the other houses I'd flown over, this place was jumping with activity, too. Dozens of cars were parked along a cleared edge of the field. Music, spooky sound effects, and voices floated up to me. A closer look revealed that the maze had costumed people threading through it.

It was a Halloween celebration with families and children, for crying out loud. This better not be the place Kramer had picked out for his gruesome little event.

"Open your eyes," I said, giving Sarah a rough shake. "Is this it?"

She only needed to slit her eyes before she nodded. "Yes. Take us to the second field west of the maze."

"West? Tell me right, left, top, or bottom," I snapped. It had been hard enough finding the place considering I was too high up to see street signs. What was probably only a forty-minute car ride from Grandview Park had taken me over an hour because I wasn't used to navigating by the equivalent of satellite imagery. I'd looked at enough maps of the areas surrounding Sioux City to know that Orange City was up and to the right of it, but all my repeated flyovers hadn't been stalling. It had been me being lost.

"You don't know where west is?" Sarah asked with disbelief.

I wasn't going to drop her to the ground. I was going to *throw* her. "Do I look like I have a compass on me?"

Sarah waved a hand at the sky. "Can't you use the stars to navigate?"

"I'm twenty-nine years old, not two hundred and twenty-nine. I navigate by GPS, MapQuest, or TomTom. Not the fucking stars, 'k?"

She sighed in exasperation. "Try the second field on the right of the maze. If that's not it, we'll walk until he finds us."

Her thoughts were still too scattered for me to detect whether or not she was lying. If Kramer really was here, I didn't need her anymore; but in case this was some sort of test, I'd keep her alive. Stupid woman didn't realize that my killing her would be doing her a favor.

I aimed for the second unmarred cornfield to the right of the maze and descended. Even with the people less than half a mile away, the lack of lights over this section combined with our dark clothes against the night sky should make us invisible. I slowed as best I could and rolled as soon as I hit the ground, letting go of Sarah. That rolling meant I took out ten yards of dry vegetation in my landing, but it also meant I lessened the impact. Sarah didn't roll, and a sharp cry of pain escaped her when she thudded down amidst the cornstalks.

"Baby get a boo-boo?" I asked, fighting the urge to kick her while she was writhing on the ground clutching her ankle.

"You bitch, you broke my ankle!" she thundered at me.

With the nearby music, sound effects, laughter, and screams of delight from the good-natured scares set up around that section of the farm, none of the Halloween revelers would hear her. So I had no hesitation about walking over, calmly taking her injured foot in my hand, and then snapping it to the side hard enough for me to feel the bone crack.

"*Now* I broke your ankle," I told her.

Sarah wailed in earnest, but though I wasn't worried about us being discovered, it was hurting my ears. I slapped a hand over her mouth.

"Quit crying before I really give you something to cry about."

That old parental threat worked. She stuffed back her loud sobs and tried to claw her way up my arm to stand. I debated shoving her away but decided that it would take longer to get to Kramer if she was hopping and stumbling on one foot, so I let her brace herself against me. She didn't speak, but her thoughts were a hateful mix of crazy static and delight when contemplating how I was going to burn, first on earth, then in hell.

Charming.

"Either you keep up or I leave you behind, I don't care which," I said, and started to walk. I wasn't sure if I was going in the right direction, but if Kramer was out here, he might have seen our crash landing. The ghost would know to be studying the sky, unlike the families in the maze and the surrounding farmhouse area. I hadn't seen any other lights in the field outside of where the revelries were being held, so if he was here, he was keeping a low profile.

Sarah limped beside me, her fingers digging into my arm and little yelps escaping her with every hobbled step. Between that, the crackling paper noise that the thousands of drying cornstalks made as they swayed against each other, and the merrymaking from the other section of the farm, I couldn't hear whether anyone else was out here with us.

Goddamn Kramer. I'd wondered why he would choose a place like this for his meet up. Now I knew. I couldn't focus on any telltale movements to spot him because everything around me moved. The corn was taller than I was, and it all looked the same, making me unable to tell if I even walked in circles or not. Noises were swallowed up by natural and artificial sounds, and all the people across the fields kept me from flying in low swoops above the area to see if I could locate him, Francine, or Lisa that way. My landing might not have been spotted, but a woman winging her way like a bat slow and low enough to detect anything in this huge moveable canvas eventually would be.

That was why I had no warning before white-hot pain blasted through my back. Once, twice, three times in rapid succession, turning my chest into what felt like a molten lake of agony. I staggered, knocking Sarah over, who screamed as I stepped on her ankle trying to keep myself upright. Her thrashing made me lose my balance, even my innate vampire reflexes unable to keep me from falling. I flipped over at the last moment, still hitting the ground but doing it without being facedown.

I wanted to spring to my feet but I couldn't. The unusual slowness to my limbs and the continuing burn in my chest told me I hadn't been shot with normal bullets. They were silver.

I had a split second to see a white-haired man loom over me, black monkish robes fluttering in the breeze and very corporeal hand pointing a gun at me. Then I heard another blast, felt my mind explode with pain, but couldn't see anything else.

Thirty-six

MY HEAD THROBBED LIKE SOMEONE HAD shoved firecrackers into my brain and set them off. That was the first thing I became aware of. The second was the burning in my chest, so intense it sent throbs of pain throughout the rest of my body. The third was that my hands and feet were bound to something tall and hard behind me. The fourth was the most disquieting realization of all: I was wet, and it wasn't from water. The harsh scent of gasoline filled my nostrils without my needing to take in a breath.

"Burn her. Burn her now, before she wakes up!" a familiar voice urged.

Sarah. I should've killed her when I had the chance. Hindsight always was twenty-twenty.

I opened my eyes. Kramer stood a few feet away in the middle of a triangular clearing amidst the tall cornstalks. Sarah was off to the side, but Lisa and Francine made up the other two corners of the triangle. They were chained like I was to tall metal poles dug into the ground, gags in their mouths, eyes wide with horror as they looked at me. Unlike me, though, neither of them had a large silver knife stuck into her chest. The blade seemed to emit a steady stream of acid, scalding my nerve endings and sapping my strength. But though it was close to the center of my chest, it wasn't in my heart. Either Kramer had deliberately missed because he didn't want to risk giving me an easy death, or his aim wasn't as good as he'd intended.

Kramer pulled out a large, leather-bound book from the folds of his new hooded black robe. Guess he'd gotten sick of that old muddy tunic he was stuck with when he was in vaporous form. His gaze seemed to gleam with malicious triumph as he opened the book and began to read aloud.

"I, Henricus Kramer Institoris, Judge named on behalf of the faith, declare and pronounce sentence that you standing here are impenitent heretics, and as such are to be delivered to justice," he intoned, and though the original version of the *Hammer of Witches* had been in Latin, he made sure to speak English so we would understand it.

I didn't have a gag, probably because Kramer knew I wouldn't bother screaming for help, but that didn't mean I was going to stay silent.

"I read that, you know. Your prose was boring and repetitive, and your overuse of capitalization for dramatic emphasis was juvenile at best. Oh hell, I'll just say it—it sucked out loud. No wonder you had to forge your endorsements."

Now his gaze gleamed with outrage. He shut the

book with a bang, stalking over to me. Writers were so sensitive when it came to criticism.

"Do you wish to die now, *Hexe*?" he hissed at me. Then he bent over, picking something up out of my line of sight. When he straightened, he had a hurricane lantern in his hand, the golden orange flame caressing the glass surrounding it as if begging to be freed.

I looked over his shoulder at Sarah, who was practically vibrating with excitement at the prospect of his setting me on fire.

"She might not know what your routine is, but I do," I said softly. "So put the lantern down. You're not burning me yet, and we both know it."

"What's she saying?" Sarah demanded, hobbling over.

His white brows drew together, and I allowed a little smile to play on my lips. "Awfully bossy with you, isn't she? Then again, it makes sense. She's got the pants on, and you're the one in the dress."

His fist flashed out, but the blow didn't land on me. It struck Sarah right as she leaned on Kramer to steady herself. She fell back, crimson spurting from her nose. Now that she'd fulfilled her usefulness, he wasn't hiding his intentions toward her anymore.

"Why?" she gasped.

Her hurt and confusion were clear on her face, but it belatedly occurred to me that I couldn't hear it in her thoughts. Same with Lisa and Francine. They had to be screaming with panic in their minds, but all I heard from them was their pounding heartbeats and short, quick gasps through their gags.

The silver bullet Kramer fired into my head hadn't

only knocked me out long enough for him to truss me up and wet me down with gasoline. It had also short-circuited my mind-reading abilities. Another round or two, and I'd be all the way dead, but of course, Kramer didn't want me dead yet. To look at the bright side, I could concentrate better without hearing everyone's frantic thoughts.

"Do not speak another word, *hure*," Kramer snarled at Sarah.

"That means whore," I supplied. "It's how he sees all women. Get used to hearing it for the rest of your short life."

That earned me a backhanded crack across the jaw, but compared to being stabbed and shot, it was a love tap. "Easy on the jostling, you don't want that silver shredding my heart and ending your fun too soon," I taunted him.

He looked at the knife in my chest and lowered his clenched fist. I didn't move a muscle, but inwardly my brows rose. My bluff had worked. *So you* don't *know it's right outside my heart instead of pierced through it. Good.*

Tears rolled down Sarah's cheeks, either from the pain in her broken nose or the realization that Kramer was everything I'd cautioned her about. I couldn't bring myself to feel sorry for her. She'd shot my best friend so many times she'd had to believe Denise was dead. Except for Denise's one-in-a-billion supernatural status, she *would* have been dead. Then Sarah had kidnapped Francine and Lisa and brought them as a present to this monster, fully expecting to watch them burn to death.

No, I didn't feel sorry that she was all teary-eyed to discover that she would also be on the receiving end of Kramer's brutality. When he landed a kick into Sarah's midsection next, doubling her over and causing her to let out an anguished cry, I still didn't pity her. That hurt a thousand times less than being burned, I knew from experience, and, considering her crimes, she had it coming.

He ground his booted foot into her broken ankle next. With her new, gasping scream and the constant crackling from the cornstalks around us, I didn't hear the bones shatter, but they probably did. She curled into the fetal position, sobbing and pleading for mercy that she'd never find from the Inquisitor. After a final kick to her rib cage, Kramer turned his attention back to me, leaving her writhing in pain on the ground.

I didn't say anything as he approached. In addition to the book, he had a satchel near the middle of the clearing, and I could imagine the various torture implements it must contain. Since Kramer left it there, he had other plans for me right now, and it didn't take mind reading to guess what those were.

"Do you confess your pact with the Devil, *Hexe*?" The words were softly spoken, almost wheedling in tone. "If you do, I may yet spare your life."

That made me snort. "Even if I didn't know better from Elisabeth, did you miss the part where I *read your book*? That includes the section where you rationalize lying to prisoners about letting them live as part of being a good Inquisitor."

His fist smashed across my jaw, making my lip

bleed before it healed. "Confess and renounce your allegiance to the Great Deceiver!"

"Judging from how surprised Sarah was when you turned on her, I'd say that label fits you to a tee, also," I noted.

His brows drew together, and he advanced until that reeking breath made me thrilled that I didn't need to breathe anymore. "You incite me as if you wish me to continue."

I shrugged as much as my bound hands would allow. I had a plan, but I wasn't about to let him in on it. Besides, as long as his attention was on me instead of Francine and Lisa, I'd take all the abuse he could dish out.

Well, within limits, I amended to myself as he grasped the center of my shirt and carefully pulled the material away from the hilt of the knife. He'd already taken my jacket off and done something with it, leaving me in my simple black button-down blouse and jeans. Once my blouse was free of the blade, he pulled it open in opposite directions with his unnaturally strong grip. The lantern cast flickering light over his face as he stared at my breasts. Impatiently, he tugged at the front of my bra where the clasp was.

I'd bet my red diamond wedding ring that a pig like him had only been able to get it up when he was human if the women had been helpless and terrified. Now that he was a ghost clad in flesh, he probably didn't have that issue; but with the look he gave me when he opened my bra, he wanted me to cringe away in shame. I didn't; only my skin was bare, but it was his soul that was exposed with these actions. I wasn't ashamed when Kramer roughly handled my breasts, avoiding the knife jutting between them. I was furious. I wanted to rip him to pieces, then burn each of them into ashes, but rage wasn't what I needed right now. In order to send out my supernatural LoJack signal, I needed something else.

It wasn't hard to tap into enough guilt and regret to make my throat tighten and moisture leap to my eyes. All I needed to do was remember a day several years ago when I'd kissed Bones, told him I loved him . . . and then betrayed him by leaving without a trace. At the time, I thought leaving him was the only way to protect him, and Don did a good job by keeping me hidden for over four long years. But all it did was make both of us miserable until Bones finally found me.

Four years. We'd been apart longer than we'd been together, and that was because I turned my back when I should have stood my ground. Bones might have forgiven me for that, but I'd never forgive myself. The memory of the one mistake I wished I could undo more than any other made that moisture leave my eyes and spill down my cheeks. The tears flowed faster, dripping down to land on his hands. Kramer stopped squeezing my flesh to look at the pink wetness with cruel satisfaction.

"Cry more of your bloody tears, *Hexe.* They only prove your tie to Satan."

"What they prove is that vampires don't have as

much water in their bodies as humans, idiot," I said, relishing the ringing slap he gave me because it drew more of that needed moisture from my gaze.

Then he ran his rancid mouth over my skin, careful of the knife, his few brownish teeth leaving grooves in my flesh. Disgust rippled over me, but I fought to ignore him, turning my thoughts from revulsion and regret to the quiet, white nothingness I'd felt the last time I tapped into the power of the grave. It wasn't right beneath surface like it had been before. I had to search. Pain from the blade and Kramer's groping lower down my body took away from my concentration, but I strained to push those things aside. I needed to find that faint spark inside. Most of my power was gone, but not all of it. It had to be within me somewhere . . .

Cool, soothing stillness seemed to brush over the throbbing from the silver and the anguish of my regrets, lessening both of them with that single caress. Despite the tears still leaking from my eyes, I smiled. *That's right.* Accessing this power meant letting go, not hanging on to emotional or physical anguish. I concentrated on the blissful emptiness that fleeting caress hinted at, and finally found the remaining ember I'd been looking for. It was only a tiny speck compared to what it had been months ago, but even still, it resonated. God, I'd forgotten how wonderful that quiet abyss was! It felt like coming home. Now the tears that fell from my cheeks were full of the most indescribable peace. If the power stemmed from brushing the edges of eternity, death truly was nothing to be afraid of.

Kramer drew back, looking at me with a mixture of degeneracy and confusion.

"Why don't you beg me to stop? Why are you so silent?"

I pulled myself away from the alluring embrace of the grave enough to hold on to the power, but still focus on him.

"You'd only like it if I begged you, and you've pegged me all wrong if you think I'd do anything you like. Know what else you're wrong about? The reason behind these tears."

That inner speck felt like it was humming now, the whiteness eating away at the pain from the knife in my chest.

"You think they're a sign of weakness. That I've given up, just like you think your flesh makes you stronger. *Wrong.* Your flesh makes you weak, and these tears are stronger than any weapon you can imagine."

He leaned closer, the stinking breath from his words falling against my face. "You enjoy crying? I will see to it that you don't stop."

Then Kramer frowned, cocking his head to the side. He ran his hand over me again, but in wariness this time.

"You feel . . . strange," he muttered.

"Do I vibrate?" I asked, my voice coming out as a throaty whisper. "Do you feel drawn like you did when you followed the line of energy that led you to me in Ohio, in St. Louis, in Sioux City, and the farmhouse? Do you know *why* you're feeling it so strongly again now?"

He reached out to swipe his hand across my face, staring at the pink wetness clinging to it with growing concern instead of triumph.

"There's something in these," he drew out.

"That's right," I said, caressing each word. "Power."

†hirty-seven

Back when I had the full force of Marie's borrowed abilities in me, I could shed my blood and call forth Remnants. But if I wanted to summon *ghosts,* I had to shed tears with my inner rallying cry. I didn't have enough of the voodoo queen's power left in me for my tears to compel ghosts near and far to rush to my side. But ghosts who were concentrating on me with all their strength to try to find me, like Elisabeth and Fabian would be doing?

Yeah, I still had enough juice in me for that. The lantern Kramer had on the ground, the one he sought to terrify us with because of that flickering flame and its ominous portent, would only make it easier for us to be found by anyone flying overhead.

Kramer recoiled, wiping his hand on his tunic as though my tears were poisonous. "I will burn them from you, *Hexe!*"

I trusted that my message had been sent, and now,

it was time to quit playing possum and kick some evil ass.

"I'd like to see you try that."

He grabbed the lantern, the look in his eyes telling me he wasn't bluffing this time. What he felt in my tears must have warned him that it wasn't worth the risk to rape and torture me first. But because he'd been off by a centimeter or so when he stabbed the silver knife into my chest, I didn't hesitate to wrench my arms down, breaking the metal cuffs restraining me. It jostled the knife, but not enough to shred my heart, and before Kramer could correct that error, I yanked the blade out. Two hard jerks were my feet ripping free of the restraints, leaving nothing but the dried cornhusks at the bottom of the empty pole to catch fire when Kramer threw the lantern at me.

They went up with a whoosh, the gasoline Kramer doused me with having soaked them, too. I'd leapt back far enough to avoid any fumes on me igniting, but he'd spilled gasoline on Lisa and Francine, too. And the cornstalks around us, dried and crackling from the lateness of the season, were like tall, skinny matchsticks.

Kramer howled in frustration at missing me with the lantern. Sarah took one look at the flames and started to crawl away from the clearing as fast as she could. I ran to Francine, knocking her pole over with a linebacker tackle and ripping the metal off her wrists and ankles. She gasped in pain behind her gag, but Kramer hadn't given up on his grisly intentions so easily. He snatched at the burning husks on the ground and threw one at us.

The spot where her pole had been flared with the contact from those greedy orange and yellow tongues, but I yanked her away in time.

"Run!" I yelled, giving her a shove for emphasis. Lisa's muffled screams told me what I already knew—that Kramer was now focused on her. He grinned as he threw a burning husk at her, not even seeming to notice that the bottom of his robe dragged in the flames.

I didn't have time to knock her out of the way. It had taken precious seconds to free Francine and get her safely out of the sodden, flammable circle at her feet. That glowing bundle arced toward Lisa and I knew, with crystal clarity, the only thing I could do to save her. Instead of aiming for the screaming woman helplessly chained to the pole, I threw myself at the burning missile, snatching it and taking it with me as I landed outside the triangular clearing.

Flames raced up my arms, blazing into an avalanche of fire once they reached my gasoline-soaked clothes. Pain so intense it robbed me of thought scalded over me, spreading to cover my body in an instant. In the brief moments it took them to reach my face, I realized I'd vaulted myself straight up into the sky, doing the worst thing possible by flying and fanning the flames. It hadn't even been a conscious decision—all my primal mind knew was that it wanted *away* from this torture. With the willpower I had left in me, screaming as pain exploded in every nerve ending, I forced myself down into the fields and began to roll as fast as I could away from Kramer and the others.

You'll heal, you'll heal, you'll heal. I clung to that litany while my mind exploded with the agony of my flesh being eaten away by those merciless flames. I couldn't see, couldn't hear, but I could feel everything, including the excruciating inner searing when I screamed again, and it drew flames into my mouth. Every instinct urged me stop rolling over what felt like razors ripping away at what was left of my flesh. To run from the overwhelming suffering that spared no inch of me, but with the last vestiges of my sanity, I ignored those urges and kept rolling.

After what felt like a thousand years, I realized I could see again. I was tucked into the fetal position, still rolling blindly across the fields. I used my blurry vision to spot the few remaining patches of fire on my feet where my boots had melted around them, then slapped at them. The movement sent riptides of anguish on top of what was already more pain than I could ever remember feeling, but I kept swatting at the flames until they were out and all the shoe remains were off my feet.

For a dazed moment as I looked down at myself, I thought I was somehow still wearing my black jeans and blouse. But then I realized the dark tatters hanging over me weren't clothes—it was my own charred skin. In the midst of the searing pain, I wanted to vomit and scream out of sheer horror, but Francine and Lisa were still fighting for their lives against a maniac determined to murder them. No matter what I looked like or how much it hurt, I didn't have the option of panicking over the fire's ravages or waiting until I finished healing to move. I had to act now, or burning myself to crisp by running into that fiery projectile had been for nothing.

I got up, unable to stuff back my gasp at what moving did to my blackened and cracking skin. *You'll heal,* I repeated ruthlessly, then tried to force myself into the air. At the first attempt, I flopped back down immediately, cornhusks tearing into my still-partially-charred skin when I crashed. With another pained gasp, I got back up and tried again, flinging myself forward.

This time, I made it about thirty yards before I crashed, but it was enough for me to pinpoint where the deadly amber glow was. I ran in that direction, giving up on flying, the pain slowly starting to ease. Normally vampire injuries healed almost instantly, but with the extent of the damage the flames had caused both to skin and muscle, the healing was taking several minutes. Or it hurt so badly that it felt that way.

I burst into the triangular clearing right as flames licked the dry vegetation at the base of Lisa's pole. Without slowing down, I barreled into her and lifted upward at the same time. The pole stayed in the ground, but the impact ripped Lisa free of the metal bindings. When the gasoline ignited and shot up the pole, she was already several feet above it, safely free of the flames.

That didn't make her muffled screams decrease. Right before we crashed down, I saw that she stared at me with abject terror. Then I flipped so I'd take the bulk of the landing, stuffing back a shout as the impact reverberated through me, and the husks felt like they ripped all the new skin off my back.

Lisa expressed her gratitude for me sheltering her against the worst of the crash by punching and kicking me as soon as we skidded to a halt. The rough fall had knocked her gag loose, so she screamed between huge gasps of breath. Normally a human smacking and kicking me would have laughably little effect, but I fought the urge to crawl back into the fetal position and concentrated on catching her hands instead.

"Don't hit me, that really hurts right now!"

My voice was hoarse to the point of being unrecognizable. Breathing in a lungful of fire will do that to a person, even if that person is a vampire. Lisa stopped fighting me, but she still had fear reeking from her pores even over the stench of gasoline.

"Cat?" she managed, sounding like she didn't believe it.

"Who the hell else would it be?"

To make up for my sharp words, I tried to smile, but then stopped when that made her recoil. A glance at my arm showed I had a layer of soot over mostly healed skin, but there were still some grisly patches of charred flesh. Okay, so I looked like a crispy demon fresh from the pit, but it *was* still me.

A fresh river of tears spilled onto her cheeks. "B-but I saw you burn."

"As Bones would say, *right you are,*" I told her with a shudder of remembrance. "I healed. Mostly."

She still looked too shocked to believe me. "But . . . but . . ."

"No time for chatting, we need to get you out of here, and I have to find Francine," I muttered, grasping her again. This time, she didn't try to fight me off, but she did yelp when I lifted her and ran toward where my last aerial glimpse showed me the nearest stretch of road was. She'd be safer in the street, away from the fire that might start to spread even more if it wasn't put out soon.

As soon as I saw pavement, I let her go, dashing back into the cornfield. The pain was almost gone now, to my vast relief. That allowed me to run faster, trying to listen for any sounds that would lead me to Francine. But just like when I walked in here with Sarah, the natural sounds of the drying husks rubbing together combined with the crackles from the nearby fire and the confusion in the other section of the fields as people started to notice the orange lights, my senses were effectively blanketed.

I was about to propel myself over the field and try flying again when a sharp crack rang out, and the stalk next to me exploded. I whirled in time to avoid the next bullet aimed at me, charging toward Kramer with vicious intentness. He'd landed those shots before because I was walking very slowly with Sarah bracing herself on my shoulder, but he wouldn't get that lucky again.

I wrenched the gun away from him, taking ruthless pleasure in sending it sailing off as far as I could throw it. Silver bullets wouldn't hurt him, so the gun was useless to me. He snarled as he tried to force me to the ground, but I used his wide stance against him by ramming my knee into his groin with enough force to pulverize his parts.

"Who's crying *now*, motherfucker?" I spat, using that same knee to blast into his face when he doubled over. Those impacts hurt me, but not as much as they did him, and knowing that made my pain sweet. I sent another brutal hammer into his side, then another one, and another one.

Kramer fell back, unable to protect himself against the blows that came faster than he could react. The ghost had spent centuries dishing out punishment, but from his ineffective counterattacks, he hadn't spent enough time learning how to defend against it. Battle lust surged through my veins, fueled by the rage I'd held back while Kramer was pawing at me and the knowledge of all the people who'd been unable to fight back due to the superstition and unfairness of the age they lived in. My blows rained down harder and quicker, every nasty, effective trick Bones taught me bearing glorious fruit in the hoarse grunts of pain coming from Kramer as he tried to shield himself.

No, you don't get away! I thought, increasing my attack when he attempted to crawl out of range of my fists and feet. *Especially not tonight.*

Just when I was at the height of the euphoric high from delivering a well-deserved beat down, calamity struck.

. . . light over there . . . that's fire! . . . got to get out of here . . . where are the kids? . . . oh my God, the crops! . . . help, someone help me!

A hundred different voices assailed my mind at the same instant, as debilitating as a karate kick to the face. I clutched my head before I could stop myself, backing away from Kramer in a blind attempt to run before he noticed that I'd stopped beating the shit out of him. But that merciless cascade of voices chased me as I went, growing in volume as if fueled by my agitation.

Kramer launched himself at me with the same single-minded determination I'd showed with him. This time, it was me who couldn't field the blows fast enough as those voices hammered away in my mind, taking my focus away during the critical split seconds between ducking a kick or punch and having one land with devastating effect. His tackle brought me to my knees, and then a sharp crack to my back had me bent over with pain shooting up my spine. Kramer drew back his foot to kick me again—and his leg was yanked upward. He fell back and was pounced upon by a beautiful brunette who, at the moment, was as solid as he was.

"Run, Cat!" Elisabeth urged me, pounding away at her murderer.

I didn't run. I waited with overflowing gratitude while Elisabeth gave me the precious moments needed to force the voices down to levels where they didn't cripple me with distraction. By the time Kramer had regained the upper hand, throwing her to the ground and landing punishing blows to her midsection, I was on my feet, a fresh surge of determination cascading through me. If Elisabeth was here, then Bones couldn't be far behind.

I launched myself onto the Inquisitor, ripping my fangs through the back of his neck hard enough to sever every tendon. The foulest taste filled my mouth—not blood, but something damp and moldy like it had come from the ground. I spat it out but kept ripping at his neck because it made him scream with pain and stop punching Elisabeth. She vanished underneath in the next moment, appearing beside me in her usual vaporous, hazy state.

"I can't help you any more!" she said in anguish. "I don't have the strength to remain solid."

Kramer tried to get up, but I rammed my knee into his back hard enough to cripple a normal person and tore a larger hunk out of his neck, spitting it out before answering her.

"You already gave me the help I needed."

Kramer said something to her in German, unbelievably able to talk despite what I'd done to his neck. I caught the word "*hure*" amidst the others and snaked an elbow around his throat, pulling up with all my might.

I felt an abrupt lessening of tension, fell backward from my momentum and not having anything to grasp anymore, but when I sprang to my feet, Kramer was also on his. Not only did he still have a head, but the damage I'd done to his neck looked completely healed.

"You can't kill me, *Hexe,*" Kramer said, poison dripping off each word. "I am beyond your powers."

"I'm going to show you that you're not," I snarled.

"Why do you fight?" he demanded. "Though you and the others live now, you cannot run from me forever, and you will never trick me into one of your cunning traps."

I looked up at the sky behind him and smiled, feeling a familiar swell of unadulterated power wash over me.

"You're right. I'm in *no* shape to fly you 250 miles to where our new trap is." Kramer's victorious smile ebbed when I added, "But I bet my husband's up for the job."

Kramer turned around just in time to have a dark form blast into him with enough force to dig a deep furrow into the ground.

"And they say I can't land without making a mess," I commented to no one in particular.

Thirty-Eight

BONES TOOK ONE LOOK AT MY CONDITION and began beating the dark, foul-tasting substance out of Kramer. I'd done a fair job against him myself, but Bones was a lot stronger and hadn't used up most of his energy healing himself from being burned to kingdom come, let alone been overwhelmed by unexpected voices. I would have loved to keep watching, but I still had things to take care of.

"I need to make sure Francine's out of the fields," I said, speaking up to be heard over Kramer's groans of pain. "She's covered in gasoline; if she runs into the wrong section of field, it could kill her."

That wasn't a concern for me anymore. I was pretty sure any part of my skin that formerly had gasoline on it had been burned off.

"Go," Bones said, his arm so tight around the Inquisitor's throat that it would kill him if he weren't already dead. "I've got him."

I didn't waste my time running through the fields

but mustered up my sagging energy and flew, making sure to keep low enough to see. With the glow from the fire and some of my skin peeking out from under the soot, it was possible anyone looking in my direction might spot me, but hopefully they would think it was a trick of the flames.

With my new vantage point, it didn't take long at all to spot the trench carving itself into the cornfield that was caused by someone running. I swooped over, not aiming for Francine when I descended because I knew better. Sure enough, I bounced around in a landing that made her scream from fear and run in the other direction, but I got up and grabbed her before she went out of sight again.

"Francine, it's Cat!" I said, hearing from her thoughts that she didn't recognize me. After a few good shakes of her shoulders, she lost that terrified blankness in her gaze.

"Cat?" Her face crumpled, and I picked up words like "hideous" and "zombie" as she tried to absorb my appearance now with what I looked like before. "What did he do to you?"

"Burned me like a hamburger on the Fourth of July," I supplied, glad there weren't any full-length mirrors nearby. "It looks worse than it is, but we need to get you out of here."

I propelled myself into the air high enough to see which direction the road was, then dropped back down, wincing because I hadn't slowed my descent enough to make that painless.

"All right," I gritted out, cursing whatever I'd done to my ankles. "Let's go."

I carried her as I ran through the field toward the road. She could walk, but this was much faster. Once she was safely on the road, crying with relief when she saw Lisa a ways up, I headed back to Bones. This time, I didn't need to hover above the fields to pinpoint where I wanted to go. I could feel his power reaching out to me, drawing me nearer like a beacon.

When I reached him, I saw with relief that he still had Kramer in a viselike grip. While I didn't think the ghost was strong enough to wrestle himself away, I was worried about his poofing away, if he could transform himself back to vapor at will. But then I saw what was in Bones's hand and I laughed out loud at the stunned look on the Inquisitor's face.

"How do you like the Taser? That was Tyler's idea after seeing you zapped into flesh when you were fucking with our electricity."

"I don't think he fancies it much at all, do you?" Bones asked, pressing its prongs into Kramer's side. The ghost jerked, eyes bugging in a way that confirmed it hurt.

Well, then it was an effective and *fun* tool.

Bones tore the Inquisitor's black robes from him, revealing wrinkled, pasty flesh that I wished was covered back up. Kramer unleashed a torrent of curses at this, but both of us ignored him.

"Do you want to put this on?" he asked, holding the robe out to me.

I looked at it with loathing. "I'd rather stay naked."

The barest smile touched Bones's mouth. "Of course. Hold him for a moment."

I kept a solid grip on the ghost while Bones took

off his shirt. Kramer kept up with his threats against me, my family, my friends, my ancestors, and anyone else the Inquisitor could think up. With his shirt off, I saw that Bones had more Tasers strapped to his upper arms. We should have enough voltage to keep Kramer from attempting to dematerialize, if he even had that ability before the sun rose.

I'd passed Kramer off to Bones and slipped his shirt over my head when two other large objects came beaming toward us from the sky. Ian and Spade, I noted, the latter carrying Tyler. No wonder the medium looked even less pleased about flying than usual.

They landed with a smooth grace that made me jealous. Unlike Bones, who now only had on a pair of pants and boots, all three men wore long trench coats. Spade took one look at me, and his was off before he'd gone another step.

"Thanks," I said, putting it on more because I was cold than any concerns about flashing my butt if Bones's shirt rode up.

Ian, ever tactful, had another form of hello.

"Christ, Reaper, with your bald head and all that soot, you look like a mannequin someone attacked with a blowtorch."

"Ian, if I weren't holding this sod, you'd be on the ground right now," Bones gritted out.

"I'm not holding anyone," Spade said, and whacked Ian hard enough to make him stagger.

I ran my hand over my head and winced when all I felt was smooth skin. Well, what did I expect? That my hair had been fireproof?

"Please tell me there's a neat vampire trick that can help me grow this back quicker?"

"There is, and you're lovely with or without hair," Bones said, actually making it sound sincere.

Tyler held open his coat in flasher style, grinning when Kramer let out a fresh spurt of curses at him. "Look what I brought for you, ghostfriend!"

I no longer had any worries about our having enough Tasers for the long trip. Tyler's coat was stuffed with them, as were his pants pockets and the holster straps around his shirt. "That's why they brought me," he went on. "Didn't want to be packing as many themselves in case they had to fight, but I'm weighted down with them. Now that it looks like you've got things under control, let's pass these puppies out."

I took a few Tasers, filling up the folds and pockets of Spade's coat. Ian and Spade divvied up the rest, testing a few out on Kramer just for kicks, it looked like.

"We need to check on Lisa and Francine," I said.

We found them right where I had left them, far enough up the street to be away from the mass of activity that was now taking place at the entrance to PumpkinTown. I was just telling them to head over there so they could get treated by the ambulances that were arriving when I heard something crash through the fields about a hundred yards away. I caught brief snatches of yelps over the approaching sirens, crackling flames, chaos from the Halloween guests, and constant rustling noises from the cornstalks. But it was the mental screams and distinct patterns of white noise that identified who was out there.

I didn't need to see her to know that Sarah was going deeper into the fields, not toward the safety of the roads. The fire department might get here in time to save her, but then again, they might not. With Sarah's broken ankle and internal injuries from Kramer's kicks, there was a good chance she wouldn't outrun the flames or would be overcome with smoke. Sarah had looked forward to watching me, Lisa, and Francine burn, but despite its being poetic justice, I couldn't sentence her to the same fate.

"It's Sarah," I said, squaring my shoulders. "I'll go get her."

Spade was off like a shot before the last word left my mouth. A few moments later, I heard a scream. Saw a streak of movement going straight up until that scream faded away, and I couldn't follow them with my gaze anymore. And then, about a minute later, I heard a rush of panicked thoughts right before something fell from the sky at a great speed, landing in the field with a thump I more sensed than heard.

Spade came plummeting down far slower. He landed without a single hitch in his stride, a dark little smile playing about his lips.

"Turns out she doesn't need your assistance," he said, tone as casual as if he'd just helped Sarah cross a street, not dropped her from at least a mile up. Spade was usually chivalrous to a fault, but try to kill his wife, and you wouldn't have a former eighteenth-century nobleman on your hands. You'd have a lethal, avenging vampire.

If possible, Francine and Lisa turned even paler. They might have hated Sarah for what she did, but this was a little too much for them to handle at the moment.

"Tyler, can you take them to one of the ambulances so they can get treated?"

I wanted to stay and keep an eye on Kramer, though Bones had him well under control. Besides, the way I looked would draw too much attention if I got around people.

"Come on, sweethearts, let's get you fixed up," he urged, putting an arm around each of them. Then he winked at me. "Catch you later at the homestead. Spade said he'd send a car. Dexter's going to *flip* when he sees me."

"Is it over?" Francine asked, and the same question repeated in Lisa's mind.

I looked at Kramer, still muttering threats and thrashing in Bones's grip even though both got him nowhere. "It is for you two. You won't see him again. We'll take care of the rest."

With a last, long look at us, Francine and Lisa let Tyler escort them down the street to wait for one of the ambulances. I was eternally grateful that it seemed Kramer had been too busy following me and setting up his ambush to have spent it torturing them, but they were still the worse for wear. They had deep lacerations on their wrists and ankles from struggling against the metal restraints, and that was just what I could see.

"Do you feel up to coming with us, Kitten?" Bones asked. His aura wrapped around me in strong, soothing bands even though his hands were still full with a livid ghost.

I had no hesitation in my response. "I'll need someone to carry me, but I wouldn't miss this for the world."

I was still too weak from healing the many injuries I'd received to fly myself, but I wanted to be there when Kramer was sealed into his prison. Hell, I wanted to dance around it, chanting.

More noise drew my attention to the sky. I'd expected to see firemen, policemen, and ambulances descend on the farm, but I was surprised to see a military helicopter land in one of the cleared areas of the street. It was far enough away from the remaining flames for the churning air from the rotors not to fan them, but close enough that I recognized one of the men who exited it.

"Tate's here."

Bones's head whipped in that direction, lips tightening when he saw the brown-haired vampire shouting orders to the other, helmeted soldiers who exited after him. They were too far away to see us, but as if Tate could feel our stares, he turned, looking right at us.

"You go, I'll deal with him," Spade muttered.

We did need to leave. The trip to Ottumwa would take almost four hours, and if Tate was here, Madigan probably wasn't far behind, but I put a hand on Bones's shoulder.

"Let's wait a minute," I said, motioning to Tate. "If he calls anyone else over, we'll leave."

Tate trotted over after a last shouted command, slowing down to stare at Francine, Tyler, and Lisa when he drew abreast of them. Then he resumed his brisk pace, his indigo gaze flitting between me, Bones, and the cursing ghost between us.

"Cat, your hair . . ." he began.

"If you think I look like shit now, you should've seen me when I was on fire. But enough of that. Why are you here?"

His features tightened at my brisk overview of being burned, but then they turned stony at my question.

"Madigan confiscated some amateur footage a week ago of you throwing a car off yourself, so he knows you're in Iowa. He's hot to get his hands on the ghost who killed his men, and he knows you're after it, too. So we're supposed to keep a lookout for you."

"Was the footage from a cell phone video?" I wondered irreverently.

Tate nodded. "Those things fucking annoy me."

He'd get no argument from me on that one. "Someone reported seeing a flaming person fly through the air with one of the 911 calls about the fire," Tate continued. "We were deployed to investigate if it that was hysterical witness exaggerating, or if something supernatural was involved."

"You will all be thrown into the eternal lake of fire!" Kramer shouted. I slammed my elbow into his face without bothering to look at him. From the *zzzt!* sound that followed, Bones zapped him again.

"So Madigan's after me because he wants revenge for his murdered soldiers," I mused.

Tate grunted. "No. He wants you to trap the ghost, then have us steal the trap so he can use the thing later as a weapon. Stupid bastard thinks he could control it."

"And what are you intending to report to him?"

Bones asked, his aura changing to icy, warning currents.

Tate shrugged. "That I didn't see any vampires here but me."

Kramer continued with his ranting about how we were all going to suffer, burn, beg, etc. None of us paid any attention to him, which enraged him more.

"This is the ghost," I said, noting the shock that crossed Tate's expression as he looked at the very solid Kramer. "We need you to make sure your team stays here for a while so no one follows us."

The slightest smile crossed his face. "Then again, maybe I did see something suspicious on the far end of the field. Might take hours to investigate."

I smiled back. "Thank you."

He cast a final glance at Kramer before heading back toward the helicopter. The dangerous currents eased from Bones, changing into waves of determination.

"Let's finish this, Kitten."

I looked at Kramer and, for the first time, saw fear in the Inquisitor's green gaze.

"Yes, let's," I drew out with supreme satisfaction.

EPILOGUE

A CAR PULLED UP TO THE FORMER COMBINED sewage facility, no door on the driver's side. Denise sat behind the steering wheel, bundled up in a thick coat with her seat belt around the outside of it. Not a hint of the damage Sarah had inflicted on her showed anymore, as her bright smile evidenced. My mother dozed in the passenger seat, her lids fluttering when Denise parked. The sun had come up a few hours ago, and she was still noticeably feeling its effects.

"We here?" I heard her mumble.

Denise rolled her eyes at me. "Do you know how many times I had to poke her awake so she could mesmerize the cops who pulled us over into *forgetting* we were driving a car that clearly isn't street legal?"

Seeing her so chipper after the awful thing that had happened to her brightened my mood even more. She didn't say a word about my hair, which meant Spade had called her and warned her in advance. Oh well. There were always wigs if Bones had been stretching the truth about special vampire hair-growing abilities to lessen the stress I was dealing with at the time.

Spade stood, smiling at Denise in a way that made me glad my best friend was so cherished. Then again, I knew what that felt like, as Bones's arms around me and his mouth brushing my temple attested.

Elisabeth floated out of the facility, Fabian close behind her. I'd always thought she was beautiful, but today, she looked especially radiant even without the more vivid effect of being solid.

"You sure you want to stay here?" I asked her. "He's been screaming in there for hours and it's well past the time when he'd be air again. If he could've gotten out, he would have already."

"I'll wait until you seal the area off permanently. I don't know what I'll do after that."

The words seemed to sink in, and I could almost see Elisabeth realizing that her long quest for justice was finally over. She let out a laugh that was half-nervous, half-filled with wondrous joy.

"I have no *idea* what I'll do after that."

Fabian cleared his throat, which, considering he was a ghost, was as obvious as a sky-written message.

"Perhaps I might, ah, might be able to assist you with your options," he stammered, and, though it was impossible, I could've sworn he blushed.

Elisabeth's mouth dropped open, catching his meaning. Then she tilted her head in a very feminine, contemplative manner, a slow smile stretching her lips.

"Well," she said at last. "Perhaps you can."

Bones turned away so that they couldn't see his grin. "Everyone, let's leave them to their guarding," he said, the faintest wicked emphasis on that last word.

"No, I want to stay and see this," Ian protested.

Spade's hand landed heavily on his back. "Get in the car, mate."

Ian rose, shooting a last regretful look at Elisabeth and Fabian, who floated much closer to each other. "Only trying to enhance my repertoire with continuing education," he muttered.

"I'm sure it's plenty enhanced already," I noted dryly, accepting Bones's hand up. "Now get it out of here."

The car was only meant to seat five, and there were six of us, but we made it work. Spade insisted on driving, and Denise sat snuggled between him and my mom. Bones's comment that my mother could sleep quite comfortably in the trunk was met with a heavy-lidded, evil look that only made him laugh.

"What a dreary-looking day out," Ian commented as we pulled away.

The sky did have a grayish tint that hinted at an early winter. Darker clouds kept most of the sunlight at bay, but as I glanced up at them, I couldn't help but think that each looked like it had a silver lining.

Can't get enough of Cat and Bones?
Here's a sneak peek
at a special Christmas story by

Jeaniene Frost

Available November 2011

I GLANCED AT MY WATCH. TEN MINUTES TO midnight. The vampire would be back soon, and despite hours of careful preparation, I wasn't ready for him.

A ghost's head popped through the wall, the rest of his body concealed by the wood barrier. He took one look around the room and a frown appeared on his filmy visage.

"You're not going to make it."

I yanked the wire through the hole I'd drilled into the ceiling's rafter, careful not to shift my weight too far or I'd fall off the ladder I was balanced on. Fabian was right, but I wasn't ready to concede defeat.

"When he pulls up, stall him."

"How am I supposed to do that?" he asked.

Good question. Unlike humans, vampires could see ghosts, but tended to ignore them as a general rule. While this vampire showed more respect to the corporeal-impaired, he still wouldn't stop to have a lengthy chat with one before entering his home.

"Can't you improvise? You know, make some loud pounding noises or cause the outer walls to bleed?"

The ghost shot me a pointed look. "You watch too many movies, Cat."

Then Fabian vanished from sight, but not before I heard him muttering about unfair stereotypes.

I finished twisting together the wires along the ceiling. If all went well, as soon as the vampire came through that door, I'd use my remote transmitter to unload a surprise onto his head. Now, to set up the last of the contraptions I'd planned—

The unmistakable sound of a car approaching almost startled me into falling off the ladder. Damn it, the vampire was back! No time to rig any other devices. I barely had enough time to conceal myself.

I leapt off the ladder and carried it as noiselessly as I could to the closet. The last thing I needed was a bunch of metallic clanging to announce that something unusual was going on. Then I swept up the silver knives I'd left on the floor. It wouldn't do for him to see those right off.

I'd just crouched behind one of the living room chairs when I heard a car door shut and then Fabian's voice.

"You won't believe what I found around the edge of your property," the ghost announced. "A cave with prehistoric paintings inside it!"

I rolled my eyes. *That* was the best tactic Fabian could come up with? This was a vampire he was trying to stall, not a paleontologist.

"Good on you," an English voice replied, sounding utterly disinterested. Booted footsteps came to the door, but then paused before going further. I sucked in a breath I no longer needed. No cars were in the driveway, but did he sense that several people lurked out of sight, waiting to pounce on him as soon as he crossed that threshold?

"Fabian," that cultured voice said next. "Are you sure there isn't anything *else* you want to tell me?"

A hint of menace colored the vampire's tone. I could almost picture my friend quailing, but his reply was instant.

"No. Nothing else."

"All right," the vampire said after a pause. The knob turned. "Your exorcism if you're lying."

I stayed hidden behind the chair, a silver knife gripped in one hand and the remote transmitter in the other. When the sound of boots hit the wood floor inside the house, I pressed the button and leapt up at the same time.

"Surprise!"

Confetti unleashed from the ceiling onto the vampire's head. With a whiplike motion, I threw my knife and severed the ribbon holding closed a bag of balloons above him. Those floated down more slowly, and by the time the first one hit the floor, the vampires who'd been concealed in the other rooms had come out.

"Happy Birthday," they called out in unison.

"It's not every day someone turns two hundred and forty-five," I added, kicking balloons aside as I made my way to the vampire in the doorway.

A slow smile spread across his features, changing them from gorgeous to heart-stopping. Of course, my heart had stopped beating—for the most part—over a year ago, so that was my normal condition.

"This is what you've been so secretive about lately?" Bones murmured, pulling me into his arms once I got close.

I brushed a dark curl from his ear. "They're not just here for your birthday, they're staying for the holidays, too. We're going to have a normal, old-fashioned Christmas for once. Oh, and don't exorcise Fabian; I made him try to stall you. If you were ten minutes later, I'd have had streamers set up, too."

His chuckle preceded the brush of lips against my cheek; a cool, teasing stroke that made me lean closer in instinctive need for more.

"Quite all right. I'm sure I'll find a use for them."

Knowing my husband, he'd find several uses for them, and at least one of those would make me blush.

I moved aside to let Bones get enveloped in well wishes from our guests. In addition to Fabian and his equally transparent girlfriend floating above the room, Bones's best friend, Spade, was here. So was Ian; the vampire who sired Bones, Mencheres, and his girlfriend, Kira; and my best friend, Denise. She was the only one in the room with a heartbeat, making her seem human to anyone who didn't know better. Our guest list was small because inviting everyone Bones knew for an extended birthday/holiday bash would require me renting a football stadium. Therefore, only Bones's closest companions were present.

Well, all except one.

"Anybody heard from Annette?" I whispered to Denise when she left Bones's side and returned to mine.

She shook her heard. "Spade tried her twenty minutes ago, but she didn't answer her cell."

"Wonder what's keeping her."

Annette might not be my favorite person considering her previous, centuries-long "friends with benefits" relationship with Bones, but she'd be last on my list of people I'd expect to skip his birthday party. Her ties with Bones went all the way back to when both of them were human, and in fairness, Annette seemed to have accepted that her position in his life was now firmly in the "friends *without* benefits" category.

"She flew in from London to be here," Denise noted. "Seems odd that she'd decide a thirty minute car commute was too much."

"What's this?" Bones asked, making his way over.

I waved a hand, not wanting to spoil the festive mood. "Nothing. Annette must be running behind."

"Some bloke rung her right before we left the hotel. She said she'd catch up with us," Spade said, coming to stand behind Denise. With his great height, her head was barely even with his shoulders, but neither of them seemed to mind. Black hair spilled across his face as he leaned down to kiss her neck.

"Why am I the only one without someone to snog?" Ian muttered, giving me an accusatory glance. "Knew I should've brought a date."

"You didn't get to bring a date because the type of girl you'd pick would want to liven things up with a group orgy before cutting the cake," I pointed out.

His smile was shameless. "Exactly."

I rolled my eyes. "Deal with not being the center of slutty attention for once, Ian. It'll do you good."

"No it won't," he said, shuddering as if in horror. "Think I'll go to the hotel and see what's taking Annette."

Denise snorted. "Way to make do with who's available."

I bit back my laugh with difficulty. Denise's opinion of Ian—and Annette—was even worse than my own, but that didn't make her wrong. Still, out of respect for both of them being Bones's friends, I contained my snicker.

Far from offended, Ian's brows rose arched. "Just following the American adage about turning a frown upside down."

Mencheres, ever the tactful one, chose that moment to glide over. "Perhaps we should turn our attention to gifts."

Bones clapped Ian on the back. "Don't take too long, mate."

"I'll try to limit myself to an hour," Ian replied with a straight face.

"Pig," I couldn't help but mutter. Hey, I'd tried to rein myself in! If vampires could still get diseases, I'd wish a festering case of herpes on him, but I suppose it was a good thing that Ian's ability to carry or transmit STD's died with his humanity.

Ian left, chuckling to himself the whole time.

Bones's arm slid across my shoulders, his fingers stroking my flesh along the way. I'd worn the backless halter dress because I knew he wouldn't be able to resist that bare expanse of skin, and I was right. Heat spilled over my emotions in its own caress as Bones dropped his shields so I could access his feelings. The tie that existed between us wasn't only forged in love. It was also the blood deep, eternal link between a vampire and their sire.

Of course, that wasn't the only undead perk. The ability to heal instantly, fly, and mesmerize people didn't suck, either.

"Do you know how lovely you look?" he asked, his voice deepening in timber. Hints of glowing green appeared in his dark brown eyes, a visual cue of his appreciation.

I leaned in to whisper my reply near his ear. "Tell me later, when everyone's gone."

His laugh was low and promising. "That I will, Kitten."

We went into the next room where a pile of presents awaited. Vampires had been called many things, but stingy usually wasn't among them. Bones had barely made a dent in opening his gifts before his cell phone rang. He glanced at the number with a chuckle.

"Ian, don't tell me you and Annette are too occupied to return," he said in lieu of a hello.

Supernatural hearing meant that I picked up every word of Ian's tightly clipped reply.

"You need to get over here. Now."

THE NIGHT HUNTRESS NOVELS FROM

JEANIENE FROST

✠ HALFWAY TO THE GRAVE ✠

978-0-06-124508-4

Kick-ass demon hunter and half-vampire Cat Crawfield and her sexy mentor, Bones, are being pursued by a group of killers. Now Cat will have to choose a side…and Bones is turning out to be as tempting as any man with a heartbeat.

✠ ONE FOOT IN THE GRAVE ✠

978-0-06-124509-1

Cat Crawfield works to rid the world of the rogue undead. But when she's targeted for assassination she turns to her ex, the sexy and dangerous vampire Bones, to help her.

✠ AT GRAVE'S END ✠

978-0-06-158307-0

Caught in the crosshairs of a vengeful vamp, Cat's about to learn the true meaning of bad blood—just as she and Bones need to stop a lethal magic from being unleashed.

✠ DESTINED FOR AN EARLY GRAVE ✠

978-0-06-158321-6

Cat is having terrifying visions in her dreams of a vampire named Gregor who's more powerful than Bones.

✠ THIS SIDE OF THE GRAVE ✠

978-0-06-178318-0

Cat and her vampire husband Bones have fought for their lives, as well as their relationship. But Cat's new and unexpected abilities threaten the both of them.

JFR 1210

*At Avon Books, we know your passion
for romance—once you finish one of our
novels, you find yourself wanting more.*

May we tempt you with . . .

- **Excerpts** from our upcoming releases.

- Entertaining **extras**, including authors'
  personal photo albums and book lists.

- Behind-the-scenes **scoop** on your favorite
  characters and series.

- **Sweepstakes** for the chance to win free books,
  romantic getaways, and other fun prizes.

- Writing **tips** from our authors and editors.

- **Blog** with our authors and find out why they
  love to write romance.

- **Exclusive content** that's not contained
  within the pages of our novels.

Join us at
www.avonbooks.com